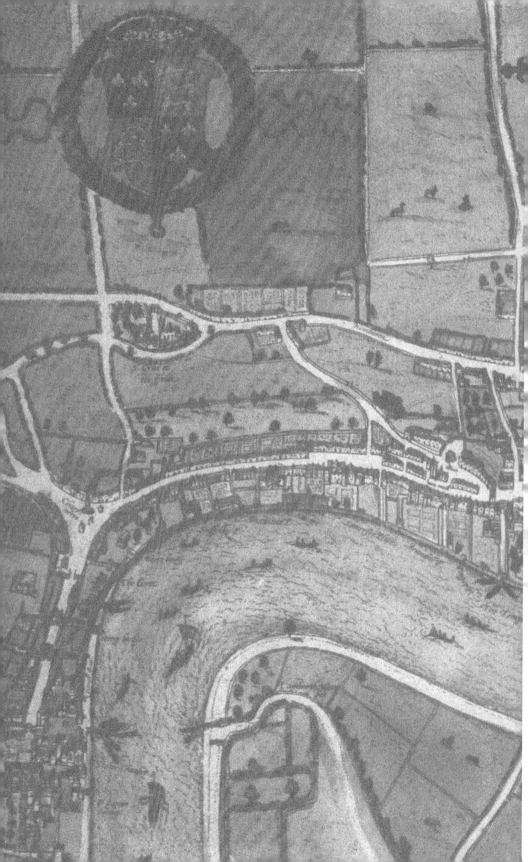

THE TUDORS

Historian's Note: Included in these pages are the first five out of ten final shooting scripts for season one of *The Tudors* on SHOWTIME. The scripts may include dialogue or even full scenes that were not in the final version of the episodes. Also, there may be elements in the episodes that were added at a later date.

SSE

SIMON SPOTLIGHT ENTERTAINMENT
An imprint of Simon & Schuster
1230 Avenue of the Americas, New York, New York 10020
Copyright © 2007 by Showtime Networks Inc. and Peace Arch Television LTD
"The Tudors" © 2007 TM Productions Limited/PA Tudors Inc. An Ireland/Canada Production. All rights reserved. © 2007 Showtime Networks Inc. All rights reserved. Showtime and related marks are registered trademarks of Showtime Networks Inc., a CBS Company.
Map art: London by Braun and Hogenberg 1541–1622 copyright © Antiquarian Images
All rights reserved, including the right of reproduction in whole or in part in any form.
SIMON SPOTLIGHT ENTERTAINMENT and related logo are trademarks of Simon & Schuster, Inc.
Designed by Jane Archer
Manufactured in the United States of America
First Edition   10 9 8 7 6 5 4 3 2 1
Library of Congress Control Number 2007921190
ISBN-13: 978-1-4169-4884-1
ISBN-10: 1-4169-4884-8

THE TUDORS

IT'S GOOD TO BE KING

Final shooting scripts 1-5 for *The Tudors*
from Showtime Networks Inc.

Created and Written by Michael Hirst
Foreword by Michael Hirst

Additional Material by
Michael Wilder

SIMON SPOTLIGHT ENTERTAINMENT
New York   London   Toronto   Sydney

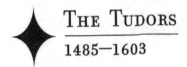

THE TUDORS
1485–1603

John of Gaunt,
Duke of Lancaster
Son of **EDWARD III**

  ✦ Katherine Swynford,
daughter of Sir Payne Roet of Guienne
(all her issue legitimated by
charter of **RICHARD II**, 1397)

Owen Tudor ✦ Katherine of Valois,
widow of **HENRY V**

Margaret Beaufort
(3rd in descent)
 ✦ Edmund Tudor,
Earl of Richmond

Jasper Tudor,
Earl of Pembroke

HENRY VII
(b. 1457, r. 1485,
d. 1509)
 ✦ Elizabeth of York,
daughter of **EDWARD IV**

Arthur,
Prince of Wales
(b. 1486,
d. 1502)
 ✦ Katherine of Aragon, (1),
Princess of Spain,
daughter of
FERDINAND V
(b. 1485, div. 1533,
d. 1536)

✦ **HENRY VIII**
(b. 1491,
r. 1509,
d. 1547)

✦ Anne Boleyn, (2),
daughter of
Earl of Wiltshire
(ex. 1536)

✦ Jane Seymour,
(3), daughter
of Sir John
Seymour
(d. 1537)

✦ Anne of Cleves, (4),
daughter of John III,
Duke of Cleves
(div. 1540,
d. 1557)

✦ Catherine Howard, (5),
daughter of
Lord Edmund Howard
(ex. 1542)

✦ Catherine Parr, (6),
daughter of
Sir Thomas Parr
(**HENRY VIII** was
her third husband)
(d. 1548)

MARY I
(b. 1516,
r. 1553,
d. 1558)

ELIZABETH I
(b. 1533,
r. 1558,
d. 1603)

EDWARD VI
(b. 1537,
r. 1547,
d. 1553)

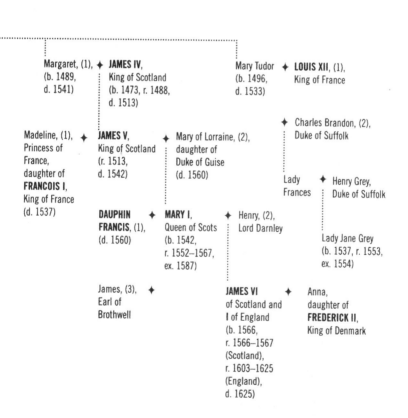

Margaret, (1), ✦ **JAMES IV,**
(b. 1489,   : King of Scotland
d. 1541)   (b. 1473, r. 1488,
                 d. 1513)

Madeline, (1), ✦ **JAMES V,**   ✦ Mary of Lorraine, (2),
Princess of   King of Scotland : daughter of
France,   (r. 1513,   : Duke of Guise
daughter of   d. 1542)   : (d. 1560)
FRANCOIS I,
King of France
(d. 1537)

                 DAUPHIN   ✦ **MARY I,**   ✦ Henry, (2),
                 FRANCIS, (1), Queen of Scots   : Lord Darnley
                 (d. 1560)   (b. 1542,
                                    r. 1552–1567,
                                    ex. 1587)

                 James, (3),   ✦   **JAMES VI**   ✦ Anna,
                 Earl of   of Scotland and   daughter of
                 Brothwell   I of England   **FREDERICK II,**
                                                     (b. 1566,   King of Denmark
                                                     r. 1566–1567
                                                     (Scotland),
                                                     r. 1603–1625
                                                     (England),
                                                     d. 1625)

Mary Tudor ✦ **LOUIS XII,** (1),
(b. 1496,   King of France
d. 1533)

            ✦ Charles Brandon, (2),
            : Duke of Suffolk

Lady   ✦ Henry Grey,
Frances   : Duke of Suffolk

            Lady Jane Grey
            (b. 1537, r. 1553,
            ex. 1554)

Contents

Foreword

Having just purchased a book called *The Tudors* it may surprise you to find that it consists of five scripts dealing exclusively with ten years in the life of the young King Henry VIII. Why not start with his father, Henry VII, who won the crown at the Battle of Bosworth Field by defeating Richard III, and founded the dynasty? Why jump forward so arbitrarily and—you may think—so irrationally, to his son's struggles to maintain and secure his inheritance?

I wish I knew. Perhaps the decision was accidental, or perhaps it was the result of hundreds of smaller decisions, many of them unconscious. Certainly when I first discussed the idea of turning *The Tudors* into a television series with my friend Ben Silverman, there were many alternate beginnings, many different and distinct ways to go. But there were other pressing factors, too: the need for this historical material to resonate with contemporary audiences, and for its themes to be relevant to our own lives. Of course I had a head start here, since I wrote the movie *Elizabeth* in the same spirit: not the story of distant kings and queens, but of a young woman propelled into a terrifying world of power and responsibility. Clearly, *The Tudors* would have to have the same human and personal core.

The more I read and thought about the Tudors, the more I came to realize that the story of young Henry VIII presented a rich and so-far-untapped vein. For one thing, he presided over the change from the medieval to the modern world. He also engineered the change in England from Catholicism to Protestantism, which was so profound that nobody had ever tackled it dramatically before, even though it underscored not only the history of the British Isles, but also the history of America! And on top of that—for God's sake—was the fact that, as a man, he was caught in an erotic triangle between his older wife and younger mistress. Granted, the stakes were a great deal higher than in most modern examples, but the reality was totally familiar, almost commonplace. Kings and queens act out, on a vast and public stage, the dramas that fill and define our own private lives.

I was asked to write a two-hour pilot. It was speculative. Nobody was sure what we were doing—least of all me! I had never properly worked in television before, nor written a soap opera! I pitched Henry as a young, glamorous, athletic, sexy . . . etc., king because I was fed up with his English iconic version as a fat, bearded monster with a vast ego and even vaster sexual appetite, and very little brain. Holbein's tyrant! He had in fact a keen intelligence—and for me there was nothing more fascinating or sexy than getting him involved in the big political and religious issues of his day. To tell you the truth, I grew to love this guy: He had everything! He was devastatingly hand-some, and he was always the best at all the physical activities—like jousting and wrestling—that he participated in. He could also speak five languages. He could play chess. He could write philosophical pamphlets. And he had absolute power. That God had given him! What a great premise for a show! For if Henry was you—what would *you* do?

Showtime liked the pilot. But they wanted to push it further. I was not to feel under any constraints to show the beauty and the violence of the period. They also liked the idea that Henry was surrounded by a group of young and handsome bucks who had no titles but who aspired to everything they could lay their hands on: titles, women, fortune, and honor. Brandon, Compton, and Knivert were the brat pack of their day, heartily disliked by the older generation of aristocrats, like Norfolk, but constantly indulged and elevated by the young king. With Cardinal Wolsey as a safe pair of hands, craftily and carefully guiding the ship of state, Henry lived a hedonistic lifestyle in the early years of his reign—a fact he guiltily admitted to later. Even so, he remained anxious to win fame and honor—if he could—on the battlefield (preferably fighting the French!) and he wanted to be a good ruler in a humanist tradition he shared with his good friend Thomas More (whose head he later cut off).

I was very happy to dramatize these extreme contradictions and events. After I had done so, there was a conference call with, among others, Robert Greenblatt, the head of programming for Showtime. Bob didn't mince his words. He told me: "Michael, we really only have one question to ask you—is *any* of this true?" It was a big moment . . . but I replied, as casually as possible, "About 85 percent." Of course the percentage was an invention—but I wanted to make the point that everything I wrote was based on historical research and historical "fact" (as reported, that is, by historians!). Naturally, as a writer, you have to shape your material for dramatic effect. You change things. Life itself is chaotic, but art—of whatever kind—has form. Yet I still wanted to cling to and express the human truths. My Henry VIII is new, in that audiences have never seen him portrayed this way, but he's not a figment of my imagination.

To make him "real" though was never totally within my gift. An actor had to come along who could not only play him, but embody him. It's ironic, given the rough history between our nations, that the man in question is an Irishman! But Jonathan Rhys Meyers, as an actor, easily transcends parochial borders. Indeed it was this refusal to accept limitations of any kind that connected him with the young king. And Jonathan recognized this, just as he instinctually recognized that Henry's love for his first wife, Katherine of Aragon, was never totally destroyed by his tearing passion for his second, Anne Boleyn. Such deep emotional attachments are not necessarily guided by the script, but have to be felt in the performance. And what I think we feel in these performances is how complicated are the relationships between men and women, and what a complex organ is the human heart.

Unlike novels, screenplays are never finished on the page. This form of expression and entertainment is collaborative, or it's nothing. So if I commend, even in an introduction to my scripts, the work of Joan Bergin, the costume designer on the series, or Tom Conroy, our designer, it's not because I feel any obligation to do so. It's because, just as much as me, they—and many others in the production—have helped create what you see on your screens. And of course we have been genuinely blessed with an unbelievably great cast, from Sam Neill's Wolsey and Jeremy Northam's More, to comparative new-comers like Natalie Dormer and Henry Cavill . . . although it's almost invidious to single out just a few names from such a talented collective.

Finally, perhaps reluctantly, I must shore myself up against the inevitable hostility of—I should imagine—mainly British academics and historians, who will find (to their secret delight) many errors of fact and detail in the work. By way of defense I should say that I was not trying to write historical biography. On the contrary, I was commissioned to write an entertainment! But there's something else, too, possibly even more important. For it seems to me that, sometimes, the desire to pursue historical "truths" can lead to the sacrifice of more human ones. To get the externals of dress and fashion, architecture, and speech absolutely correct is not the same thing as breathing life into believable, flesh-and-blood people. And although this may be heresy, I am inclined to believe that some historians, however much they have read of and about Henry VIII, King of England, have never actually *thought* of him as a human being at all, but merely an historical construct. Perhaps to do so is intended to diminish him, although I don't think so. It may be true that we can't go back in time, but that doesn't mean we should treat the past as a museum. History is a living thing. And we, no less than Henry, are living it.

MICHAEL HIRST
NOVEMBER 2006

Major Events Time Line

Henry's Life	Major World Events
1491—Henry born	
	1492—Columbus sails the ocean blue
1502—Prince Arthur dies	
	1503—Da Vinci paints the *Mona Lisa*
	1508—Michelangelo begins painting the Sistine Chapel
1509—Henry ascends the throne	
1511—Katherine bears a son who dies a month later	
	1512—Ponce de León claims Florida for Spain
1516—Princess Mary is born	
	1517—Martin Luther nails his criticism of the Catholic Church on the Wittenberg Cathedral
	1519—Magellan sets off to sail around the world. He dies in 1521, but his crew completes the circumnavigation
	1519—Hernando Cortés conquers the Aztec capital, Tenochtitlán, completing his conquest of Mexico
1520—The Field of the Cloth of Gold	
	1524—Verazzano discovers the New York Bay
1526—The start of the King's Great Matter	1526—First Battle of Panipat—Zahir ud Din Babur defeats much larger army led by Delhi's sultan and founds the Mughal dynasty in India

Henry's Life

1530—Cardinal Wolsey dies

1533—Henry marries Anne;
    Princess Elizabeth born

1536—Anne beheaded; Henry
    marries Jane Seymour

1537—Prince Edward born;
    Jane dies

1540—Henry marries Anne of
    Cleves in January, gets
    annulment, and marries
    Catherine Howard in July

1542—Catherine Howard executed

1543—Henry marries Catherine Parr

1547—King Henry dies

Major World Events

1531—Pizarro conquers Peru, ending
    the Incan Empire

1534—Cartier claims Canada for
France

1542—De Soto discovers the
    Mississippi

1542—First European visitors arrive
    in Japan

1543—Copernicus claims Earth
    revolves around sun, directly
    contrasting the accepted
    theory that everything circled
    the Earth

1547—Ivan the Terrible has himself
    crowned the czar of Russia

The Start of
THE TUDOR DYNASTY

T he Tudor dynasty began the day Henry VII defeated Richard III at the Battle of Bosworth Field, effectively ending the War of the Roses and finally providing stability to the throne. Up to that point, a power struggle had waged between the Houses of York and Lancaster. For more than thirty years, the War of the Roses had caused upheaval, as the balance of power swung back and forth between the two houses and England reeled from lack of leadership. Henry VII acted to change that.

Henry VII's claim to the throne was tenuous. His mother was a descendant of Edward II, but her bloodlines, although legitimate, had been barred from succession because her grandfather had been born out of wedlock. Yet Henry's victory on the battlefield gave him the crown, as most of his rivals were in no position to contest him. He married Elizabeth of York in order to unite the two houses under the throne, strengthen his claim, and ensure his offspring would be of royal blood. Not wanting further battles, Henry turned his attention to restoring faith in the monarchy.

Henry VII © Antiquarian Images

Still dealing with claimants to the throne, the new king worked to quell any uprisings. He was content to allow the nobles their regional influence if they were loyal and as long as they operated within the law. Others, perceived as possible threats, were fined and laws were passed to limit the power of the different royal houses. In addition, in order to replenish an inherited bankrupt treasury and rebuild the monarchy, he enacted ruthless taxation against the nobility. Known to be a stingy monarch, Henry VII worked toward his goal of maintaining peace and creating economic prosperity through effective trading and opportunities. At his death, Henry had amassed a personal fortune of £1.5 million (equivalent to $1.25 billion today), a huge increase from where he had started.

From the very beginning, King Henry VII wanted the Tudor dynasty to be one of longevity. In the naming of his first son, Henry VII established a link to an early legend of a powerful king, Arthur. Henry immediately began grooming the young Prince Arthur for his eventual ascension to the throne. One of the first monarchs to recognize Spain as a rising power, Henry VII arranged a marriage between two-year-old Arthur and one-year-old Katherine of Aragon. All hopes of extending a Tudor dynasty rested on the ultimately frail shoulders of Prince Arthur.

On November 14, 1501, at the age of sixteen, Arthur married Katherine and headed to Wales for the honeymoon, as was custom. Six months later, the perpetually ill Arthur was dead. Suddenly, Henry, the younger brother, became the heir apparent, thrust into a role his brother had been groomed to take. Prince Henry immediately took over his brother's titles. His father, wanting to maintain the alliance between England and Spain, even arranged a marriage between Henry and Arthur's widow, Katherine. This was only possible after Katherine swore her marriage to sick Arthur was never consummated; otherwise it was a sin against God for Henry to marry his brother's widow. A dispensation from the pope, obtained in haste, helped give validity to the future nuptials. Over the years, Henry VII soured on maintaining a relationship with Spain, as both sides balked at paying money toward the agreement. The marriage was delayed until 1509, when Henry VII passed away and Prince Henry succeeded his father, the first peaceful transition of power since before the War of the Roses. Two months later, the new king took Katherine as his wife, and the reign of King Henry VIII began.

The Sweating Sickness:
A Tudor Disease

Hopes for the Tudor dynasty began with the frail Prince Arthur, but Arthur died at a young age from a mysterious illness. Was it the infamous Tudor disease?

It began suddenly with a general sense of apprehension. Then came the cold shivers, sometimes violent; giddiness; headache; and severe pains in the neck and shoulder. These symptoms lasted from a half hour to three hours before the characteristic sweat overtook the victim. After the sweat poured out, palpitation and pain in the heart, delirium, and an overall weakness flooded over the victim's body. Finally there was the desire for sleep, which usually meant certain doom.

This was the sweating sickness, a disease that ravaged England five times before disappearing forever. It first appeared at the beginning of the reign of King Henry VII, right before the Battle of Bosworth Field. It may have been carried over by the French mercenaries who fought alongside Henry, as they seemed to be immune to it. Regardless, it arrived before the battle and broke out in the capital seven days later, following Henry's arrival and coronation. It was regarded as being quite distinct from the plague, the pestilential fever, or other epidemics previously known, not only by the special symptom that gave it its name, but also by its extremely rapid and fatal course. One survived attack did not offer immunity, and a person could suffer several bouts with the sickness before succumbing. As sweating sickness seemed to be more virulent among the rich than the poor, unlike other epidemics, outbreaks caused tremendous fear within the royal houses. After 1485, the disease disappeared but resurfaced in 1507, although to a lesser degree. The year 1517 brought another outbreak, more severe than the others. Although some cases appeared in Calais and Antwerp, sweating sickness seemed to stay mostly confined to England. This time proved to be very fatal, as some areas reported half the population to have perished.

In 1528 the disease recurred for the fourth time, and with great severity. It first showed itself in London at the end of May, and speedily spread over the whole of England, although Scotland and Ireland were spared. Many people in Henry VIII's court fell sick and Henry developed a morbid fear of contracting the disease himself. He would change residences every other day in an effort to avoid coming in contact with those of his court who had become infected.

The most remarkable fact about this epidemic is how rapidly it spread over Europe in a few weeks, appearing suddenly first at Hamburg, and causing more than a thousand deaths. Then the terrible sweating sickness started on a destructive course, causing fearful mortality throughout Eastern Europe. It spread quickly, arriving at Switzerland in December, heading northward to Denmark, Sweden, and Norway, eastward to Lithuania, Poland, and Russia, and westward to Flanders and Holland. The epidemic, which declared itself simultaneously at Antwerp and Amsterdam on the morning of September 27, may have come from England directly. In each place affected it prevailed for a short time only, generally not more than a two-week span. France, Italy, and the southern European countries were remarkably spared. By the end of the year it had entirely disappeared, except in eastern Switzerland, where it lingered into the next year; and the terrible English sweat disappeared again. One last outbreak occurred, in 1551, before eventually vanishing from the continent forever.

Sweating sickness wreaked havoc in Henry's court. The disease may have claimed Prince Arthur's life, possibly affecting both him and Katherine during their honeymoon. Anne Boleyn had a bout with the sickness in 1528, and Charles Brandon's two sons from his final marriage died in the span of three hours during the 1551 outbreak. Remarkably, Thomas Wolsey survived multiple attacks throughout his lifetime.

It's still not known what caused the disease. By all accounts, it appeared in the summer months and infected the country until winter brought relief. Blame has been placed on the general hygiene and sewage problems of the time and some reports link it to relapsing fever, spread by lice and ticks. Whatever the case, it plagued the land for the whole of Henry VIII's reign and is forever linked with the Tudor dynasty.

THE CONSTANT COMPANION:
Charles Brandon

Charles Brandon, was, perhaps, the only person in all of England to successfully retain Henry's affection over a span of forty years. King Henry VIII wanted what he wanted, and although loyal, turned on those who defied him. His reign is littered with the lives of trusted advisors who disappointed him, either accidentally or deliberately, and lost their standing, their lives, and sometimes their heads. Thus it was rare for someone to remain in his favor for any length of time.

Orphaned at an early age, Charles Brandon grew up in the royal court with Arthur and Henry. His mother died in childbirth, and his father, a standard bearer for King Henry VII, lost his life during the Battle of Bosworth Field, reportedly at the hands of Richard III himself. Although Charles Brandon had neither titles nor great wealth, he held something much greater: the affection of the king. Henry recognized the loyalty Brandon's father had shown and rewarded the deceased man by raising the boy under his own roof.

Although seven years older than Henry VIII, Charles shared many of the future king's most prominent characteristics: natural athleticism, robust physical health (unlike the delicate Arthur), and a devotion to all sports (wrestling, hunting, tilting, and jousting, to name a few). During these adolescent years, the two boys laid the foundation for a lifelong friendship. When Henry became king, Charles's rise to prominence began.

Early on, Charles displayed an ambitious and callous streak. The first sign of this became apparent in 1505, following his engagement to

Anne Brown, a woman of impressive lineage. He and Anne slept together, as evidenced by the child she bore in 1506, but Charles refused to marry her. He instead married her aunt, a wealthy widow. The marriage was not taken seriously due to its mercenary nature and the legal action undertaken by Anne's family. Eventually the marriage was annulled and Charles honored his wedding agreement and married Anne. They had one more daughter before Anne died in 1510 and soon after, Charles moved on to his next conquest.

By late 1512, Charles contemplated yet another union. His new betrothed was an eight-year-old orphan, the heiress to Lord Lisle of Sparsholt in Berkshire. It was common practice for the Crown to assume guardianship of an orphaned minor child with inherited property and then sell the guardianship to the highest bidder, often the child's own relatives who wanted to receive the property revenues until the child came of age. Charles had been given the wardship of Elizabeth Grey and this, along with various offices, grants, and pensions, was a mark of Henry's continued favor. In early 1513, Charles announced his engagement to the girl and the king created him Viscount Lisle, in right of his betrothed wife. Charles Brandon finally had a noble title.

Always a ladies' man, Charles caused an incident when he publicly flirted with Margaret, the daughter of the Roman Emperor Maximillian, causing her great embarrassment. Henry had to apologize for his friend, despite having been complicit in helping translate the conversation between Margaret and Charles. Yet rather than being annoyed by the incident, Henry went an opposite direction. He named Charles the duke of Suffolk, a huge honor. It meant that he was one of only three dukes in the entire kingdom. Suddenly the poor orphan boy was on equal or greater footing than anyone in the whole realm.

Emboldened by his new position, Charles appeared untouchable. The king, seeking to solidify his standing with France, arranged a marriage between his younger sister, Mary, and King Louis XII. His sister, distraught by the arrangement, agreed to the marriage on one condition: After Louis died, as he was old and sickly, she could pick her next husband. Henry agreed, possibly to make her trip to France easier. Mary, who some say admitted Charles was the man she loved, went quietly to her wedding and three months later King Louis was dead, possibly from an inordinate amount of bedroom activity during his marriage. Henry sent Charles to negotiate with the new king, Francis I, on repayment of dowry and to bring the new dowager queen home. However, Henry demanded Charles go as an official of the king and leave behind his personal feelings. Fearing Henry would force her to remarry for political reasons, Mary confessed her love for Charles to Francis I. Francis, worrying the king would use Mary to form an alliance with the Romans and wanting to keep her dowry in France, convinced Mary she should marry Charles immediately to block her brother from doing his own wishes. When Charles arrived, Mary gave Charles an ultimatum: now or never. Brandon found himself in a dif-

Henry VIII's Sister Mary and Charles Brandon, Duke of Suffolk
© Antiquarian Images

ficult position. On the one hand, he knew the king was his meal ticket, the man who had given him everything. Yet, here was Mary, arguably the most beautiful woman in the royal court and the king's sister, demanding that they marry. Ever ambitious, Charles recognized that marrying the princess would solidify his position for the rest of his life, if they could overcome the king's wrath. He knew that Mary was a great prize; after all, he harbored no overt dynastic ambitions but six years of marriage had produced no living child for Henry VIII. Perhaps Charles and Mary would create a new royal line. And she was a royal princess and queen, just twenty years old and madly in love with him.

Charles, swayed by tears and ambition, agreed, and sometime in February 1515, they married secretly at the Cluny chapel. When the king learned of their act, he was not happy, feeling Brandon had betrayed his orders and went behind his back. Plus, this was Henry's sister, and Brandon had married her without the consent of the king. The king, at first, would not see them, and Mary sent word that as his loyal subject she would wait in Calais until he sent for them. Charles wrote to Wolsey, hoping for his help in improving the situation. Wolsey responded that the king could not believe his friend had betrayed him and the newlywed couple would have to pay a stiff penalty—literally. When Henry finally did allow them to return, he met with them in private. Henry was willing enough to forgive his best friend and favorite sister, *after* she turned over all her jewels and plate from France and signed a contract to repay the money spent on her first marriage in annual installments of 4,000 pounds. It was obvious that Henry was not surprised by the marriage; he was mostly angry at Charles for breaking trust. A new wedding was held at Greenwich Palace in May, and once again Brandon had escaped unscathed.

Brandon continued to serve the king for the rest of his life, and was present for all the major events. He attended the Field of the Cloth of Gold, brought down Wolsey by authority of the king, and pleaded unsuccessfully with Katherine on Henry's behalf to accept the break with Rome and her new title of princess dowager. After Mary died in

1533, he remarried once again for the final time, this time to a wealthy young baroness, and lived happily with her. He attended all the momentous events of the 1530s—he sat at the trials of Thomas More and Anne Boleyn; he was even present at the scaffold when she was beheaded. He helped lead forces to end the Pilgrimage of Grace, one of the most serious problems of Henry's reign. When Henry finally got the son he always hoped for, Prince Edward, Brandon acted as god-father to the new addition. As the landscape of England changed, Charles Brandon, the duke of Suffolk, remained loyal to the king. When Charles died suddenly in 1545, at the age of sixty, King Henry demanded a grand funeral. The funeral was an emotional event for the king as he laid to rest the one constant companion of his entire life. The last influence Brandon ever had on the Tudor dynasty surfaced years later when his daughter by Princess Mary, Lady Jane Grey, held the throne for nine days after Edward VI's death before Princess Mary took her rightful place, executing Jane at the Tower of London.

THE FAILURE OF KATHERINE OF ARAGON

Katherine of Aragon © Antiquarian Images

It seemed a perfect match. Two rising nations, looking to form a lasting alliance, would be linked by the marriage of Prince Arthur of England and Princess Katherine of Aragon. Katherine, after some trouble with weather, finally arrived in England for the much-anticipated wedding, which went off flawlessly. The young couple headed for Wales and a new life together, but the bad weather that had slowed Katherine's arrival into England turned out to be an omen for her stay in the country.

Her new husband, Arthur, never a robust child, took ill within months of their marriage and died soon after. Katherine, suffering from the same virus, stayed bedridden until after the funeral, which custom forbade her from attending anyway. Katherine returned to London as soon as she was healthy enough to travel. Her parents, Ferdinand and Isabella, wishing to keep the alliance with England, moved to have her engaged to Henry VIII, Arthur's younger brother. Ironically, Henry VIII had just walked Katherine down the aisle to "give her away" at her wedding to Arthur. Because Katherine's first marriage wasn't consummated, according to her, the wedding was permissible under the eyes of God. Katherine's claim about consummation held validity, in light of both Arthur's already sickly condition and Katherine's own devout piety. To be sure, both sets of parents requested a papal dispensation from the pope to allow the marriage. It looked as if the alliance would be preserved.

The pope took longer than expected for the dispensation, and during that time Katherine became deathly ill once again. Suffering from fever and fits of shivering, it was widely feared she would die. Strangely, despite her royal position, she lived in poverty, as Henry VII cut off her allowance. Henry VII had soured on the union, awaiting the remaining dowry to be paid. He felt, also, that he could find a better match for his son. He even ordered the prince to make a secret but formal protest against marrying his brother's widow. The reason Henry VII did not break off the engagement publicly, though, was because he did not want to repay the first installment of her dowry from her marriage to Arthur. Ferdinand, finally obtaining the papal dispensation, sped up the process to get the marriage under way, yet

Henry continued to balk, demanding payment of the second dowry installment. He also claimed that Prince Henry was underage at the time of the agreement and thus, nothing was binding. It seemed that the wedding would never happen. Katherine began to get better. She had been too sick to spend much time with her betrothed, but now they were able to see each other. Despite the seven-year age difference, they discovered they truly enjoyed each other's company. A worried Henry, still desiring a better match for the prince, sent Katherine to the country. He gave Ferdinand a deadline for the dowry payment, but then extended the deadline indefinitely. In April 1509, Henry VII died of tuberculosis and Prince Henry was named the new king. Urged by the privy council to marry Katherine, Henry VIII visited the princess and privately asked her to become his wife. They had a secret ceremony on June 11, 1509, keeping the marriage quiet as Henry was still in mourning for his father. On the June 15, Katherine made her first appearance in court as the new queen of England, after a long and arduous eight years.

The new couple brought liveliness to the court, a vast difference from Henry VII's austere rule. They were a loving and affectionate couple, a departure from the typical royal marriages, with obvious displays of public affection and declarations of love and respect. A month into the marriage, Katherine announced her pregnancy, resulting in a stillborn daughter. Although disappointing to the king and queen, this was a common occurrence for the first pregnancy. In May 1510, Katherine was pregnant again, and on January 1st she gave birth to a son, naming him Henry. The kingdom rejoiced as Katherine fulfilled her main duty as queen. She had given Henry a male heir, especially important since Henry was the only surviving male Tudor. Guns fired from the Tower of London and bells rang the good fortune. The new

Prince Henry was christened at Richmond Palace. A month later the infant prince died. Henry, devastated, held a lavish funeral for his son and buried him in Westminster Abbey.

It was two years before her next pregnancy, as Henry left to fight in France. This third pregnancy brought the premature birth of a son who died shortly after his first breath. A year later brought another pregnancy and another disappointment, a stillborn son. A year and half later, another pregnancy gave way to another stillborn son. Katherine had now lost four babies in the span of five years. Suddenly Katherine's seven-year seniority over the king began to be a major concern. Pregnancy number five brought little optimism, and even when Princess Mary arrived, the celebration, although genuine, was tinged with despair. The long-hoped-for boy seemed an impossible dream, although Henry still believed if Katherine could produce a healthy girl, then surely a boy would follow. Yet he was wrong, as the sixth child was a weak baby girl who died in a couple of days. The queen was now thirty-two years old, her body showing signs of the stress and miscarriages over the years.

The king no longer desired her, and when his mistress gave birth to a healthy baby boy, Henry knew Katherine would never produce. She could not be his queen. Nevertheless Katherine would not grant him the annulment he craved, sticking by her Catholic faith and ideals. Even as Henry's new love, Anne Boleyn, gained higher standing in the court, Katherine hoped for reconciliation with the king. Henry would not be denied his divorce and eventually, by breaking with the Roman Church, got his wish. In 1533 after six years of turmoil, Henry married Anne, the new queen, and Katherine was once again known as the dowager princess of Wales, Arthur's widow.

Katherine spent the rest of her years living in exile from court, referred to by her new title, but, in her mind, always Queen Katherine. Sad and lonely, she died in 1536, after living in a succession of dank and foul castles. She supposedly died of cancer, as her heart had turned black. There were rumors that she had been poisoned, perhaps by Anne, but in reality the stress and disappointment of her position led to her deathbed. Sadly, the poor queen never even knew her one last contribution to history. In the end, her inability to bear Henry a male heir led to another failure. Katharine, the devoted and pious Catholic, unintentionally brought England the Reformation.

THE FORCE BEHIND THE THRONE:
Cardinal Thomas Wolsey

The man who ruled England in the early days of King Henry VIII's reign was not the king. That responsibility fell on the shoulders of Cardinal Thomas Wolsey. The son of a butcher, Wolsey had achieved the title royal chaplain under Henry VII through great intellect, work ethic, and his lowly background. Since Henry VII distrusted the nobility, he deliberately sought to favor those from more humble backgrounds for positions of prominence. When the new king cleared the counsel, Wolsey remained in the employ of the new king. The new king trusted the cardinal from the beginning, as Thomas supported Henry's ideas for the new regime. Early on, King Henry VIII cared more for jousting, hunting, gambling, and feasting than he did for the political operations of office, spending little time on government business. Wolsey worked diligently behind the scenes, running the day-to-day operations for the king.

Henry made Wolsey lord chancellor in 1515, a great honor made even greater by the fact that he was a commoner. As Wolsey tasted power, he hungered for more, gaining great wealth and political influence over the king. As always, he kept the interests of the king foremost in his mind, and looked to work those interests to his advantage. Wolsey continued to be the real power behind the throne without ever let-

King Henry VIII talking with Cardinal Thomas Wolsey
Heritage Image Partnership © Art Resource/NY.
Guildhall Art Gallery. London. Great Britain

ting Henry realize who was truly running the country. The young king followed Wolsey's advice unhesitatingly. The cardinal's true ambition was to become pope, so he constantly steered Henry toward aligning with France, as this gave him the best chance to assume the title. Yet Wolsey was careful not to push too hard. Henry had a natural rivalry with the country and its king, so it took careful maneuvering by the cardinal to bend Henry to his will. Also, Wolsey had to contend with Katherine. Henry's love of Katherine, as well as her ties to Rome and her nephew, Charles the emperor, were constant obstacles. However, as time and failed pregnancies went by, Katherine gradually lost her influence over Henry, giving Wolsey almost total power.

By 1520, Wolsey's status nearly rivaled the king. His residence, Hampton Court Palace, was a magnificent structure built on the Thames River. He had great wealth and privilege. He enjoyed a close relationship with the king, a closeness rivaled only by Charles Brandon. Wolsey's tremendous standing coupled with his modest beginnings gave him many enemies within the court. Since the king trusted him completely and gave him free reign, Wolsey was able to keep those jealous rivals at bay. Katherine herself despised Wolsey, as she felt he had turned the king against her. Try as she might, she could not sway the king. Wolsey was untouchable, having never failed Henry in his years of service. When Anne Boleyn entered the court, Wolsey was not readily impressed. In fact, he broke up her romance with Henry Percy in 1522, an act that forever earned him her hostility. Although it is romanticized that the king ordered this breakup for his own selfish reasons, it is not known if Henry even had noticed her at this time. It is very likely that Percy's father, the earl of Northumberland, did not approve of the match and requested it broken off. Anne's return to court would soon prove the undoing of Wolsey. As Henry and Anne began their romance, Wolsey started to lose his hold over the king. Attempting to keep favor, Wolsey gave the king expensive gifts, including the Hampton Court Palace. Henry took up residence there in 1525, although the cardinal continued to live in some of the apartments.

Even though Wolsey's relationship with Henry was weakening, the king still depended on his top advisor. Doubting the validity of his marriage, Henry wanted a divorce and he charged Wolsey with making it a reality. Wolsey favored the idea, as he had always viewed Katherine as an adversary. He opposed the idea of Anne as queen, and as he went about securing the annulment, he intended to marry the king to a French princess.

Unfortunately for the cardinal, he could not get the annulment, try as he might. Wolsey's failure caused Henry to turn on his trusted advisor. Until then Wolsey could do no wrong, but facing off against the pope, the very title he coveted, turned out to be an unenviable position. Wolsey worked tirelessly to obtain the annulment for his king, but he was fighting against the queen's nephew, the pope, and his own religion. The glaring spotlight shone on him, and as the case dragged on for years, Henry became impatient. Making matters worse for Wolsey was that Anne Boleyn blamed him for the delay, and although he had successfully overcome Katherine's disdain, he was no match for the influence Henry's new love had over the king.

Failure swiftly brought about Wolsey's downfall. The king used Charles Brandon, the same man who had once turned to Wolsey for help during his marriage scandal, to openly attack the cardinal in court. Charles was also sent with the duke of Norfolk to demand the great seal from Wolsey, ultimately stripping the cardinal of his offices and wealth. Having already given the Hampton Court Palace to Henry, he was now forced from the premises. In 1530, Wolsey was arrested for high treason, but his case never made it to court. He died of illness on his way to the Tower of London. The man who had risen to the highest ranks, who once had the ear of the king, died without fanfare or dignity. His one failure, the one obstacle he could not overcome, was only the first casualty in the bloody trail of Henry's desire for a son.

THE FIELD OF THE CLOTH OF GOLD:
Much Ado About Nothing

The balance of power in Western Europe rested precariously between France and Rome, both courting English favor to gain strength over the other. King Henry, looking to make a name for himself and his reign, was unsure whether France or Rome offered him the best chance at personal and national gain, so for a time he navigated the middle, hoping whichever nation ascended power would benefit England. His court was likewise torn; his chief advisor, Cardinal

Francis I © Wonderstock/wonderstock.net

Wolsey, favored France while Katherine maintained strong ties to her nephew, Emperor Charles of Rome.

The Field of the Cloth of Gold was to be a great meeting between two monarchs. In 1520, Wolsey persuaded Henry to forge an alliance with the new king of France, Francis I. Wolsey set up the meeting between the two young kings at a location near Calais, a stretch of unremarkable countryside just outside the English territory in France. Both kings were of similar age and dashing reputations, rivals both personally and politically. The purpose of the meeting was to attain mutual respect and peace between the two enemy countries. Also, the rulers hoped to be thought of as Renaissance princes—princes who chose peace from a position of power.

The meeting began on June 7, 1520, and what followed was indeed a sight to behold. Henry, traveling with his wife and virtually the entire English court, set up camp on one side of the valley in Calais while Francis settled on the other side with his full complement of subjects. The two kings met in the middle. To make sure both nations were on equal footing, the kings' first meeting in the valley was on artificially leveled land, so neither side rose above the other. As both sides prided themselves on the splendor of their courts, no expense was spared in showing off. The camps each occupied more than two acres of land. The silken tents were richly decorated with cloths of gold and precious gems, as were the throngs of courtiers and ladies-in-waiting. There was even a fountain built with three separate spouts for spice wine, water, and claret. Reports claimed that more than 2,200 sheep were consumed in Henry's camp alone. In the fields beyond the castle, tents were erected for less distinguished visitors. Gorgeously clad ladies cheered on knights from each country as jousts and competitions took place amid this exquisite scene. The ostentatious display of wealth and power earned the meeting place between Francis and Henry the title "The Field of the Cloth of Gold."

Lasting for three weeks, the effort to impress and outdo each other placed a tremendous amount of financial strain on both nations. The days were spent in tournaments and banquets, an endless stream of competition between the two countries. At the end, Henry and Francis agreed in principle to an alliance and after Wolsey oversaw a mass for the assembled people, the courts parted ways. It seemed to be a huge success. Yet, only two weeks later, Henry entertained Charles in England and they agreed to not enter into any alliance with France. No one is sure what caused Henry to rethink his position, although some reports indicate that he was embarrassed after losing a wrestling match to Francis. It may have been that he could not abide by an alliance with such a rival, a rival that matched him in splendor and standing. Two years later, Henry declared war on France and his new ally, Emperor Charles, joined in the battle. Then, in 1525, Charles broke his treaty with Henry, which did not help Katherine's already declining standing in the royal court. A treaty was signed with France, starting anew the jockeying among the three nations, which continued for the rest of Henry's reign, and gave fire to Henry's eventual break from the Roman Church.

ANNE BOLEYN:
The Anti-Queen

Whether she knew it or not, Anne Boleyn had been training for her place in history from birth. Her father, Thomas Boleyn, was an ambassador for England, and raised Anne abroad in various foreign courts. At an early age, she joined her older sister in the service of Queen Mary, Henry's younger sister, in the French court. When King Louis died, Mary Boleyn returned to England with Mary Tudor, while Anne became an attendant of Claude, the new French queen. Her stay in France developed her taste for fashion and the arts. After six years, Anne returned to London in 1521, primed to make a huge splash.

Anne became a lady-in-waiting for Katherine in 1522, perhaps at the suggestion of Mary Tudor, who was very close to the queen. A personal romantic upheaval forced Anne to leave the court, and it wasn't until 1526 that Henry finally noticed the woman who would dominate the next ten years of his life.

The surprising aspect about Anne was her appearance, as she was never thought of as the most exquisite woman. She was considered moderately pretty, but not a great beauty. Anne was the opposite of the blonde-haired, blue-eyed, pale image of beauty. She had dark olive skin, thick, dark brown hair, and dark brown eyes, which often appeared black. Those large dark eyes were often singled out in descriptions of Anne. Some rumors suggest that she had six fingers on one hand and a mole or goiter on her neck. These reports may have sprung up after the fact as a way to disparage her character, since Anne was not popular with the English subjects, who had openly favored the solemn piety of Katherine during the annulment case. Plus, the mention of a sixth finger, at the time considered the sign of the devil, didn't appear until the next generation, and it seems highly unlikely that the very particular Henry would overlook such deformities.

Anne's wit and vitality, her skill as a dancer, and her charisma played a crucial part in attracting the king. Her exotic looks certainly helped, and people were intrigued by her eyes, which mesmerized. Anne was everything Katherine was not: feisty, fun, and although religious, not overly pious. Her fashion sense inspired trends within the court, and the more Henry saw of her, the more he wanted her. Anne had learned from her sister Mary's mistake, though. Mary had become a mistress to the king years earlier, tarnishing her reputation and leaving her with nothing. Anne did not want to go through the same process and refused the king's advances. She did not want to be his mistress; she wanted to be his wife. Clearly smitten, Henry showered her with attention and began to pursue an annulment from his wife. Over the course of a few years, Anne's standing in the court rose, as the king clearly favored her over the queen, even before the annulment. They often dined in private and Henry showered her with expensive gifts and wrote her many love letters. After Wolsey's disposal, he moved Anne into the cardinal's vacated apartments. Henry was so blinded by love that even his closest companions were afraid to disparage the situation. His sister Mary, who was close to Katherine, refused to accompany Henry and Anne on a trip to France, and Charles Brandon did voice concern that Anne may have slept with the poet Thomas Wyatt. For the most part, though, they kept their criticisms in check.

Anne Boleyn, 1534 (oil on panel) by English School, (16th century) © Hever Castle, Kent, UK/ The Bridgeman Art Library

As the court case went on without resolution, Anne finally gave in to Henry, physically. She became pregnant and they secretly wed to ensure the child would be legitimate. This forced Henry to break from the church and make himself head of the English Church. Thus he was able to get his annulment and Anne, a commoner, became the new queen of England.

This new union was not looked upon lightly by the English people, who blamed Anne for Katherine's disposal. This was not entirely fair. Although Anne clearly had influence over the king, Henry made his own decisions and steadfastly believed that his marriage to Katherine was a sin. Still, it was easier to blame this manipulative girl than the beloved Tudor king. Henry did not care, as he now had what he wanted: a young wife to bear him an heir, a woman with whom he could grow old. Henry's affection for Anne was real and after she gave birth to a healthy young girl, he was confident she would soon produce his much-desired son. Henry's mistaken marriage to Katherine had been rectified and all had been set right, or so he thought.

After two and half years and two failed pregnancies, Anne's favor with the king was fading. He had rid himself of a wife who couldn't give him a son, and now he was saddled with the same problem. He started doubting this new marriage. When Katherine died, coupled with Anne's final miscarriage, Henry saw an opportunity to start afresh. To do that, Henry decided that Anne could not just live in exile. Henry's fate for her would be much more final, as he realized that if both former queens were no longer alive, the acceptance of his next queen would be much easier. On May 19, 1536, Anne Boleyn was beheaded on charges of adultery, leaving behind one child, Elizabeth. Her daughter, the heir Henry did not want, would eventually sit on the throne for longer than her father, a Boleyn offspring put there by her mother's determination.

The Tower of London

Tower of London © Antiquarian Images

Originally built in 1078, the Tower of London was a fortress, a prison, and a symbol of William the Conqueror's power after seizing the crown. Twenty years after construction began, the tower was completed. Nearly one hundred feet high with walls fifteen feet thick in places, the tower was protected by a wide ditch, stone walls, and the Thames River—all means to keep prisoners from escaping. Inside housed a chapel, apartments, guardrooms, and crypts.

Around 1240, King Henry III made the tower his home, building it up to a beautiful palace. The actual tower remained a prison, home to several imprisoned monarchs over the years. In 1485, King Henry VII took up residence there, the last king and only Tudor to use the tower as a place of residence.

During King Henry VIII's reign, the tower served as both a place of celebration and execution. Henry VIII married Anne Boleyn on May 19, 1533, and for eleven days, the tower hosted partying and feasting. Exactly three years later Anne Boleyn was executed at the tower on her wedding anniversary, along with her brother and three other accused men. Catherine Howard, Henry's fifth wife, also lost her head at the tower. Henry's one-time close advisors Thomas More and Thomas Cromwell were also executed on the Tower Green.

The tower stayed in business after Henry's death. Queen Mary imprisoned Elizabeth there for two months when she felt Elizabeth was a threat to her throne. Elizabeth was released on May 19, 1554, exactly eighteen years after her mother, Anne, was beheaded. Elizabeth spent three more days at the tower for her coronation as queen, left to be crowned at Westminster Abbey, and never returned. In 1603, the year Elizabeth died and the Tudor dynasty ended, the crown jewels were put on display in the tower.

THE MISCONCEPTION OF HENRY VIII

Henry VIII dancing with Anne Boleyn
© Antiquarian Images

The prevailing image of King Henry VIII depicts an overweight, philandering monarch, capable of cruel and atrocious acts to serve his own selfish desires. Yet this crude portrayal does not describe the king—at least not his early years. As the first English monarch to be educated during the Renaissance, Henry was well learned and knew the teachings of the Bible almost as well the pope himself. Not only scholarly, Henry was also an accomplished musician, linguist, and athlete. As he had not been the first in line for the throne, he spent his youth hunting, playing tennis, and jousting. After the death of his brother, the burden of extending the Tudor dynasty fell squarely on his shoulders. As he was a larger-than-life character, a tall sturdy man, his succession to the throne was met with universal acclaim. England excitedly welcomed this energetic and extravagant new king, so different from his serious and miserly father.

Henry brought a new vivaciousness to the court, a spirit of celebration and gaiety. However, one of Henry's first acts as king revealed his darker side. Wanting to gain public approval, Henry beheaded his father's most trusted and ruthless tax collectors on trumped-up treason charges. A popular move at the time, this act foreshadowed his later years when he executed those who got in the way, manipulating the law for his own personal gain.

Although Henry did not take much early interest in politics, he anxiously wanted to make a name for himself. Henry joined forces with Ferdinand to attack France in 1513, hoping to emulate his ancestors Henry V and Edward II. While he was away, the Scots attacked England, led by Henry's brother-in-law, James IV. The Scottish army was defeated and James killed in the battle. Henry returned to England in 1514, after defeating France in the Battle of the Spurs. Frustrated by Ferdinand's dissolution of the English alliance and Katherine's miscarriages, Henry suddenly began to question his marriage. His doubts evaporated, however, when the youthful and antagonistic King Francis succeeded his father, King Louis XII, in France. Ferdinand and Henry, reacting to this new threat, restored their alliance, and Henry had renewed hope for a male issue when Katherine gave birth to Mary.

Henry took his first public mistress, Elizabeth Blount, in 1514. Although Henry had mistresses, a common practice for monarchs of the day, he was, in fact, not the womanizer he was often portrayed as. Actually, he was quite a prude in comparison to his contemporaries.

When taking a mistress, he often remained loyal to her. This held especially true when he courted Anne Boleyn, remaining celibate until finally consummating their relationship after six years.

In 1519, Elizabeth bore him an illegitimate son. To Henry, this proved the problem of issue did not lie with him. Initially, he had loved and respected his queen, but now he wondered if their marriage was a sin against God. His knowledge of the Bible provided his proof, as it stated that any man who married his brother's wife would remain childless. Granted, he had fathered a daughter with Katherine, but Henry regarded Katherine's failure to birth a son a punishment from God. Adamant in his belief, he implored Katherine to accept that their union was unholy and grant him an annulment. She refused, steadfastly denying the charge that she had consummated her relationship with Arthur. Unfazed, Henry decided to pursue the matter in court. Thus began the next chapter in his life: The King's Great Matter. Little did he know this would take many years and lives to settle, costing Henry valuable time to sire an heir.

As the years passed, Henry grew impatient. He longed for the day he could marry Anne, his love, and father the son he knew she would bear him. The delays mounted and the pope refused to grant him his annulment. The frustrated Henry decided on another course of action: If the church would not recognize his situation, then he would no longer recognize the church's authority. He broke from Rome and became the Supreme Head of the Church of England. Thus, in 1533, he obtained his divorce from Katherine and legally married Anne.

By the time the matter was settled, Henry was in his early forties. Pregnant Anne issued him a daughter and then suffered two miscarriages. Betrayed by Anne's failure, Henry had her beheaded and ten days later married Jane Seymour. His new queen, although she never had a coronation, bore him the male he had so long desired. As the sole woman to give him a son, Jane Seymour was the only woman he claimed to truly love. She died shortly after childbirth, leaving behind a far different Henry. He had what he so desperately wanted, but in the process, the young king had been transformed. In his place was the overweight tyrant better known today, the man remembered as a ruthless, bloodthirsty, gluttonous monarch.

Yet, this same man, bright and physically powerful, helped bring England out from underneath the Roman church rule. His personal desires established a more unified country, a country saved from religious civil war. A strengthened England was started on a new course of history. And since his actions stemmed from his singular pursuit for a son, they also led to the great irony of his legacy.

The Great Irony of Henry

King Henry VIII wanted a male heir. Like his father, he believed a woman could not successfully hold the crown. As the last remaining male Tudor, he craved a son to continue on his dynasty. This obsession drove him from wife to wife, all in an effort to have that elusive heir. He had three children in all: Princess Mary, Princess Elizabeth, and Prince Edward. Six wives gave him three surviving children, and only one boy.

When Henry died in 1547, he was succeeded by the son for whom he had strived so hard, King Edward VI, the first Protestant king of England. Only nine years old at the time, Edward ruled until the age of fifteen, dying before he could have any offspring. He was followed by Mary, a devout Catholic, who tried to return England to her mother's religion. She ruled for five years before dying, and Elizabeth, the last of the Tudors, ascended the throne.

Henry's biggest fears were realized. The Tudor dynasty was in the hands of a woman, and she was the last remaining heir. The crown King Henry VII had won and worn would pass to another family, for no woman could successfully rule England. And yet Elizabeth proved a powerful queen, ruling for forty-five years, seven years longer than her father. In that time Elizabeth successfully enforced the religious changes Henry started. Eventually her influence surpassed that of her father as she led England from an impoverished country torn apart by religious squabbles into a golden age of prosperity. When she died in 1603, England was regarded as one of the most powerful and prosperous countries in the world.

Henry's certainty that a daughter could not successfully succeed him had been mistaken. Unfortunately for the Tudor name, Elizabeth's death still ended the dynasty. Having never married, the last of the Tudor monarchs left no successor. There are many theories as to why she remained the virgin queen, but two prevailing thoughts link back to Henry VIII. The first is that she had witnessed the brutal treatment of Henry VIII's wives and forever remembered her mother's unfortunate end. The second is that she knew that she would lose her power and

Queen Elizabeth
© Antiquarian Images

wealth to her husband if she were to wed, and she had no intention of relinquishing her control to any man. Her father's behavior had taught her well. Henry's callous and brutal actions, meant to keep the dynasty intact, eventually caused it to die, on the head of the daughter he did not want.

THE TUDORS

Episode 1

Created and Written by
Michael Hirst

FINAL SHOOTING SCRIPT
July 12, 2006

EXT. DUCAL PALACE - URBINO - DAY

TITLE: URBINO, ITALY

On the ground floor there are raised voices as the English ambassador, EDWARD COURTENAY, EARL OF DEVON, is led inside by two of the duke's officials, BEDOLI and SARTO.

> SARTO
> Mr. Ambassador.

> COURTENAY
> This is really most humiliating, Signore Bedoli.

> BEDOLI
> Prego, Excellency, prego.

> COURTENAY
> What could possibly be so important that you drag me from my bed before seven o'clock in the morning?

> SARTO
> The duke has called an early meeting of the Council. He wanted you to attend.

Ducal SECRETARIES and GUARDS throng the lower floor, but as they mount the grand staircase Courtenay sees a group of armed MEN wearing very different clothes. They part to let him through. The CAPTAIN bows to him.

> CAPTAIN
> Monsieur.

They go on up.

> COURTENAY
> Why are the French here?

                    BEDOLI
               (quietly)
          That is what His Grace wants to talk to
          you about.

                                              CUT TO:

INT. CORRIDOR - DAY
Halfway down the corridor, Courtenay sees the same
group of Frenchmen. He is uneasy as he passes them
and quickens his pace towards the door of the
duke's cabinet.

He is aware that they have fallen in behind him.

                    CAPTAIN
          Excellency.

Courtenay whirls round to face them. The captain
stabs him with a dagger.

He tries to free his sword - but the hilt has
become entangled with his cape. And as he
struggles to free it, he is stabbed again and
again.

                    COURTENAY
          Bastards! You French bastards!

But he is a powerful man, and hampered and wounded
though he is, he drags his assailants this way and
that across the lobby, smearing its marble floor
with blood, while they go on lunging at him with
their daggers.

With a sudden convulsive movement he shakes the
pack loose and stands alone, swaying, blood
pouring from his wounds. He takes a step forward -
and falls headlong to the ground, stone dead.

                                              CUT TO:

EXT. WHITEHALL

Establishing shot.

INT. COURT - WHITEHALL PALACE - LONDON - DAY

The king's secretary, RICHARD PACE, walks through
the court, watched enviously by some of the young
COURTIERS.

He is joined by a man of an older generation,
THOMAS MORE (36), dressed soberly in black.

                    MORE
          Mr. Pace.

                    PACE
          Mr. More.
                    (beat)
          His Majesty wants Council this
          afternoon to be brief.

                    MORE
          Where is the king?

Pace lowers his voice a little.

                    PACE
          He's in seclusion and not to be disturbed.

More knows what he means, frowns with disapproval.
They walk on, through grand rooms.

                    MORE
          How is he?

                    PACE
          With regards to . . . ?

                    MORE
          With regard to Italy. What the French are
          doing in Italy. What other regard is there?

                    PACE
          His Majesty is counselling patience.

                    MORE
          Yes, but you are his secretary. You see
          him every day.

Pace stops, not far from the doors to the king's
private apartments, guarded by YEOMEN OF THE GUARD
armed with long battle axes.

Outside the doors, a milling CROWD OF PETITIONERS wait
impatiently, desperate to gain the king's attention.

Pace speaks confidentially.

                    PACE
          In private he's mad with grief. Almost
          inconsolable.
                    (beat)
          I think you ought to remember it was his
          uncle they murdered!

INT. PRESENCE CHAMBER - DAY

Henry enters. Councillors bow.

Henry is presiding over a meeting of his Council.
The COUNCILLORS - apart from Pace and More - are
the great lords of England, men like the DUKES OF
BUCKINGHAM and NORFOLK, scions of ancient families
with vast wealth and estates.

                    CRIER
          The king.

                    HENRY
          My lords -

CHANCELLOR THOMAS WOLSEY, a man with soft, almost
effeminate features, is dressed in the red robes
of a cardinal.

                    HENRY (cont'd)
                  (he sits)
We meet to consider questions of great
moment. The king of France has demonstrated
to the world his aggressive policies. He's
already overrun five or six city-states in
Italy. He's a threat to every Christian
nation in Europe - yet he bullies the
pope into declaring him Defender of the
Faith!
                  (beat)
On top of that, to prove that nobody can
touch him, he has our ambassador in Urbino -
and my uncle - murdered in cold blood.

There are large murmurs of outrage and disgust
around the room.

                    HENRY (cont'd)
My Lords, I believe these are all just
causes for war.

Now there are even louder mutterings of agreement -
vigorous nodding of heads. Henry turns to
Buckingham. Although he is England's highest-
ranking nobleman, Buckingham - with his fat, red
face - actually looks more like a butcher. Even
so, his clothes are richer, more ostentatious, more
bejewelled than the king's.

                    BUCKINGHAM
                  (proud and haughty)
Your Majesty is certainly right. You have
every reason to prosecute a war. Indeed
I warned you a year ago about French
ambitions - though it has taken this
personal tragedy for Your Majesty to
accept my word!

                    HENRY
Thank you, Lord Buckingham.

Henry frowns at the open criticism, but says nothing
further - looks towards another of his great nobles.

                    HENRY (cont'd)
          Norfolk?

                    NORFOLK
          I agree with my lord Buckingham. The king
          of England has an ancient and historic
          right to the French throne, which the
          Valois have usurped. It's high time we
          kicked them out!

There is some laughter, more nodding of heads.

                    NORFOLK (cont'd)
          We should attack France with all our might.

Henry, quietly pleased, looks slowly around at his
councillors. He pauses at More, but More pretends
to be writing a note.

Henry's gaze finally falls upon his chancellor.

                    HENRY
          What say you, Wolsey?

Wolsey pauses before replying. Buckingham glares at
him with the deepest and most aristocratic disdain.

                    WOLSEY
          I concur with Your Majesty. These are
          indeed just causes.

Henry smiles, claps his hands together.

                    HENRY
          Good!
                    (rising)
          Then it is settled. We are to war with
          France. Your Eminence will make all the
          arrangements.

Wolsey obediently lowers his head.

                    WOLSEY
          Majesty.

                    HENRY
          Now I can go play.

They all bow as Henry quits the chamber. Then the
councillors fall into their own little groups and
cliques, whispering, as they exit.

WOLSEY and MORE remain behind a moment.

                    MORE
          You really think we should go to war?

                    WOLSEY
          I think we should try to do what the king
          wants us to do.

A beat.
                    MORE
          What if the king doesn't know what's in
          his best interest?

                    WOLSEY
          Then we should help him to decide.

Wolsey moves on past.

                                        CUT TO:

INT. HENRY'S BEDCHAMBER - JERICHO - DAY

On a vast bed, in a well-appointed chamber, this
young KING who is "mad with grief" and "almost
inconsolable" is in fact making passionate love to
his latest mistress, the beautiful and blonde
ELIZABETH BLOUNT.

HENRY VIII, King of England, is 25 years old:
tall, athletically built, and extremely handsome:
by reputation "the handsomest prince in
Christendom."

INT. OUTER CHAMBER - JERICHO - DAY

In the very next room, Henry's GROOMS, SERVANTS, and
BODYGUARDS await him. The king is never truly alone.

They can hear very distinctly the creaking of the
wooden bed and Elizabeth's mounting moans of
pleasure - but they sit without expression, as if
they can't hear anything at all.

                                    CUT TO:

INT. HENRY'S BEDCHAMBER - JERICHO - DAY

Passion spent, Henry rolls off. There's a long
beat. She can't speak before he does.

                    HENRY
          How is your husband?

                    ELIZABETH
          My husband is - extremely jealous.

Henry turns towards her, smiles gleefully, puts
his hand back on her breast.

                    ELIZABETH (cont'd)
          He's threatening to make a scandal. He
          says he'll put me in a nunnery.

Henry runs his hand down her taut, naked body.

                    HENRY
          That would be such a waste.

Elizabeth smiles back at him.

40

CUT TO:

EXT. HAMPTON COURT PALACE - DAY

Beyond the pond, the clipped hedges and lawns, and
marble statues, is Wolsey's mellow, redbrick,
clock-towered palace: one of the most beautiful
houses in England.

We see a carriage arriving.

CUT TO:

INT. WOLSEY'S PRIVATE APARTMENT - DAY

Wolsey, as ever in his red robes, his red cardinal's
hat visible behind him, rises from a desk piled with
business and official papers, in his book-lined
chamber.

                    SECRETARY
          His Excellency the French ambassador and
          Bishop Bonnivet.

                    WOLSEY
          Gentlemen, welcome.
                    (beat)
          Your Excellency.

He offers his hand and they both kiss it. He makes
a gesture for them to sit.

                    WOLSEY (cont'd)
          What happened in Urbino - the butchering
          of our ambassador - was most unfortunate -
          especially for me. Your Excellency is
          well aware of my sentiments towards your
          country. I have laboured long and
          consistently in French interests. But -
          how to explain this? The murder of my
          king's uncle.

                    AMBASSADOR
          Frankly it was not done on my master's
          orders. And those that committed the crime
          have been punished.

Wolsey shrugs.

                    WOLSEY
          No. You must understand, we are well
          beyond that. King Henry is a young man.
          He has an appetite for war. And on
          this occasion it will be hard to
          appease him.

                    AMBASSADOR
          Then, by all means - let us have war.

A beat.

                    WOLSEY
          With the greatest respect - you don't mean
          that.

                    BONNIVET
          Well . . . I believe that everything
          humanly possible should be done to avoid a
          war between our two countries. It would do
          England no good to get involved in our
          European squabbles. Far better she stands
          above them. I'm sure Your Eminence has
          ways of pacifying the young lion.

A beat. Wolsey smiles at them.

                                        CUT TO:

INT. REAL TENNIS COURT - DAY

Henry plays "real" tennis with his close friend
CHARLES BRANDON. Brandon is the same age as the
king, physically very similar.

It's a doubles match. Their opponents are two
young men we shall also get to know better -
ANTHONY KNIVERT and WILLIAM COMPTON.

The game they are playing is not like modern
tennis but a fast, more aggressive version, played
with racquets and a hard ball in a confined space.
The ball SLAMS off black-painted walls and sloping
roofs, and there are galleries filled with
SPECTATORS.

Henry and Brandon wear shorts, soft shoes, and
fine-textured shirts, through which their fair
skins glow. They play hard and physical.

                    HENRY
          Play on!

Henry plays a winning shot - to great applause
from the galleries.

                    HENRY (cont'd)
          Our game, I think, Anthony.

                    KNIVERT
          Your Majesty knows we're just letting
          you win!

                    COMPTON
          Actually, I'm playing as hard as I can!

Henry grins.

They start playing again.

                    BRANDON
          Now, there is someone I have to try. Look
          over there: middle gallery, blue dress. See
          her? See that exquisite, virginal face?

                    HENRY
          Who is she?

Brandon CRACKS the ball, unplayably, off three angles. And grins.

                    BRANDON
          She's Buckingham's daughter.

Henry glances up at the sweet face of the girl, then at Buckingham, proud and haughty.

                    HENRY
          A hundred crowns you don't succeed.

                    BRANDON
          Done.

                                        CUT TO:

INT. HENRY'S PRIVATE CHAMBERS - OUTER CHAMBER - DAY

Music is quietly playing.

Buckingham has the honour of serving the king, while Lady Elizabeth Blount serves the queen. They sit at a table beneath a canopy of cloth-of-gold, embroidered with roses and the entwined initials H & K.

The Spanish-born KATHERINE OF ARAGON, once beautiful, is still attractive and dignified, but worn out by constant miscarriages. She picks at her food and waves most of it away. Henry eats with relish.

                    HENRY
          How is our daughter?

                    KATHERINE
               (still with traces of her
                Spanish accent)
          She is well. Her tutors say she has
          exceptional talents, especially for music.
          Your Majesty should be proud.

                    HENRY
        I am. You know I am, Katherine. Mary is
        the pearl of my world.

He gestures. Buckingham, with a bow, presents
another dish: a large fish complete with head,
then moves away. Henry tucks in with his knife and
fingers.

                    KATHERINE
                  (after a beat)
        You have not answered my nephew's letters.

                    HENRY
        Just because your nephew is the king of
        Spain, does he think I have nothing better
        to do?

                    KATHERINE
        You know he advises you to sign a treaty
        with the emperor, recognizing France as
        your mutual enemy.

Henry, his mouth full of fish, doesn't answer.
Katherine is quietly insistent, leaning closer.

                    KATHERINE (cont'd)
        He also advises you not to heed everything
        Wolsey tells you, since Wolsey is so
        biased for the French.

Henry glances at her.

                    HENRY
        Since when are you a diplomat?

                    KATHERINE
        I am my father's daughter!

                    HENRY
        You are my _wife_! You are not my minister,
        you are not my chancellor, but my wife.

A beat. They both smile for the sake of the
watching COURTIERS.

                    KATHERINE
                  (whispers)
            And I should like to be your wife
            in every way. Will you not visit my
            bedchamber, as you used to?

                    HENRY
            Eat.

                                        CUT TO:

INT. HENRY'S BEDCHAMBER - NIGHT

The GROOMS of the bedchamber finish preparing the
king for bed: tying up his nightgown, pulling back
the curtains around the bed, and removing the
warming pans.

A jewelled crucifix is presented to Henry, who
kisses it devoutly, crosses himself.

A silver bowl of fruit is offered to him. Henry
picks out a pomegranate and slices it in half. For
a moment he stares at the rich, moist, ruby flesh
inside, plump with glistening seeds. It reminds
him of nothing so much as a -

                    HENRY
            Gown.

As Henry sucks out the fruit with relish, the
servants busy themselves again, fetching a
dressing gown, taking flaming torches from the
walls. A hidden door is opened into the secret
passage that connects Henry's private apartments
to Katherine's.

                                        CUT TO:

46

INT. PASSAGE - NIGHT

By the light of the flickering torches, Henry
walks through the passage.

                                        CUT TO:

INT. QUEEN'S PRIVATE BEDCHAMBER - NIGHT

Taken by surprise, the queen's LADIES OF THE
BEDCHAMBER hurry to greet the king. They curtsy low
and flustered. Among them is LADY JANE HOWARD. Up
close she seems even younger, and more beautiful,
her skin milky white, her hair tousled, her pert
young breasts easing from her dress.

                    HENRY
          Where is the queen?

                    LADY JANE
          Her Majesty is still at prayer, Your Majesty.

A beat. Henry stares at her. He's changed his mind.

                    HENRY
          Tell Her Majesty that I came to offer my
          love and devotion, as her true husband.

                    LADY JANE
          Yes, Your Majesty.

Henry turns away, but as he does so he catches the
eye of one of his SERVANTS, who understands
immediately. As Henry withdraws, the servant goes
over and whispers something into Lady Jane's ear.

                                        CUT TO:

INT. CHAPEL ROYAL - NIGHT

Alone in the small beautiful chapel, filled with
candles and icons, Katherine kneels on the stone

floor, as she does for hours each day. On the altar before her is an image of the Holy Virgin holding the baby Jesus in her arms.

                                        CUT TO:

INT. HENRY'S BEDCHAMBER - NIGHT

Lady Jane is escorted into Henry's bedchamber. She curtsys. With a gesture, Henry dismisses his servants then gently lifts her.

                    HENRY
          Jane.

                    LADY JANE
          Your Majesty.

                    HENRY
          Do you consent?

                    LADY JANE
          Yes, Your Majesty.

Henry touches and kisses her, gently, her mouth, cheek, and throat. As she arches back he tears open the front of her gown and kisses her breasts.

Lady Jane sighs.

                                        CUT TO:

EXT. TILTYARD - DAY

A fallen rider is lifted off the ground by three STRONG MEN.

Henry and Katherine sit under a coloured awning, watching the jousters with several of her LADIES.

ANNOUNCER
Charles Brandon is entering the list.

Trumpets announce Brandon's arrival in the list.
He rides up to the dais on which Henry and
Katherine are sitting. He bows to the queen.

BRANDON
Your Majesties.

Then his eyes search: settle on Lady Jane a
moment, pass on . . . settle again on Buckingham's
daughter, ANNA.

BRANDON (cont'd)
My lady Buckingham, would you do me the
honour of letting me wear your favours
today?

Anna appears to hesitate, blushes . . . then
shyly nods, stands up and gives Brandon a piece
of material dyed with her colours.

ANNOUNCER
Charles Brandon, jousting against Lord
Hallam.

Brandon and Hallam face each other astride their
horses.

CLOSE ON: Anna Buckingham.

A pageboy lowers a flag - the riders charge
towards each other.

Lord Hallam is knocked to the ground.

Applause.

ANNOUNCER (cont'd)
A match between Lord Buckingham and the
duke of Cornwall.

The pageboy lowers the flag once again.

The riders charge towards each other.
With the splintering crash of Buckingham's lance,
the Duke of Cornwall is thrown to the ground.

Bloodied, the duke is carried off the field.

CUT TO:

INT. WOLSEY'S CHAMBER - HAMPTON COURT PALACE - NIGHT

Wolsey with the two Frenchmen, eating dinner.

> AMBASSADOR
> Does Your Eminence have a plan? A way to
> avoid war?

Wolsey pushes a sheaf of papers across the table.

> WOLSEY
> This is the outline of a new peace treaty
> uniting the English with the French.

The ambassador reaches for the paper.

> AMBASSADOR
> May I?

Wolsey stops him.

> WOLSEY
> No. I want you to take it away and read
> it very carefully. I believe it represents
> something new in the world of diplomacy.
> If your king accepts it, in principle, he
> can sign without any loss of face. Indeed,
> he can rejoice. My master can rejoice. We
> can all - rejoice.

A beat. The ambassador lightly touches the
document, as if it were a poisoned chalice.

50

                    AMBASSADOR
          In which case - what does Your Eminence
          want in return?

                      WOLSEY
          Nothing.

                    AMBASSADOR
          Nothing?!

                      WOLSEY
          Nothing from you.

Wolsey looks at the bishop.

                  WOLSEY (cont'd)
          What I want, Your Grace . . . only you
          can give me.

                                        CUT TO:

EXT. TILTYARD - DAY

Cheers and applause.

Once more the Black Knight - Buckingham - enters
the list.

                    ANNOUNCER
          Lord Buckingham has entered the list.

Henry's friends Knivert and Compton. watch on
horseback.

                      KNIVERT
          He's won ten courses already! What is he
          trying to prove?

                      COMPTON
          I'm going to take him.

                                                  51

                    BRANDON
          No. I will. I'd love to damage
          Buckingham's pride.

Trumpet fanfare.

                    ANNOUNCER
          The king will face Lord Buckingham.

Henry rides into the list. The very appearance of
the king of England, in armour, on horseback, in
the flesh . . . elicits an audible thrill of
excitement, a gathering of breath, an expectancy.

As Henry rides over to the dais, Compton leans
closer to Brandon.

                    COMPTON
          Here we go again.

                    BRANDON
          Claim or no claim, Buckingham is not
          the king.

                    COMPTON
          Not all of the court is as loyal as
          you, Charles.

Henry approaches the dais, stops in front of
Katherine, and bows.

                    HENRY
          My lady.

Katherine smiles, walks over to him . . . and ties
her colours to his lance. At the same time, out of
the corner of his eye, Henry catches Lady Jane's eye.

But he bows once more to Katherine, canters back
to the end of the list. Both he and Buckingham are
given their shields and helmets.

Henry puts on his helmet and closes the visor. The crowd roars. Buckingham's horse hurtles towards Henry's.

An EXPLOSION of NOISE, a sickening sound of high-speed collision, a lurching, shattering . . . like some high-speed auto crash.

Applause.

Henry's lance is shattered and he throws it aside. Buckingham is lying on the ground. The people are cheering. He rides back, watches as Buckingham's PAGES remove his helmet, sit him upright.

Henry stares down at him for a moment, without a word - then rides off to enjoy his triumph.

CUT TO:

EXT. RIVER THAMES - DAY

It's a beautiful summer's day. The king's ornate barge is rowed upstream from Whitehall to Chelsea, a small village outside the city walls.

Villagers in a small rowboat suddenly become aware of what is passing in front of them: a barge with liveried OARSMEN beating time, with the royal flags fluttering, and the king himself sitting beneath a canopy of red and gold.

They lower their heads in respect and reverence.

CUT TO:

EXT. MORE'S HOUSE AND LANDING STAGE - CHELSEA - DAY

Thomas More and his extended FAMILY await the arrival of the royal barge at his private landing stage. As the boat docks, Henry leaps ashore and embraces More with obvious affection.

                    HENRY
          Thomas.

                    MORE
          Your Majesty.

More indicates the large gathering.

                    MORE (cont'd)
          This is my family. My wife, Alice.
                    (to his wife)
          Alice, won't you kiss the king?

Alice, a rather plain woman, comes hesitantly forward, but kisses Henry on the mouth, in the English fashion.

                    HENRY
          Mistress Alice.

                    ALICE
          Your Majesty.

                    HENRY
                    (to More)
          Shall we walk by the river, Thomas? I like walking.

More smiles, indicates the path. They walk on together.

                    HENRY (cont'd)
          Why won't you come and live at court?

                    MORE
          You know perfectly well why: I don't like it. My legal practice and my life are here. The court is for more ambitious men.

A beat.

                    HENRY
You didn't say much in Council last month.

                    MORE
About what?

                    HENRY
Going to war with France.

More is silent a while. The wide river slips past.

                    MORE
As a humanist I have an abhorrence of war.
It's an activity fit only for beasts - yet
practiced by no kind of beast so constantly
as by man.

A beat.

                    HENRY
As a humanist I share your opinion. As a
king I am forced to disagree.

More smiles a little.

                    MORE
Spoken like a lawyer.

                    HENRY
You should know. You taught me!

                    MORE
Not well enough, it seems.

                    HENRY
Are you finished?

                    MORE
Yes!
          (calls out)
Harry!

The king pauses, surprised. More catches up to him.

> MORE (cont'd)
> Instead of spending ruinous amounts of
> money on war, I think you should spend it
> on the welfare of your people.

Henry nods.

> HENRY
> Thomas, I swear to you I intend to be a
> just ruler. But tell me this: Why is
> Henry V remembered? Because he endowed
> universities and built alm houses for the
> destitute? No. He is remembered because
> he won the Battle of Agincourt. Three
> thousand English bowmen against sixty
> thousand French. The flower of French
> chivalry destroyed in four hours. That
> victory made him famous, Thomas. It made
> him immortal!

And More, sadly, bites his lip and looks back at
Henry.

> CUT TO:

INT. COURT - NIGHT

A crowded court. Buckingham and Norfolk observe
it. Buckingham is drunk.

> BUCKINGHAM
> He has no right to any of this.
> His father seized the crown on the
> battlefield; he had no real claim to
> it, only through a bastard on his
> mother's side.

> NORFOLK
> Your Grace's family is more ancient.

                         BUCKINGHAM
         I am a direct descendant of Edward II.
         This is my crown, and this is my court.
         Not his crown or his court.

Norfolk looks around carefully.

                         NORFOLK
         That's treason, Your Grace.

                         BUCKINGHAM
         It's the truth. And one day we shall make
         it come true.

He looks at Norfolk, who doesn't deny it.
Buckingham smiles, and moves away.

As he walks through the court, COURTIERS bow and
ostentatiously make way for him. One or two even
lean forward to kiss his hand. Buckingham, this
glittering figure, is like a king in waiting.

                                              CUT TO:

**INT. BUCKINGHAM'S PRIVATE APARTMENTS - WHITEHALL
PALACE - NIGHT**

No sooner is BUCKINGHAM inside, when he hears the
VERY LOUD sounds of lovemaking from an adjoining
room.

A beat. Then Buckingham throws open the doors.

On the bed, Brandon is making love, doggie-
fashion, to Anna, Buckingham's daughter.

                         BUCKINGHAM
             What is this? Brandon!

                         BRANDON
         This is what it looks like - Your Grace.

                    BUCKINGHAM
          You have violated my daughter.

                    BRANDON
          No. No, she begged.

                    BUCKINGHAM
                (drawing his sword)
          You've taken her honour.

                    BRANDON
          I swear to Your Grace I have not. Someone
          else was there before me.

The girl can't help laughing. Buckingham is
puce.

                    BUCKINGHAM
          Son of a whore.

Brandon meets his gaze squarely.

                    BRANDON
          Yes, that is true, Your Grace.

                    BUCKINGHAM
          I should kill you for this.

Buckingham lowers his sword.

                    BUCKINGHAM (cont'd)
          Get out.

Brandon leaves.

Buckingham walks over to the bed. He hits Anna so
hard in the face that her nose explodes with
blood.

                                        CUT TO:

INT. WOLSEY'S CHAMBER - HAMPTON COURT PALACE - DAY

Wolsey works at his desk, carrying on the affairs of state while his master sports, a couple of lean dogs at his feet.

                    SECRETARY
          Eminence - Lady Blount is here.

A beat. Wolsey seems irritated then nods.

                    WOLSEY
          Very well.

Elizabeth is shown in, curtsys.

                    ELIZABETH
          Your Eminence.

                    WOLSEY
          What can I do for you, Lady Blount?

A beat. She is somewhat unnerved.

                    ELIZABETH
          I am - with child, Your Eminence.

                    WOLSEY
          Yes . . .

                    ELIZABETH
          It is - His Majesty's child.

Wolsey is suddenly all attention. Puts down his quill. Looks at her searchingly.

                    WOLSEY
          You are certain?

                    ELIZABETH
          Yes.

A beat. Wolsey thinks.

                    WOLSEY
          Have you told the king?

She shakes her head.

                    WOLSEY (cont'd)
          Good. I will inform His Majesty in due
          time. But for the time being you will say
          nothing to anybody - on pain of death. Do
          you understand?

A beat. She nods.

                    WOLSEY (cont'd)
          When you are no longer able to hide your
          condition, you will be removed to a
          private place for your lying-in. There
          you can give birth to your bastard.

A beat. He's finished.

                    ELIZABETH
          Thank you, Your Eminence.

Wolsey is once more writing his correspondence.
Elizabeth quietly leaves his chamber.

                                        CUT TO:

EXT. WHITEHALL PALACE - DAY

Wolsey rides on a mule into the palace grounds,
just as Christ rode a mule to enter Jerusalem. But
there the (deliberate) comparison ends. Christ
came in poverty. Wolsey is preceded by two CROSS
BEARERS on horseback bearing aloft two silver
crucifixes, and followed by four liveried FOOTMEN
carrying gilt poleaxes. And his mule is decked out
in velvet cloth!

But he makes a great impression and creates a great stir, drawing CROWDS OF PEOPLE who stare in awe at the chancellor of England.

CUT TO:

INT. COURT - DAY

Holding an orange hollowed out with spices and herbs to his nose, to protect him against the stench of humanity, Wolsey proceeds through the palace. Hordes of PETITIONERS swarm around him, his SERVANTS pushing them back, his USHER walking in front.

> USHERS
> (shouting)
> Oh my lords and masters, make way for His Lord's Grace. Make way for His Eminence, Cardinal Wolsey!

Still the petitioners wave their suits in his face and call out beseechingly:

> PETITIONER 1
> Eminence, I beg you, read my petition!

> PETITIONER 2
> Read mine, for pity's sake!

> PETITIONER 3
> All I ask, sir, is justice! For the love of Christ, for my poor wife and children, I beg Your Eminence . . . Please, sir . . .

Among them, we see a spotty youth: starved and ill, he is still too reticent to thrust himself forward.

Wolsey is joined by Pace, as the anguished petitioners are kept back.

                    WOLSEY
                   (quietly)
          Mr. Pace, I trust you are keeping a good
          eye on my interests?

                    PACE
          Of course, Your Eminence. Like an eagle.

                    WOLSEY
          I don't want an eagle, Mr. Pace. They can
          soar too high. Be a pigeon - shit on
          everything!

                    PACE
          Yes, Eminence.

Wolsey moves on.

                    WOLSEY
          Where is the king?

                    PACE
          Out hunting.

                    WOLSEY
          Good. It keeps him in good humour. Send
          word when he returns.

                    PACE
          Yes, Eminence.

Pace bows as Wolsey walks away. The petitioners
continue to call out. Pace looks over - and for
some reason recognizes the spotty youth. He
signals to him. Looks him up and down.

                    PACE (cont'd)
          What is it you want?

The youth fumbles inside his shirt.

                    YOUTH
        I - I have letters of introduction sir. I -

He pulls them out, hands them over. Pace, almost
suspiciously, regards them.

                    PACE
        But - these are from the dean of
        Canterbury Cathedral!

The youth lowers his eyes in embarrassment.

                    YOUTH
        Yes, sir.

                    PACE
        Why did you not present yourself?

The young man just looks back at him shyly.

                                        CUT TO:

EXT. COUNTRYSIDE - DAY

Henry's hunting party roams the countryside.

INT. CHAPEL ROYAL - PALACE - DAY

The shy youth is ushered into the small chapel,
where a group of YOUNG CHORISTERS are rehearsing,
under their master, WILLIAM CORNISH. The sacred
music contrasts with the violence of the field.

Cornish's attention is drawn to the new arrival.
With some irritation he stops the rehearsal, walks
over - is given the letters. Is surprised, looks
at the spotty youth.

                    CORNISH
        Thomas Tallis.

                    TALLIS
        Yes, sir.

                    CORNISH
        And you can play, it says, the organ
        and the flute, and can sing more than
        moderately well.

Tallis flushes with desperate embarrassment.

                    CORNISH (cont'd)
        Anything else?

A beat.

                    TALLIS
        Yes, sir. I - I compose a little.

                    CORNISH
            Indeed. Well, if the dean commends your
        talents - we shall have to see, won't we?

                                        CUT TO:

INT. HENRY'S PRIVATE CHAMBERS - OUTER CHAMBER - NIGHT

Henry with Wolsey and More. Henry, loose-limbed,
relaxed, bites into an apple, walks around.

Of course, such big spaces at night are jet-black -
only fitfully, here and there, lit by candles, like
pools of light into which Henry comes and goes.

                    HENRY
        Thomas.

                    WOLSEY
            I trust Your Majesty enjoyed hunting today.

Henry nods, amiably. Moves briefly into a pool of
light.

                         HENRY
          How are the preparations going?

                         WOLSEY
          Very well. Both your army and fleet are
          assembling. Provisions and stores are
          being laid in. You could go to war in a
          matter of weeks.

Henry beams.

                         HENRY
          Excellent. I knew I could depend on you.

                         WOLSEY
          I am grateful to Your Majesty.

A beat. Wolsey, always a great actor, seems to
hesitate.

                         HENRY
          What is it?

                         WOLSEY
          Your Majesty, wars are expensive. To pay
          for them you must raise taxes. That's not
          always popular.
                    (beat)
          What if Your Majesty could gain more power
          and prestige by other means?

                         HENRY
          Other means?

                         WOLSEY
          Peaceful means.

Henry pulls a face.

                         HENRY
          What! No battles? No glory?

He glances at More, who in turn glances at WOLSEY.
They are in this together!

                    MORE
          I think Your Majesty should hear him out.

Henry sits down with obvious reluctance, and nods.

                    WOLSEY
          In the past few weeks, I have conducted,
          on Your Majesty's behalf, an intense
          round of diplomatic talks. Not just with
          the French ambassador - also with
          representatives of the emperor, with
          envoys from Denmark, Portugal, the
          Italian states . . .

                    HENRY
          What for?

                    WOLSEY
          To make a treaty.

Beat.

                    HENRY
          What kind of treaty?

                    WOLSEY
                 (after a pause)
          A Treaty of Universal and Perpetual Peace.

Henry, despite himself, is intrigued. Gets back to
his feet, and paces around again.

                    HENRY
          How is it to be effected?

                    WOLSEY
          In several stages. In the first place
          there will be a summit meeting between the
          kings of France and England. At the

summit, Your Majesty's daughter will be
betrothed formally to the French Dauphin.
And at the end of the summit, you will
both sign the treaty.

                    MORE
The treaty is entirely new in the history
of Europe, committing all its signatories
to the principle of collective security
and universal peace.

                    HENRY
How would it be enforced?

                    WOLSEY
Should any of the signatory countries suffer
aggression, all the others would immediately
demand that the aggressor withdraws. If he
refuses, within one month all the rest would
declare against him . . . and continue until
peace is restored.

                    MORE
The treaty also envisages the creation of
pan-European institutions.

HENRY mulls it over.

                    HENRY
In some ways I like it. I recognize
it . . .
          (looks at More)
And so do you, Thomas.

                    MORE
Indeed.

                    HENRY
It's the application of humanist principles
to international affairs.
          (beat)
Your Eminence is to be congratulated.

                        WOLSEY
        I don't seek praise. Your Majesty will be
        known as the architect of a new and modern
        world. That would be reward enough.

                        HENRY
        Always be assured of our love.

Wolsey beams. HENRY, in good spirits, claps MORE
on the back, as a nervous GROOM enters.

                        HENRY (cont'd)
            What is it?

                        GROOM
        Your Majesty, the duke of Buckingham
        insists upon an audience.

Henry pauses, grimaces - then reluctantly nods.

                        HENRY
        Your Grace.

                        BUCKINGHAM
        Your Majesty ought to be made aware that I
        have discovered Mr. Charles Brandon in
        flagrante delicto with my daughter.

Henry looks at him.

                        BUCKINGHAM (cont'd)
        Mr. Brandon has brought shame to my
        family. I demand that Your Majesty banish
        him from court - with whatever other
        punishment Your Majesty sees fit.

Henry rises.

                        HENRY
        There will be no punishment. Unless your
        daughter accuses Mr. Brandon of raping
        her. Does she so claim?

A long beat. Buckingham struggles with his anger.

                    HENRY (cont'd)
          Does your daughter claim that Mr. Brandon
          raped her?

                    BUCKINGHAM
          She doesn't need to. The offence is
          against me and against my family.

                    HENRY
          As far as I know, there has been no
          offence. So there is no need for any
          punishment.

A long beat. Still Buckingham struggles with his
emotions. Then briefly bows.

                    BUCKINGHAM
          Your Majesty.

                    HENRY
          Your Grace.

And walks out. More and Wolsey emerge from the
shadows.

                    MORE
          Be careful of Buckingham, Harry. He may
          well be stupid, but he is richer than you
          are, and he can call upon a private army.
                    (beat)
          Not even your father crossed him.

Henry looks back at him and Wolsey.

                                        CUT TO:

INT. CORRIDOR - COURT - NIGHT

Wolsey walking in company with Bishop Bonnivet
down a shadowy corridor. They speak quietly.

                    WOLSEY
          I'm very happy that the king of France
          has agreed to sign the treaty and to
          host the summit.

                    BONNIVET
          His Majesty is delighted there will
          be no war. As we all are.

                    WOLSEY
          What about the other matter we
          discussed?

A beat.

                    BONNIVET
          Which - other matter, Your Eminence?

Wolsey stops - and with surprising strength
suddenly seizes the bishop and SLAMS him against
the wall.

                    WOLSEY
          I saved your master's arse. I want my
          reward. And you can arrange it. Do you
          understand?

Bonnivet nods.

                                        CUT TO:

INT. BEDCHAMBER - BRANDON'S CHAMBERS - NIGHT

Brandon gently examines the scar on Anna's nose.

                    BRANDON
          Poor you.
                    (beat)
          Now - where were we, when we were so
          rudely interrupted?

His hand begins to trace her body. She moans a
little, excitedly . . . fearfully.

                    ANNA
                  (whispers)
         Charles, we shouldn't! My father will
         kill you!

Brandon lifts her skirts.

                    BRANDON
         Then I shall die a happy man.

                                        CUT TO:

INT. MORE'S HOUSE - CHELSEA - NIGHT

Holding candles, More's CHILDREN - a BOY, two
NATURAL DAUGHTERS, and an ADOPTED DAUGHTER, all
teenagers - come forward to wish their father good
night. Smiling, he embraces them in turn.

                    MORE
         Now, have you all finished your reading?

                    CHILDREN
                  (one by one)
         Yes, Father.

                    MORE
         Very well. May God and his angels bless
         you and keep you this night - and always.
                  (turns to his wife)
         Good night. Good night, children.

Alice curtsys to her husband, moves away with her
children.

More enters his closet.

                                        CUT TO:

INT. MORE'S CLOSET - CHELSEA - NIGHT

The small room is more like a monk's spartan cell
than a bedroom. It is dominated by the silver

crucifix, which glows in the candlelight. There is
an iron cot, a wooden table, a washstand.

More removes his shirt - and reveals beneath it
the filthy, lice-ridden hair-shirt which he never
takes off. The skin around it is lacerated and
raw, with weeping wounds.

More kneels down to pray.

                                          CUT TO:

EXT. WHITEHALL PALACE - ESTABLISHING - DAY

INT. HENRY'S PRIVATE CHAMBERS - OUTER CHAMBER - DAY

Henry being shaved by his BARBER, while at the
same time dictating a letter to Pace.

                    PACE
          Your letter to King Francis, Your Majesty.

                    HENRY
          My dearest royal cousin . . . No. Make
          that - My beloved cousin. We send you our
          love. We love you so much it would be
          impossible to love you better.

A beat. He catches Pace's eye . . . and the
suggestion of a grin.

                    HENRY (cont'd)
          Make all necessary arrangements so we may
          meet face to face. Nothing is now closer
          or more dear to my heart than this Treaty
          of Universal Peace.

He pauses to let the barber shave under his chin.

                    HENRY (cont'd)
          As a token of my good will, my commitment
          to this treaty, and my love for Your
          Majesty, I have decided . . .

He pauses again to let the barber finish and gently wipe his face. Then Henry strokes his clean-shaven jaw reflectively.

> HENRY (cont'd)
> . . . I have decided - I have decided not to shave again until we meet. My beard will be a token of universal friendship, of the love between us.

CUT TO:

INT. WOLSEY'S CHAMBER - HAMPTON COURT PALACE - DAY

Bishop Bonnivet kisses Wolsey's hand.

> BONNIVET
> I have some news for Your Eminence. His Holiness, Pope Alexander, is desperately ill. It cannot be long before he is summoned to God's House.

Wolsey crosses himself, mutters an invocation.

> BONNIVET (cont'd)
> In view of Your Eminence's well-known piety, as well as your great learning and diplomatic skills - I can assure Your Eminence of the support of the French cardinals at the conclave to elect a successor. With the votes of your own cardinals - and if it is pleasing to God - you will be elected pope, bishop of Rome - our new Holy Father.

Wolsey's face somehow manages to express his total satisfaction. Nevertheless, he crosses himself devoutly again.

> WOLSEY
> Thank you, Your Grace. You make me feel truly humble.

CUT TO:

INT. QUEEN'S PRIVATE BEDCHAMBER - PALACE - NIGHT

Katherine is undressed by two of her ladies -
Elizabeth Blount and Lady Jane. As they unfasten
each article of clothing (dresses were made up of
many interchangeable parts), she catches their
eyes - but says nothing. Maybe she knows, and
maybe she doesn't. But her feminine intuition
probably tells her something.

Elizabeth moves away from her, suddenly has a
stomach cramp. She touches her stomach - and
Katherine sees her doing it.

                    KATHERINE
          Are you ill, Lady Blount?

                    ELIZABETH
          No, Your Majesty.

She moves away.

                    KATHERINE
          No, stay.

Elizabeth turns, curtsys again. Katherine
indicates that she can kneel beside her, and
dismisses Lady Jane.

There's a long beat.

                    KATHERINE (cont'd)
          I have not talked to anyone for a long
          time. Cardinal Wolsey dismissed my Spanish
          confessor and most of my Spanish ladies,
          in case they were spies. And I cannot
          trust my English confessor.

A beat. She plays with her rosary.

74

KATHERINE (cont'd)
But I can trust you, though, can I not,
Lady Blount?

ELIZABETH
(after a beat)
Yes, Madam.

KATHERINE
What is my sadness? It is this: that I
cannot give the king a living son. I gave
birth to a baby boy once . . . a sweet
boy . . . but he died in my arms, after
just four weeks of life.

She pauses, overcome.

KATHERINE (cont'd)
The king blames me. I know. He thinks it
all my fault! He does not know how much I
suffer, how much I pray . . .

Katherine weeps bitter tears. Elizabeth cannot
watch, and lowers her eyes.

CUT TO:

INT. CONFESSIONAL - NIGHT

Henry sits alone in the small and dark confessional.
He looks very somber. This is a different Henry, not
just thoughtful but troubled.

HENRY
I have been thinking about my brother.
Arthur. He died. It was decided that I
should marry Katherine. I think my father
didn't want to lose the dowry. Or the
prestige of a Spanish marriage. In any
case, Katherine swore the marriage was
never consummated. That's why a papal
dispensation was granted.

In the darkness, Henry can hear the soft, close breathing of the priest.

> HENRY (cont'd)
> So I married her. And since then we have had five stillborn children, a boy who lived for twenty-six days, and a single living daughter.

Another pause. There is real pain in Henry's eyes.

> HENRY (cont'd)
> What if their marriage was consummated?

> PRIEST
> She has sworn before God that it was not.

> HENRY
> What does it say in the Gospels? If a man should marry his brother's wife . . .
>   (beat)
> Tell me!

> PRIEST
> In Leviticus it says: "If a man marries his brother's wife, they will die childless."
>   (beat)
> But you have a child.

> HENRY
> But not a son! I have no son.

                                    CUT TO:

INT. BUCKINGHAM'S CHAMBERS - OUTER CHAMBER - PALACE - DAY

One of Buckingham's RETAINERS - a man called HOPKINS - accompanies Boleyn as he walks through the duke's gilded rooms. He passes Anna, who is reading a book, a bandage over her nose. She turns away self-consciously.

Hopkins finds his master.

                    HOPKINS
          Sir Thomas Boleyn, Your Grace.

Buckingham makes a languid gesture. Boleyn walks
in, bows, and kisses his hand.

                    BUCKINGHAM
          Sir Thomas. I hope you didn't find my
          invitation presumptuous. I heard you had
          been recalled from France.

                    BOLEYN
          I'm here for a short while, Your Grace.

                    BUCKINGHAM
          They tell me you are an excellent
          ambassador.

                    BOLEYN
          Then, whoever they are, they are very kind.

There's a pause. Buckingham dismisses Hopkins and
his other SERVANTS with a gesture.

                    BUCKINGHAM
          You come from an old family.

                    BOLEYN
          Though not as ancient, nor as grand, as
          Your Grace's.

                    BUCKINGHAM
          The king chooses to surround himself with
          commoners, men of no distinction, new men,
          without pedigree or titles. How does that
          help the prestige of his crown?

                    BOLEYN
                 (in dangerous waters)
          Your Grace, I -

                    BUCKINGHAM
     His father only acquired the crown by
     force - not by right!

                    BOLEYN
     Your Grace, no one wants to return to the
     evil days of civil war. What is done is
     done. The king is the king.

A long beat. Buckingham searches Boleyn's eyes.
Plays his games.

                    BUCKINGHAM
     The king is the king.
                (beat)
     Wolsey. A man of the cloth with a mistress
     and two children. How do you like this
     fellow?

Boleyn seems relieved to be let off the hook.

                    BOLEYN
     Not at all.

Buckingham smiles.

                    BUCKINGHAM
     We shall talk again.

                                        CUT TO:

INT. PRIVATE CHAMBERS - OUTER CHAMBER - EVENING

Henry and Boleyn sit opposite each other at a
table, playing chess.

                    HENRY
     Tell me about King Francis, Sir Thomas.

                    BOLEYN
     He is twenty-three years old.

                    HENRY
          Is he tall?

                    BOLEYN
          Yes.
                    (beat)
          But ill-proportioned.

He moves a pawn.

                    HENRY
          How about his legs? Are his calves strong,
          like mine?

                    BOLEYN
          Majesty, <u>no one</u> has calves like yours.

                    HENRY
          Is he handsome?

                    BOLEYN
          Some people might think so. He certainly
          thinks so himself.

                    HENRY
          He's vain?

                    BOLEYN
          Your Majesty - he's <u>French</u>!

They both laugh.

                    HENRY
          What about his court?

                    BOLEYN
          It has a reputation for loose morals and
          licentiousness, which the king, by his own
          behaviour, does nothing to dispel.

                    HENRY
          You have two daughters, Sir Thomas. How do
          you protect them?

                        BOLEYN
        I keep a watchful eye on them. But I also
        trust in their goodness and virtue.

He moves a pawn to block the bishop. Henry looks
at him.

                        HENRY
        You will return immediately to Paris. I am
        entrusting you with all the diplomatic
        negotiations for the summit.

Boleyn inclines his head.

A beat. Henry nods. Moves his knight.

                        HENRY (cont'd)
        Checkmate.

                                            CUT TO:

INT. COURT - DAY

Henry strides through the court accompanied by
COURTIERS and SERVANTS.

The doors to the queen's private chambers open,
and a dark-haired, very pretty LITTLE GIRL of
about six emerges, with her GOVERNESS.

                        HENRY
        Mary!

                        MARY
        Papa.

                        HENRY
        Aren't you beautiful? Aren't you the most
        beautiful girl in the world?

He hugs and kisses her, and Mary smiles and kisses
him back, much to everyone's delight.

                    MARY
            I don't know.

                    HENRY
            Yes, you are. How do you feel?

                    MARY
            Well.

                    HENRY
            Well? Papa's busy.

Then Henry hands her back to her governess.

                    HENRY (cont'd)
            Be good. Do everything you are told.

Katherine has also appeared.

                    KATHERINE
                  (quietly)
            May we speak?

                    HENRY
            Continue, my lady.

                                        CUT TO:

INT QUEEN'S PRIVATE CHAMBERS - OUTER CHAMBER - DAY

Katherine and Henry enter. Katherine's ladies
curtsy, exit.

                    KATHERINE
            I don't like it.

                    HENRY
            What don't you like?

                    KATHERINE
            Your beard.

Henry grins ruefully, touches the result of
several days' growth.

                    KATHERINE (cont'd)
          Nor what it represents.

                    HENRY
                (warning)
          Katherine.

                    KATHERINE
          You are giving my daughter away to the
          dauphin and to France. You did not even
          consult me. The Valois are the sworn
          enemies of my family.

                    HENRY
          She is mine to do with as I see fit. It
          is a great marriage.

                    KATHERINE
          I see Wolsey's hand behind this. Though I
          love Your Majesty, and am loyal to you in
          every way, I cannot disguise my distress
          and unhappiness.

Henry looks at her, rather coldly.

                    HENRY
          Well, you're going to have to.

                                        CUT TO:

EXT. FRANCE - ESTABLISHING - DAY

INT. CHAMBER - AMBASSADOR'S HOUSE - PARIS - DAY

A FRENCH SERVANT greets Boleyn as he enters.

                    SERVANT
          Bonjour, Ambassador. Il y a des messages
          pour vous. Une demande d'une audience avec
          le roi.

                    BOLEYN
        Très bien. Merci -
             (calling out)
        Where are my daughters?

Continuing onward, he enters a room. Two young
women approach him excitedly.

                    BOLEYN (cont'd)
        I have some exciting news. There is to be
        a summit between King Francis and King
        Henry near Calais. I am to arrange it.
             (beat)
        That means you will both have the
        opportunity to meet the king of England!

Boleyn looks at the first girl, hands her a glass.

                    BOLEYN (cont'd)
        Mary.

Then turns to Mary's sister, a younger girl with
dark hair and compelling eyes.

                    BOLEYN (cont'd)
        . . . and Anne. Boleyn. To your futures!

Anne Boleyn smiles.

                                        CUT TO:

**INT. HENRY'S PRIVATE CHAMBERS - OUTER CHAMBER -
PALACE - DAY**

Henry, is being fitted for a suit by his TAILOR.

The fabrics are beautiful, expensive, and richly
coloured. Many have jewels sewn into them.

                    SERVANT
             (announcing)
        His Eminence Cardinal Wolsey.

Wolsey enters, bows. Henry gestures him over.

                    HENRY
          I want your opinion. Do you like this cloth?

                    WOLSEY
          I think it suits Your Majesty very well.
          Perhaps, I might suggest - with these.

He picks out some accessories carefully - gloves,
shoes, chain, and then an over-jacket lined with
black fur. Henry is pleased.

                    HENRY
          Do you think Francis will have anything as
          fine as these?

                    WOLSEY
          Only if he steals them.

Henry laughs.

                    HENRY
          Come. Let's eat together. We can talk.

He walks from the room, all the courtiers and
servants bowing. There are still more in the next,
larger chamber, with a dining table already laid
and food ready to be served.

Buckingham is also in the chamber, ready to serve
the king. He has been given the privilege of holding
the silver basin for the king to wash his hands in.

Without really thinking, Henry dips his fingers
into the basin, then removes them to be dried.
Buckingham is about to take the basin away.

                    WOLSEY
          Hold.

Wolsey puts his own fingers into the basin.
Outraged that he is waiting upon the son of a

butcher, Buckingham tips the whole basin of water over Wolsey's shoes.

Everything stops.

> HENRY
> Your Grace will apologize.
> (beat)
> I said, you will apologize.

> BUCKINGHAM
> I apologize if I have offended Your Majesty.

A beat. Henry nods a little.

> HENRY
> Your Grace may leave us.

Buckingham bows, withdraws. Henry looks to one of his grooms.

> HENRY (cont'd)
> Boy, fetch the chancellor a new pair of shoes!

CUT TO:

INT. BUCKINGHAM'S CHAMBERS - NIGHT

Buckingham storms into his chambers in a rage.

> BUCKINGHAM
> (shouts)
> Hopkins! Hopkins!

His servant, HOPKINS, turns. Buckingham knocks a glass of wine from his hands and continues onward to the inner chamber. There, we find already assembled his coconspirators: Norfolk, Boleyn, and two other councillors.

Buckingham regards them all.

                              NORFOLK
          Your Grace.

                            BUCKINGHAM
          It's time.

                                                    CUT TO:

INT. HENRY'S PRIVATE CHAMBERS - OUTER CHAMBER - NIGHT

Henry and Wolsey sit at table, wine is poured.
Henry is in great spirits.

                              HENRY
               Speak to me.

                              WOLSEY
               Yes. Well, everything is prepared for the
               summit. It will take place in the Pale of
               Calais - English territory. In a valley
               known as the Val d'Or - the valley of
               gold. A thousand labourers have constructed
               a palace for Your Majesty. It's known as
               the Palace of Illusions. Some say it is
               the eighth wonder of the world!

Henry soaks up the good news. Raises his glass.

                                                    CUT TO:

INT. BUCKINGHAM'S CHAMBERS - NIGHT

                             BUCKINGHAM
               You are to purchase as much cloth of
               gold and silver as you can find. It is a
               better thing to bribe the guards with.

                              HOPKINS
               Yes, Your Grace.

                             BUCKINGHAM
               Then I want you to proceed to our
               estates and do as we discussed, just

                    making some noise that we're only
                    raising men to defend ourselves.

                              HOPKINS
                    Yes, Your Grace.

                                                 CUT TO:

INT. HENRY'S PRIVATE CHAMBERS - OUTER CHAMBER - NIGHT

                              WOLSEY
                            (quietly)
                    Lady Blount is with child.

                              HENRY
                    Lady Blount?

A long beat. Henry thinks about it.

                              WOLSEY
                    If you want her to keep the child, I will
                    arrange for her to be moved to the house
                    at Jericho. I will also deal with her
                    husband.

HENRY doesn't respond - a sign of his approval.

                                                 CUT TO:

INT. BUCKINGHAM'S CHAMBERS - NIGHT

BUCKINGHAM picks up a thin dagger from his table,
stares at it.

                              BUCKINGHAM
                            (after a long beat)
                    My father once told me how he had planned
                    to assassinate Richard III.

Abruptly BUCKINGHAM seizes hold of HOPKINS
with a rough hand. Stares at him with
malevolence - as if HOPKINS had turned into
Richard III.

BUCKINGHAM (cont'd)
He would come before him - with a knife
secreted about his person.

BUCKINGHAM suddenly drops to his knees before HOPKINS,
the knife now hidden among the folds of his clothes.

BUCKINGHAM (cont'd)
(hissing)
Your Majesty!

HOPKINS, trying to play his part in this charade
moves to raise BUCKINGHAM - but we see fear in his
eyes, and alarm in those of the watchers. With an
abrupt, almost savage movement, BUCKINGHAM rises
and thrusts the dagger into HOPKINS'S chest!

BOLEYN gasps. There's a beat. Then BUCKINGHAM
opens his hand. It's empty. He shakes his sleeve
and the dagger drops out.

BUCKINGHAM grins.

CUT TO:

INT. HENRY'S PRIVATE CHAMBERS - OUTER CHAMBER - NIGHT

HENRY
(after a beat)
I can't wait for this summit! It will
change the world forever.

WOLSEY
That is my dearest hope and my ultimate
belief.

HENRY
Nothing will ever be the same, Your
Eminence. You and I will be immortal.

End of Episode 1

THE TUDORS

Episode 2

Created and Written by
Michael Hirst

FINAL SHOOTING SCRIPT
September 6, 2006

EXT. VAL D'OR - DAY

CAPTION: FIELD OF THE CLOTH OF GOLD. FRANCE.

We see an empty and grassy ridge. We HEAR, faintly
at first, the sound of horses' hooves - and then
suddenly Henry, King of England, breasts the
ridge, dressed magnificently in cloth of gold and
silver and riding a bay horse hung with gold bells
that jangle as he rides.

Beside him are his formidable YEOMEN OF THE GUARD,
carrying the fluttering pennants and banners of
England, the Lion Rampant. And then behind them,
in glittering array, come Henry's COURTIERS and
great NOBLES, first ambitious Buckingham then
Boleyn and Norfolk.

And then they reach the top of the ridge - and the
whole world changes! Down below them in the valley
is a truly fantastical sight: a vision of brightly
painted tents and pavilions and a fairy-tale
palace: the Field of the Cloth of Gold.

                    HENRY
          There it is! The Val D'Or: the Valley of
          Gold.

COMPTON and KNIVERT ride up together.

                    KNIVERT
          What if the French don't show?

A beat.

                    COMPTON
          Oh, they'll show. They'll just be a little
          fashionably late.

A beat. RIDERS begin to appear on the ridge
opposite.

                    COMPTON (cont'd)
                    (indicating)
         Your Majesty, look! There they are.

Escorted by a large party of his impressive SWISS
GUARDS, FRANCIS I, KING OF FRANCE, appears at the
crest: young, tall, dark, with a long priapic
nose, but still devilishly handsome.

Streaming out behind him, members of his own
glittering NOBILITY, the flags and pennants of
France, the fleur-de-lis.

The two parties stare across at each other, warily.
Knivert eases his horse closer to the king's . . .
as the French KNIGHTS begin to stream down the
heavily wooded slope.

                    BRANDON
         What is the plan?

                    HENRY
         I was to ride down alone and meet
         the king.

THEY WATCH THE HOST OF THE FRENCH DESCEND THROUGH
THE TREES IN GLITTERING FILES.

                    KNIVERT
                    (quietly)
         What if it's a trap? What if they
         mean to lure you down there, to
         kill you!

A long beat. Henry stares across at Francis . . .
then abruptly urges on his horse.

                    HENRY
                    (shouts)
         All of you! On pain of death! Stay!

He rides down swiftly into the valley, just as
FRANCIS and his guards emerge from the trees. It
looks for all the world like a trap.

They watch edgily as HENRY reaches the bottom of
the valley. At the same time FRANCIS gallops away
from his guards, both kings converging on the
magnificent French pavilion.

BUCKINGHAM, alone, looks disappointed at the happy
outcome.

                                        CUT TO:

EXT. FRENCH PAVILION - DAY

The pavilion is made of gold damask and guarded by
a statue of St. Michael.

Henry and Francis ride slowly towards each other.
On meeting they doff their caps and embrace, full
of smiles . . . and admire each others' full
beards, with a laugh of recognition.

                    HENRY
          Cousin.

                    FRANCIS
                 (in French)
          Cousin. Welcome to France.

They turn and ride together towards the doors of
the pavilion - where they pause.

                    HENRY
          After you.

                    FRANCIS
          Mais non. After you!

                                            93

The impasse lasts a moment or two, then laughing, they ride inside together.

                    HENRY
          How do you like my beard?

                    FRANCIS
          You almost look French, you know?

                                        CUT TO:

INT. PAVILION - DAY

The inside of the pavilion is lined with blue velvet embroidered with fleurs-de-lis.

This is a formal reception, with the French on one side and the English on the other.

Henry is supported by Queen Katherine, by Wolsey, More, and many members of his nobility. Beside Francis is his beautiful young wife, QUEEN CLAUDE, and several DUKES and PRINCES OF THE CHURCH.

All these people are fashion victims. It's like the Oscars, except it's both men and women who have dressed up like peacocks to impress and dazzle. The competitiveness of the whole occasion is already just so obvious.

But no one dazzles more than the two kings. Their clothes simply glitter with jewels.

Trumpets sound. An ENGLISH HERALD steps forward to read a proclamation.

                    HERALD
          Hear ye! Hear ye! I, Henry, by the Grace
          of God, King of England, Ireland, and
          France, do hereby . . .

                    HENRY
                  (loudly)
     Stop.

Henry looks at Francis.

                  HENRY (cont'd)
          I cannot be that while you are here, for
          I would be a liar. During this summit I
          am simply Henry, King of England.

He smiles, and applause ripples through the pavilion.

                    FRANCIS
          And I am just Francis, King of France -
          and Burgundy.

There is more applause. But already, beneath the
conviviality, both kings are sparring.

                    WOLSEY
          Your Majesties, may I ask you each to
          place a hand upon the Holy Bible and swear
          before God and these princes and lords
          here gathered, that you will be true,
          virtuous, and loving to each other.

He holds out a large, gold-tooled Bible. Both
Henry and Francis manage to put their hands upon
it at the same time.

                    HENRY
          I so swear.

                    FRANCIS
          Oh, moi aussi. I swear too. Of course.

From another entrance CARDINAL LORENZO CAMPEGGIO
enters accompanying the eight-year-old DAUPHIN of
France and six-year-old PRINCESS MARY. Both
children are dressed like adults, and the DAUPHIN
even wears a miniature sword.

They are applauded.

> WOLSEY
> Princess Mary, may I introduce Prince
> Henry Philip, your future husband.

There is more applause - and smiles all round.

MARY looks her future husband up and down with a child's unaffected curiosity.

> MARY
> Are you the dauphin of France?

> DAUPHIN
> Oui.

> MARY
> Then I want to kiss you.

There is some genial laughter as she tries to do this . . . but the dauphin, small and rather feeble, is patently terrified, tries to escape from her clutches.

> DAUPHIN
> Mama! Mama!

Disgusted by this performance, Mary pushes him away and he sprawls on the floor. Amusement turns to horror.

> FRANCIS
> Mon Dieu!

> HENRY
> Mary.

The dauphin, now weeping, is consoled by several of his COURTIERS. Personally, Henry finds it hard to disguise a little smile of satisfaction.

CUT TO:

EXT. PAVILION - DAY

Outside the pavilion great crowds of French and
English SERVANTS and RETAINERS have gathered. They
have already been served free wine or beer and are
also in a party mood.

Compton fills his wine mug from a fountain.

                    COMPTON
          I have got to get one of these.

                                        CUT TO:

EXT. PALACE OF ILLUSIONS - DAY

Henry and several of his party approach the
specially constructed palace. From the outside it
looks like a genuine building, constructed of
brick and stone, with a gatehouse and battlements,
with lawns in front of it, an "ancient" Roman
fountain, and striped poles with the king's carved
heraldic beasts atop them.

Henry surveys the effect. Looks at More.

                    HENRY
          The Palace of Illusions. What do you think?

                    MORE
          It's - it's incredible, Your Majesty.

Henry laughs, puts his hand against the solid
wall - and shakes it!

                    HENRY
          Only painted canvas.

Most of the others look on, genuinely amazed.
Brandon dismounts and walks over to the fountain,

97

cups his hands, and drinks from the free-
flowing liquid.

                    BRANDON
          But real wine!

Everyone laughs.

                    HENRY
          Don't drink too much of it, Charles!

                                        CUT TO:

EXT. PALACE OF ILLUSIONS - ESTABLISHING - LATER

We start to HEAR the clash of arms.

                                        CUT TO:

INT. PALACE OF ILLUSIONS - NIGHT

Another beautiful illusion. The "hall" has a
ceiling of green silk studded with gold roses, a
taffeta carpet.

In between the crowd of standing COURTIERS and
the long dining table at which the kings, queens,
and the most important nobles are sitting, is a
space in which English and French soldiers are
demonstrating their fighting prowess with staves
and pikes. French and English voices in the crowd
urge on their champions - to laughter, which does
not disguise the sharp competitive undertow.

The contests finish - to applause.

                    FRANCIS
          And now I have a gift for you.

A FRENCH NOBLE takes a gift to Henry.

The gift is revealed - a magnificent bracelet of
diamonds. There are genuine gasps of amazement and

admiration: Clearly it's worth a great deal more
than Henry's gift. But Henry manages to smile
graciously.

                    HENRY
          You embarrass me, brother. And all I can
          offer you in return is . . . this pastry.

He gestures. His CHEF carries a large brown pie
across to Francis. Its crust is shaped like a
cockerel - but it is, after all, only a pie! Some
of the French COURTIERS audibly snigger.

The chef bows, places it before the French king
and - oddly - offers him a sharp hunting knife.

Amused, slightly puzzled, Francis takes the knife
and cuts into the elaborate pastry. Almost at once
the whole dish trembles, the crust cracks open,
bright wings flutter - and a dozen small ortelon
birds burst from the pie and fly around the tent.

There is general amusement, and much applause for
Henry's little trick. Only Francis seems completely
unimpressed.

                    FRANCIS
          Très amusant!

Now, music returns - this time played by French
TROUBADOURS. Wine continues to flow freely. We
favour BRANDON, COMPTON, and KNIVERT.

                    COMPTON
          What are you thinking, Charles?

                    BRANDON
          I'm thinking that, while I'm here, I
          should behave like the king of France.

                    KNIVERT
                 (puzzled)
          Which means?

BRANDON looks at him.

> BRANDON
> Which means I shall slip readily into the
> gardens of others and drink the water from
> many fountains.

They laugh.

Now again we favour HENRY and FRANCIS as the two
kings embrace in a show of amity.

> FRANCIS
> (whispers)
> Do you see that young woman over there?
> Dressed in purple and gold?

HENRY locates her and nods.

> FRANCIS (cont'd)
> Her name is Mary Boleyn, the daughter of
> your ambassador, with her sister, Anne. I
> call Mary my English mare because I ride
> her so often.

He laughs softly and having scored a point, moves
away again.

HENRY looks after him angrily.

> CUT TO:

EXT. FRENCH PAVILION - ESTABLISHING - NIGHT

INT. FRENCH PAVILION - NIGHT

Boleyn makes his way into the huge pavilion, where
everyone, of course, is speaking in French. He has
an easy familiarity with the language, and is
recognized by several FRENCH NOBLES as he makes
his way through the throng, into the far reaches
of the pavilion.

Here, in candlelit gloom, the atmosphere changes. It is suddenly charged with a kind of eroticism. The beautiful YOUNG WOMEN that Philip has brought with him as ornaments are being flirted with and seduced by members of the FRENCH NOBILITY. There are card games, there is drinking, there is laughter, and touching and whispering and lingering glances. Who will go to bed with whom tonight - is the obvious text, the meaning behind these blatant flirtations. Perhaps this beautiful CREATURE must decide between the three young and well-dressed MEN who pay such close attention. Or perhaps she will choose all three.

The beautiful creature is Boleyn's daughter Mary. He smiles as he draws her gently away from her admirers. She kisses him.

                    MARY
          Papa.

                    BOLEYN
                 (whispers)
          King Henry noticed you today. He wants to
          see you.

He starts to lead her away.

                    MARY
          Wait! I must go and tell Anne.

MARY walks into the crowd.

They part before her - and she finally catches sight of her younger sister. ANNE, too, is besieged by FRENCH ADMIRERS . . . and enjoying their attentions. One YOUNG FRENCHMAN is kissing her beautiful neck . . . even as MARY approaches.

ANNE is not embarrassed. It's normal. Her sister signals her, and whispers into her ear.

ANNE is amused by the information.

We move in tight on ANNE's face - as we start to hear a beautiful song sung by a single male voice.

CUT TO:

EXT. PALACE OF ILLUSIONS - HENRY'S WINDOW - NIGHT
INT. KING'S APARTMENTS - PALACE OF ILLUSIONS -
NIGHT

Thomas Tallis's face is bathed in candlelight, like a Caravaggio - as he sings for Henry.

Henry sits in a chair, being shaved by his BARBER while listening with pleasure to the haunting and spiritual song.

The song finishes.

> HENRY
> What's your name, boy?

> TALLIS
> Thomas Tallis, Your Majesty.

> HENRY
> Tallis.
> (beat)
> A good voice. Take a sovereign for your song.

> TALLIS
> Thank you, Your Majesty.

Tallis bows and is shown out by a GROOM.

CUT TO:

INT. PRIVATE SPACE - PALACE OF ILLUSIONS - NIGHT

By candlelight, Wolsey talks quietly to Boleyn.

                    WOLSEY
          What of Buckingham?

                    BOLEYN
          In my presence he has railed against Your
          Eminence, calling you a necromancer, a
          pimp, accusing you of using evil ways to
          maintain your hold over the king.

                    WOLSEY
          And what did Lord Buckingham say about
          the king?

A long beat.

                    BOLEYN
          He told me he has a greater claim to the
          throne, and that as His Majesty has no
          male heirs, and will have none, that he,
          Buckingham, will succeed to the throne.
                    (beat)
          But he also told me once that he has
          considered bringing that eventuality
          forward more quickly.

Wolsey leans forward.

                    WOLSEY
          In what way?

                    BOLEYN
          By assassinating His Majesty.

A beat. Wolsey nods.

                    WOLSEY
          You have done well to come to me.

He offers his hand, and Boleyn kisses it.

                    WOLSEY (cont'd)
          But I must warn you, say nothing of this
          to anyone.

CUT TO:

INT. PALACE OF ILLUSIONS - NIGHT

Here, there is organized violence! The royal
parties and their courtiers watch WRESTLING
MATCHES between English YEOMEN OF THE GUARD and
some FRENCH BRETONS.

Many of the drunken revellers from outside now
begin to push their way past the hapless guards
into the palace, where their raucous shouts just
add to the heightened tension and drama.

Francis is visibly delighted by the success of one
HUGE BRETON who tosses a YEOMEN out of the ring
like a straw man.

>   FRANCIS
>   You see that, brother? In most things, we
>   French excel you. We have the greatest
>   painters, the greatest musicians, the
>   greatest poets . . . most of whom, by the
>   way, live at my court. The greatest
>   philosophical minds, architects, engineers.
>   And, of course, we have the most beautiful
>   women. You won't deny that, will you?

He laughs - but he means it! More, sitting beside
Henry, watches his master's face contort with anger.

>   FRANCIS (cont'd)
>   Even our wrestlers are better than yours!

A beat.

>   HENRY
>   Are you sure?

His voice is heavy with threat.

>   FRANCIS
>   What?

104

                    HENRY
          I said, are you sure? Are you sure all
          your wrestlers are better than mine? Do
          you want to prove it?

Henry stands up - and everything around them
abruptly STOPS, and GOES QUIET.

                    FRANCIS
          What are you suggesting?

                    HENRY
          I am challenging you to a wrestling match -
          brother.

There is general astonishment - also a frisson of
excitement. Francis's ADVISORS immediately surround
him, shaking their heads, pleading with him (in
French) not to respond.

                    HENRY (cont'd)
                 (to Francis)
          You're a coward.

Furious, Francis springs up.

                    FRANCIS
          Merde!
                 (beat)
          I accept your challenge. Let's do
          it now.

                    HENRY
          Groom!

                    MORE
          Your Majesty . . .

                    HENRY
          No.

The two kings walk down to the ring. There is an
almost incredulous silence as their GROOMS disrobe

them, until they are practically naked. Both are
fit men, well toned; they like showing off.

They walk into the ring towards each other.

                    HERALD
          Your Majesties . . . gentlemen . . .
          the rules are . . . as follows: The
          first man to throw his opponent to the
          ground shall be declared the winner. Are
          you content?

                    HENRY
          Yes.

                    HERALD
          Then fight on!

And suddenly the whole pavilion EXPLODES with
noise, the French shouting and screaming for their
king, the English doing the same, all decorum
abandoned.

In the ring the two young men begin cautiously to
circle each other, making feints, looking for
places to attack. First one attacks, then the
other. Brief, hard, repulsed.

The SPECTATORS are mesmerized, excited. Who could
have expected such a thing?

                    KNIVERT
          What bet will you lay?

                    COMPTON
          Two kings . . . two queens - and a fool.

                    KNIVERT
          Who's the fool?

                    COMPTON
          I don't know yet, but it's a full house.

Brandon leans over, has to shout above the noise.

>   BRANDON
>   Henry's going to win.

But More shakes his head.

>   MORE
>   No, whatever happens, he's not going
>   to win.

They look on - people are yelling themselves
hoarse. Already both men have worked up a sweat,
are panting slightly, still looking for that
opening, that vital chance.

The queens watch on, white-faced. Katherine gently
takes Claude's hand in hers.

Boleyn catches his daughter's eye - and smiles at
her, knowingly.

Wolsey stares across at Buckingham.

In the ring Francis seems to be blowing harder -
and Henry goes for him, big time. He gets the
French king in a deadly grip . . . and the contest
seems virtually over.

But in the last second, as if finding some
inner strength, Francis suddenly powers his body
upwards. Henry is caught off balance. He loses
his grip on Francis's sweaty flesh, seems to hang
in the air a long time . . . but then crashes to
the floor.

Francis has won.

The French go delirious. Grooms and servants of
both men pile into the ring and surround them.
Among the English there's a palpable sense of
disbelief.

Henry, with only his ego truly bruised, is quickly
back on his feet. He tries to shove his way
through the throng to Francis.

> HENRY
> (shouting)
> I want a rematch!
> (beat)
> Can you <u>hear</u> me? I want a rematch. Are
> you afraid of a rematch?

Francis at least pretends to be angry and up for
it again. He even pretends to try and reach
Henry.

> FRANCIS
> Are you calling <u>me</u> afraid? Of what am I
> supposed to be afraid?

> HENRY
> Of me!

> FRANCIS
> Let's have it then . . .

But Henry is obliged to see Francis being hustled
away, the victor, applauded, fawned upon, slapped
on the back, kissed, cheered by his supporters.

HENRY, angry and humiliated, starts to leave. MORE
joins him.

> HENRY
> I'm not going to sign the treaty!

> MORE
> That's understandable. But, still -

> HENRY
> No, I won't sign it. Go and tell them.

                         MORE
          If that's what you want.
                    (beat)
          But perhaps Your Majesty -

HENRY raises his voice angrily.

                         HENRY
          I said - go and tell them.

A long beat. More nods.

                         MORE
          All right. If you want the world to
          think that the king of England is
          easily changeable, shallow, intemperate,
          incapable of keeping his word - then,
          of course, I'll go and tell them. After
          all, I am merely Your Majesty's humble
          servant.

A beat.

Then HENRY walks out.

                                             CUT TO:

INT. KING'S APARTMENTS - NIGHT

The beard is off. The BARBER shows HENRY his
face in a small mirror. Then HENRY catches the
reflection of BRANDON and a YOUNG WOMAN in the
glass.

He dismisses the BARBER with a gesture.

He looks round. The YOUNG WOMAN has a hood drawn
over her face.

Brandon nods, smiles, and withdraws, leaving them
alone.

Henry gently pulls off the hood, revealing the
beautiful face of MARY BOLEYN. He stares at her.

                    HENRY
          Lady Mary.

                    MARY
          Your Majesty.

He touches her face.

                    HENRY
          I have heard a lot about you. You have been
          at the French court for two years. Tell me -
          what French graces have you learned?

                    MARY
          With Your Majesty's permission?

                    HENRY
          Granted.

She sinks to her knees in front of him. We see
this from behind, but it's clear she unfastens and
takes off his codpiece, takes his cock in her
mouth.

CLOSE ON: Henry's face. He is surprised, disgusted,
and thrilled - all three at once! He glances down
at her bobbing head, then closes his eyes in
pleasure.

                                        CUT TO:

INT. PALACE OF ILLUSIONS - DAY

We are close on HENRY's face. He looks very
miserable - and casts an almost angry glance
across at MORE.

Meanwhile a choir - including TALLIS - sings
beautiful choral music.

110

Courtiers, the two QUEENS, watch the signing of
the treaty.

> WOLSEY
> And now I ask His Gracious Majesty, the King
> of England, in good faith, to also sign the
> Treaty of Universal and Perpetual Peace.

Henry signs the treaty - and is embraced by a
smiling FRANCIS as the audience applauds. WOLSEY
hands both men small copies of the Gospels, bound
in velvet with gold leaf - and embraces them both
as the applause goes on.

> SUDDEN CUT TO:

INT. KING'S APARTMENTS - PALACE OF ILLUSIONS - DAY

The choral music continues over this scene. HENRY
stands alone in his beautiful apartment, holding
the Gospels in his hand.

A long beat, then he hurls the book across the
chambers, smashing something. Then seizing an
ornamental axe from the wall, he starts to destroy
the apartment. Because everything is so flimsy
(the walls made of canvas and only painted to look
like brick), it is easier for him to wreak havoc.

He tears the illusion to bits, his cold fury so
great and terrifying as he hacks about him that
no servant or groom dares approach. They back
off, disappear . . . while HENRY grunts with
concentration, destroying the dream.

> CUT TO:

EXT. PALACE OF ILLUSIONS - DAY

The party is over. The Palace of Illusions is being
dismantled. It's surprisingly easy. Two workmen

unfasten ropes at either end - and seconds later
the whole canvas face falls to the muddy earth.

CUT TO:

INT. KING'S APARTMENTS - PALACE OF ILLUSIONS

Eventually when everything has been destroyed,
smashed, splintered, obliterated, Henry stops.

CUT TO:

EXT. PALACE OF ILLUSIONS - DAY

CUT TO:

EXT. GROUNDS AND PARK - WHITEHALL PALACE - DAY

CAPTION: WHITEHALL PALACE. LONDON

We look out upon a wintry scene. A harsh wind
blows.

CUT TO:

INT. HENRY'S BEDCHAMBER - PALACE - DAY

We are CLOSE ON Henry's face. His eyes are open,
he seems to be thinking.

A long beat. As we pull back slightly, Mary
Boleyn's face comes into vision. They are clearly
in bed together.

With pouted lips, she starts to rake Henry's
chest, gently and teasingly, with her fingernails.

She gets slightly bolder. Henry has not reacted at
all - now he turns his face towards her.

                    HENRY
        Leave.

Mary leaves the bed.

                    HENRY (V.O.) (cont'd)
          The queen's nephew has been elected emperor.

                                          CUT TO:

INT. HENRY'S PRIVATE CHAMBERS - OUTER CHAMBER - DAY

Henry moves away from the leaded window.

                    HENRY
          Now he is no longer just Charles V, King
          of Spain, but also the Holy Roman Emperor.
          His dominions are vast, his wealth
          extraordinary.
                    (beat)
          And he's only twenty years old.

A beat. He focuses on WOLSEY.

                    HENRY (cont'd)
          You will make arrangements to visit him at
          Aachen. Personally. It may suit us better
          to do business with him than with the
          French. I don't trust them.

HENRY's eyes are challenging - but WOLSEY doesn't
blink. He bows.

                    WOLSEY
          Yes, Majesty.

                                          CUT TO:

INT. PENSHURST - PANELLED ROOM - DAY

Boleyn is ushered into Buckingham's stern
presence. The duke is flanked by two heavily
armed, warlike retainers.

                    HERALD (V.O.)
          Sir Thomas Boleyn, Your Grace.

Boleyn almost quails at the sight of them.

>   BOLEYN
>   Your Grace . . .

Buckingham stares at him, walks slowly and
threateningly around him.

>   BUCKINGHAM
>   What did you think of that performance?

Boleyn is both frightened and confused.

>   BOLEYN
>   I . . . I . . .

>   BUCKINGHAM
>   Don't be stupid! You're not stupid. The
>   king's performance! At the summit! How did
>   it strike you?

Boleyn relaxes.

>   BOLEYN
>   Personally - I would have wished to see a
>   greater - a more powerful man - upon the
>   throne of England. Someone whose very
>   presence would have made the French sit up
>   and come to heel.

A beat. Buckingham nods.

>   BUCKINGHAM
>   I have the way and the means to crush the
>   usurper of my throne - as one would crush
>   a revolting spider!
>   (beat)
>   I will make him wish that he had entered
>   the church after all - and left the affairs
>   of state to those who are born to rule.

He moves closer to Boleyn - again threateningly.

                    BUCKINGHAM (cont'd)
          If you betray me, Boleyn, I will feed your
          body to my dogs.

                                          CUT TO:

INT. HENRY'S PRIVATE CHAMBERS - OUTER CHAMBER

A beat. HENRY paces about again. His voice is
different - more confidential.

                    HENRY
          What have you discovered here?

                    WOLSEY
          I have it on good authority that the duke
          of Buckingham is raising an army. He tells
          everyone that it's to protect him when he
          tours his Welsh estates, since he's
          unpopular there. But -

Henry glances at him.

                    WOLSEY (cont'd)
          He's also been borrowing large sums
          of money.

Henry moves thoughtfully about.

                    HENRY
          Buckingham. Invite him to court, for
          the New Year. But don't say anything
          to alarm him.

                                          CUT TO:

EXT. ROYAL BARGE - THAMES - DAY

On a freezing day, Henry is travelling with More
on the busy Thames. They are escorted, discreetly,
by yeomen of the guard, who keep their distance in
a following boat.

                    HENRY
          How are your children?

                         MORE
               Well, thank you, Your Majesty. I encourage
               them all at their studies. Even the girls.

Henry smiles.

                         HENRY
               Always the idealist.

                         MORE
               At some point, I imagine, it will be
               considered ordinary enough, and nothing
               strange, for a girl to be educated.

A long beat.

                         HENRY
               I've had a gift. From the duke of Urbino.
               A book called The Prince, written by a
               Florentine called Niccolo Machiavelli.

                         MORE
               Yes, I know it. It's about political
               opportunism.

Henry laughs.

                         HENRY
               It's true it's not like your book Utopia.
               It's less . . . utopian. Nevertheless, he
               asks the important question: whether it's
               better for a king to be feared or loved.

A beat. MORE glances at HENRY, He has stopped
smiling and looks out across the water, deep in
thought.

Then HENRY says, in a voice so quiet that MORE
barely catches it.

                    HENRY (cont'd)
         Buckingham is going to try and kill me.

                                        CUT TO:

INT. OUTER CHAMBER - JERICHO - DAY

Big with child, Elizabeth Blount moves slowly into
the main chamber, accompanied by two of her
ladies, where Wolsey is waiting.

                    ELIZABETH
         Your Eminence.

Wolsey offers his hand, and she kisses his ring.

                    WOLSEY
         Lady Blount. You are full term?

                    ELIZABETH
         In a little while.

                    WOLSEY
         You are well?

                    ELIZABETH
         As can be expected.
              (beat)
         Have you some message from His Majesty?

                    WOLSEY
         No. None. But from your husband.

Elizabeth's face falls.

                    ELIZABETH
         My husband.

                    WOLSEY
         I have spoken to him. He finds that he is
         reconciled to your condition.

                              ELIZABETH
            Then he won't send me to a nunnery?

                               WOLSEY
            He will be made an earl, and given estates.

                              ELIZABETH
            And my child?

                               WOLSEY
            That is for the king to decide - whether
            he will recognize the child. I'm afraid I
            can offer you no more comfort than that.

                              ELIZABETH
            Will you tell the king of my love for him?

Wolsey doesn't react, or reply. Merely bows a
little, and walks away down the long hall, and out.

                                               CUT TO:

EXT. PENSHURST PALACE - DAY

Horsemen pass in front of us riding towards
Buckingham's magnificent ancestral home: a massive
fortified castle, with a deep moat and tower. The
duke's banners fly from the flagpoles.

                                               CUT TO:

INT. GREAT HALL - CASTLE - DAY

Buckingham sits on a throne beneath an awning
of cloth of gold - just like a king. Servants
in his livery are in evidence all around the
great hall.

A line of local NOBLES and KNIGHTS wait to pay him
obeisance, each in turn kneeling before him and
kissing his hand.

                    NOBLE
     My lord, I hereby pledge my allegiance to
     you and your house, and do swear to serve
     you, even unto death.

Buckingham smiles at each, raises each man up, and
kisses his cheeks.

                    BUCKINGHAM
     We thank you from the bottom of our hearts.
     And in due course, you will find your
     loyalties richly and properly rewarded.

                                   CUT TO:

INT. WOLSEY'S CHAMBER - HAMPTON COURT PALACE - DAY

Wolsey with More. Wolsey, as usual, with his desk
piled high with official business.

                    WOLSEY
     I thought I should tell you. I am being
     sent to meet the new Holy Roman Emperor.
     The king has asked me to draw up a new
     treaty, uniting us against the French.

                    MORE
     You must be very disappointed.

                    WOLSEY
     I am very realistic.

                    MORE
     Then I am disappointed.

                    WOLSEY
     Our dreams were very unrealistic.

                    MORE
     Maybe so. But I will continue to dream
     them, even if I am alone in doing so.

A beat. Wolsey smiles a little.

                    MORE (cont'd)
          I fear His Majesty no longer trusts or
          cares for me as he once did.

There's a long beat. Wolsey fixes his gaze.

                    WOLSEY
          Thomas, let me offer you some advice. If
          you want to keep the love of a prince,
          this is what you must do: You have to be
          prepared to give him the thing you most
          care for in all the world.

A beat.

                    MORE
          But the thing I care for most is my
          integrity.

A beat. Wolsey meets his gaze.

                    MORE (cont'd)
          And what is it that you care for most in
          the world, Your Eminence?

Wolsey's expression is inscrutable.

                                        CUT TO:

EXT. WHITEHALL PALACE - NIGHT

Torchlight red on sweaty faces. A cold night.
Great wooden gates are opened to allow inside a
large body of HORSEMEN.

Buckingham and his retinue clatter into the
courtyard.

                                        CUT TO:

120

INT. PRESENCE CHAMBER - PALACE - NIGHT

Henry, in apparent good humour, stands next to
Katherine beneath a canopy, receiving New Year
gifts from his nobles. He is flanked by his close
friends BRANDON, COMPTON, and KNIVERT.

Each gift is displayed, then removed by the palace
chamberlain and placed upon a table with the rest,
for comparison. Each noble tries hard to impress.

                    USHER
          Your Majesty - the duke of Norfolk.

NORFOLK kneels at HENRY's feet. He kisses Henry's
coronation ring.

                    NORFOLK
          I hope Your Majesty will accept this
          humble gift for the New Year.

His RETAINER comes forward with a solid gold
goblet (worth a complete fortune).

                    HENRY
          We are very grateful to Your Grace. Your
          generosity overwhelms me. As always.

NORFOLK bows again, moves away.

                                        CUT TO:

INT. BEDCHAMBER - JERICHO - NIGHT

ELIZABETH BLOUNT is in the last stages of labour.
She is attended by MIDWIVES and other WOMEN.

The contractions are quickening. The midwives
sponge her sweating face as she groans aloud.

                                        CUT TO:

INT. PRESENCE CHAMBER - NIGHT

BUCKINGHAM enters the chamber with Hopkins in
attendance. COURTIERS bow to him. MORE glances at
WOLSEY - who makes a small, discreet signal.
GUARDS move quietly and unobtrusively into
position just outside the doors.

A space is cleared. BUCKINGHAM walks slowly towards
HENRY. MORE stiffens. BRANDON, KNIVERT, and COMPTON
move close about the king protectively.

BUCKINGHAM meets HENRY's gaze for a long moment,
before sinking to his knees before him . . . just
as he had once kneeled in mockery before HOPKINS -
who is also watching intently.

HENRY holds out his hand.

BUCKINGHAM kisses HENRY's ring.

                    HENRY
      Your Grace.

                   BUCKINGHAM
      Your Majesty.

BUCKINGHAM's hand moves - but only to gesture
to HOPKINS, who comes forward with a gift - a
clock!

Its casing is inlaid with jewels.

                BUCKINGHAM (cont'd)
      It has some words engraved on it.

                    HENRY
      Give it to me.

He is handed the clock. Reads the engraving.

                    HENRY (cont'd)
          "With humble, true heart."
                    (smiles)
          Your Grace overwhelms me. Your words touch
          me. They are the greatest gift; greater
          than any riches.

He puts his hand out to raise BUCKINGHAM to his feet.
If anything is going to happen, now is the moment.
BRANDON actually takes a step forward, but HENRY
shakes his head imperceptibly and BRANDON holds.

BUCKINGHAM is back on his feet, bows, moves away,
and joins NORFOLK.

HENRY catches MORE's eye, then turns away.

                                            CUT TO:

INT. BEDCHAMBER - JERICHO - NIGHT

ELIZABETH is beyond endurance.

                    MIDWIFE
          It comes! Push, my lady! Push!

ELIZABETH screws her eyes shut, and pushes and pushes.

And the baby gushes out.

                                            CUT TO:

EXT. WHITEHALL PALACE - DAWN

It is barely light, and freezing cold, as
Buckingham and his large group of retainers ride
to the palace gates.

Then, spurring on his horse, he rides out through
the gates, his men streaming out behind him.

                                            CUT TO:

INT. HENRY'S PRIVATE CHAMBERS - OUTER CHAMBER - NIGHT

Henry stares at his new jewelled clock - as the hands approach the hour of midnight. When they join, the clock begins sweetly to chime.

                    HENRY
              (quiet, sarcastic)
        With true and humble heart.

                                    CUT TO:

INT. ELIZABETH'S BEDCHAMBER - JERICHO - DAWN

ELIZABETH lies in bed, her new baby all wrapped up so only its face is visible, beside her, fast asleep. She looks absolutely exhausted but happy.

                                      CUT TO:

EXT. ROYAL PARK - DAY

Buckingham and his huge party ride in glittering array through a landscape of field and ancient oaks, back towards his estates.

Suddenly and unexpectedly, another PARTY OF HORSEMEN appear through the trees - and ride down to cut them off. At the head of this party - who wear the king's colours - are Knivert and Compton. Nevertheless it's a much smaller party than Buckingham's, and Buckingham is not unduly impressed or concerned.

They stop close.

                  BUCKINGHAM
       What do you want?

                    COMPTON
        Your Grace is arrested on suspicion of
        treason. I am ordered by the King's
        Majesty to take you to the tower.

Buckingham's MEN draw their swords. Compton and
Knivert are clearly outgunned, and for a few
moments everything seems to hang in the balance.

                    BUCKINGHAM
        If you take my advice, gentlemen, you will
        let us pass.

                    KNIVERT
        By no means. And if any of your men
        should strike one of His Majesty's
        servants in pursuit of his duty - that is
        treason, too, as Your Grace should know.

A beat. Buckingham considers - then gestures for his
men to put away their swords. He rides closer to
Compton and Knivert, regarding them contemptuously.

                    BUCKINGHAM
        You are only new men. You don't know
        anything. If I am accused of treason, I
        must be tried by a jury of my peers, not by
        the dogs of butchers. And there is no lord
        in England who will ever find against me!

No one answers him. Horsemen close around
Buckingham and escort him away.

                                        CUT TO:

INT. HENRY'S PRIVATE CHAMBERS - OUTER CHAMBER - DAY

Henry attends to some business, reading and
signing documents.

Wolsey waits.

                    HENRY
               (after a long beat)
     I have instituted a Court of High Steward
     to judge Buckingham's case. Twenty peers
     will be appointed to the court. Norfolk
     will be first among them.

He seals and hands Wolsey the necessary documents.
Wolsey doesn't move.

                    WOLSEY
     Your Majesty, if I may . . .

                    HENRY
     What?

                    WOLSEY
     It would be dangerous to find the duke
     guilty of treason.

                    HENRY
     Even if he is?

                    WOLSEY
     Yes. Even if he is.
               (beat)
     On the other hand, he could be found
     guilty of some lesser offence, heavily
     fined and banished from court. In that way
     he would be disgraced but his allies and
     friends would have small cause or occasion
     to rise against you.

                    HENRY
     And that would be the best outcome?

                    WOLSEY
     I believe it would.

                    HENRY
     And you could make the court come to that
     decision?

126

WOLSEY smiles.

                    WOLSEY
         I have every confidence.

Henry smiles, puts his hand on Wolsey's shoulder.

                    HENRY
         As I have in Your Eminence.

But as we go tight on HENRY, we see his expression
abruptly harden.

                                        CUT TO:

INT. TENNIS COURT - DAY

HENRY and BRANDON play a singles match, HENRY
playing seriously and hard.

From the gallery they are watched by spectators -
including KATHERINE, BOLEYN, and MARY BOLEYN. They
applaud a good shot by HENRY. We favour him as the
players change ends, pausing at the net to wipe
the sweat from their faces.

                    HENRY
                  (quietly)
         Wolsey will set up the court. Norfolk will
         head it. I want you to remind His Grace
         of his responsibilities.

Brandon nods, also seriously - and they move apart.

Now we favour BOLEYN. He glances at KATHERINE -
then at his daughter.

                    BOLEYN
                  (quietly)
         Does the king still call for you
         at night?

A long beat. Then Mary, rather embarrassed, shakes
her head.

                    MARY
        No, Papa.

                                        CUT TO:

INT. COURT - DAY

Norfolk walks through, in good humour, accompanied
by three of his servants, and a YOUNG BOY with his
tutor.

Brandon approaches the party, bows.

                    BRANDON
        Your Grace.

Norfolk's good humour melts away.

                    NORFOLK
        What do you want?

                    BRANDON
                  (mildly)
        Only to pass on His Majesty's love. He
        appreciates the role you will play at my
        lord Buckingham's trial, and for all the
        care you have for His Majesty's well-
        being.
                  (beat)
        He also sends you this.

He hands Norfolk a small package. Inside is a large
gold ring bearing a ruby seal. Norfolk reacts -
draws Brandon a little away from the others.

                    NORFOLK
        This is my father's ring. He was executed -
        by His Majesty's father, you know that?

> BRANDON
> His Majesty thought you might like to wear it.

A beat. He looks over at the young boy.

> BRANDON (cont'd)
> Is this your son?

> NORFOLK
> Yes. He is to be received by his godfather -
> the king.

> BRANDON
> Your Grace should have a care for his
> inheritance. It would be terrible, for
> example, if some action of yours were to
> deprive him of a father, a title . . .
> and a ring.

A beat.

Brandon bows again.

> BRANDON (cont'd)
> Your Grace.

And walks off.

> CUT TO:

INT. COURT - WHITEHALL PALACE - DAY

The court is arraigned. The great NOBLES OF
ENGLAND sit on plump chairs, with Norfolk in their
midst - waiting for Buckingham to be brought in.

Buckingham himself looks easy and confident as he
approaches his peers.

Buckingham takes his seat in front of the bench.
Glances around at the gallery, sees Wolsey.

Then looks back at Norfolk, smiles a little in anticipation.

                    NORFOLK
          Your Grace has been accused of treason,
          and with imagining and plotting the death
          of the King's Majesty.

A beat. Norfolk shuffles his papers - and begins
to cry. Buckingham at last begins to look uneasy.

                    NORFOLK (cont'd)
          This - this court of High Steward, after
          reviewing all the evidence against Your
          Grace . . . finds Your Grace guilty of
          the charges against you.

                    BUCKINGHAM
          No.

Norfolk goes on.

                    NORFOLK
          And so . . . sentences Your Grace to
          death, at His Majesty's pleasure.

Buckingham, pale with anger, leaps to his feet and
points to Wolsey.

                    BUCKINGHAM
          This is your doing! You butcher's dog!
          It's all your doing.

Wolsey shakes his head . . . as yeomen of the
guard come forward to restrain the hysterical duke.

                                        CUT TO:

INT. CELL - TOWER OF LONDON - NIGHT

Broken in spirit, BUCKINGHAM is pushed with rough
hands into a small, dark cell. The door is closed
and locked. Footsteps fade away.

He is left in utter isolation. But not total
silence. In the darkness he begins to hear
something - the ticking of a clock!

He finds it - lifts it - and sees it is the same
clock he gave to HENRY: "With humble, true heart."

Now it ticks away the last hours of BUCKINGHAM's
life.

                                        CUT TO:

EXT. ROYAL PARK - DAY
It's a beautiful sunny day. Dressed all in
yellow - the colour of rejoicing - HENRY rides
a splendidly accoutred mare through a beautiful
mustard field.

                                        CUT TO:

EXT. TOWER GREEN - DAY

We see everything from Buckingham's POV - as he is
led out of the tower and walks across the path to
the scaffold. He passes lines of people, but does
not really see them.

He is in a state of collapse. He hangs from the
arms of his ATTENDANTS and moans and drags his
feet. He is not at all ready for death.

                                        CUT TO:

EXT. JERICHO - DAY

Henry arrives. Dismounts.
                                        CUT TO:
EXT. TOWER GREEN - DAY

Ahead of him, on the platform, Buckingham can see
the hooded EXECUTIONER and the BISHOP and his
PRIESTS.

It doesn't make it any better. He trembles
violently as he is helped onto the platform.

                                        CUT TO:

INT. BEDCHAMBER - JERICHO - DAY

Henry ducks his head under the low lintel as he
enters the bedchamber, where there are two
MIDWIVES, Elizabeth Blount, and a wooden cradle
covered with a velvet cloth.

                                        CUT TO:

EXT. SCAFFOLD - DAY

Sunlight glints on the executioner's axe as he
kneels before Buckingham.

                     EXECUTIONER
          Do you forgive me?

Buckingham's mouth opens as if to reply, but
no words come out. He is cold in his shirt,
and afraid. His eyes are full of tears, and
his body trembles uncontrollably. Glancing aside,
he sees his daughter ANNA among the small crowd
come to watch him die. Their eyes meet. She is
weeping. BUCKINGHAM cannot bear it, and looks
away.

A PRIEST mutters the Orisons. Then pauses, looks
at the distraught duke, and whispers:

                     PRIEST
          Your Grace must lie down.

Buckingham groans. Someone helps him to lie down,
and puts his head upon the block.

                                        CUT TO:

132

INT. BEDCHAMBER - JERICHO - DAY

The midwives sink to their knees as Henry slowly
approaches the cot. He looks down at the dear face
of a little baby, though without expression.

                                              CUT TO:

EXT. SCAFFOLD - DAY

                    EXECUTIONER
        When you stretch out your arms, I will
        strike! Stretch out your arms.

He raises the axe. BUCKINGHAM has not stretched
out his arms.

Suddenly KNIVERT steps forward from the small
group of watching DIGNITARIES.

                                              CUT TO:

INT. BEDCHAMBER - JERICHO - DAY

Henry signals. One of the midwives gently pulls
back the silk sheet that covers the baby's body.
The baby is naked beneath it, and Henry can easily
see its sex.

He makes the sign of the cross.

                    HENRY
        I have a son.
                (beat)
        I have a son.
                (beat)

                                              CUT TO:

INT. CHAMBER - THE TOWER OF LONDON - DAY

Knivert seizes BUCKINGHAM's hands and pulls his
arms straight towards him.

The axe thumps down.

CUT TO:

EXT. JERICHO - DAY

Henry rides out, calls to the skies.

> HENRY
> I have a son. I have a son, God, can you
> hear me? I have a son.

CUT TO:

EXT. WHITEHALL PALACE - NIGHT

A firework explodes in the sky with a whumph,
followed by streams and traces of silver light,
bursting over the palace in celebration.

CUT TO:

INT. COURT - PALACE - NIGHT

An EXPLOSION of noise and gaiety! Henry has thrown
a big party to celebrate the birth of his son.
Outside the (guarded) doors, crowds of PEOPLE have
gathered, excitedly watching the great LORDS and
LADIES sweeping down the hall and entering the
court, and trying to peep in at the festivities
within.

Brandon and Knivert swagger in together, like
celebrities enjoying the press of people around
them, the envious stares. Norfolk enters, beside
his WIFE, with greater pomp and ceremony.

And More tries to slip in unnoticed.

CUT TO:

INT. COURT - NIGHT

Drink is flowing. Henry drinks and laughs with great gusto, clearly enjoying himself. There is no sign of Elizabeth Blount.

Wolsey enters the gallery and makes his way towards him, bowing.

> WOLSEY
> Your Majesty is to be congratulated on this happy event.

> HENRY
> Thank you, Your Eminence.
> (beat)
> The lady is upstairs.

He indicates an adjoining room. Wolsey bows again and makes his way towards it.

> BRANDON
> Henry, congratulations.

A beat. Henry stops smiling, momentarily.

> HENRY
> Thank you, Charles. I always knew it wasn't my fault.

> BRANDON
> No.

CUT TO:

INT. SMALL CHAMBER - PALACE - NIGHT

Elizabeth sits in semidarkness, listening to the festivities, bolt upright on a chair, her hands folded.

Wolsey stares at her a moment.

> WOLSEY
> His Majesty has decided to recognize his
> son. He will be known for the present as
> Henry Fitzroy, and he is to have his own
> establishment at Durham House, with a
> chaplain, officer, and retinue befitting
> his station.

A long beat. Elizabeth's face twitches with emotion.

> ELIZABETH
> (quietly)
> Thank you.

> WOLSEY
> You should write and thank His Majesty. I
> only do his bidding.

He walks out.

                                          CUT TO:

INT. COURT - PALACE

There's a pause. The level of noise has gone down
suddenly. Henry stares towards the far end of the
gallery. Katherine has come in, accompanied by two
ladies. They curtsy.

Katherine looks dark-eyed - but still very regal.
She takes a glass of wine - raises it toward
Henry, and sips from it, in celebration. Then,
handing back the glass, she goes out again.

> HENRY
> To my son!

Applause.

                                          CUT TO:

EXT. THE VATICAN - ESTABLISHING - DAY

CAPTION: ROME

INT. BEDCHAMBER - VATICAN - DAY

Attended by two or three red-robed CARDINALS,
and Bishop Bonnivet, the weak and elderly POPE
ALEXANDER lies on his deathbed. A PRIEST recites
the last rites in a sonorous voice.

Four great candles burn at the four ends of the
bed. The Holy Father holds a crucifix between his
folded hands. His eyes flicker.

Cardinal Campeggio - whom we last met at the Field
of the Cloth of Gold - whispers to Bonnivet.

> CAMPEGGIO
> What was your deal with Wolsey?

Bonnivet whispers back. The last rites go on.

> BONNIVET
> In return for England not going to war with
> France, I promised him the French vote.

Campeggio - a very devout-looking man - nods,
rather seems to ignore the last suffering of the
dying Holy Father. A wafer is prepared for him.

> CAMPEGGIO
> The fact is, Wolsey has gone to Aachen to
> meet the new emperor. He obviously means
> to break the treaty with your king.

> BONNIVET
> In which case, we are no longer obliged to
> deliver our side of the bargain.

The priest meanwhile puts a wafer on the pope's
tongue.

                    CAMPEGGIO
        In any case, we don't want an English
        pope! We had one once. He was insane!
        Never again. The pope must be an Italian.
        That is God's will.

                    PRIEST
                  (crying)
        Your Holiness must swallow it.

                    CAMPEGGIO
            Push it!

Shocked, but desperate, the priest pushes the
wafer down the pope's gullet. Alexander's mouth
twitches in a little smile.

Then he dies.

Campeggio and Bonnivet remove their caps, cross
themselves, and kneel with great devotion beside
the corpse.

A bell begins to toll.

                                        CUT TO:

EXT. SLIPPER CHAPEL - WALSINGHAM - DAY

It's a bitter day. Rain is falling. About half
a mile away is the small Slipper Chapel of Our
Lady of Walsingham, the most famous shrine in
England.

A coach draws up. Her ladies help Katherine out.
Then, like any other pilgrim, Katherine removes
her shoes - and starts to walk barefooted and
bare-headed, through the rain, towards the
chapel.

                                        CUT TO:

EXT. SLIPPER CHAPEL - DAY

Drenched, Katherine passes alone into the small chapel.

                                        CUT TO:

INT. CHAPEL - DAY

It's dark and cold inside. But hundreds of candles
illuminate the image of the Virgin and Child.

Katherine crosses herself, and sinks to her knees
on the stone floor. She stares up at the lovely,
compassionate face of Mary, holding the baby Jesus
in her arms.

Tears form in Katherine's eyes, spill onto her
cheeks.

                    KATHERINE
                  (whispers)
        My Lady, full of Grace, I pray you . . .
        I beseech you . . . in all humility . . .
        for the love I bear for you, and for your
        son Jesus Christ . . . I pray you . . .
        give me a child. A son to fill my empty
        womb. I beg you . . .

Weeping, she presses her face against the cold,
unforgiving stone.

                                        CUT TO:

INT. WOLSEY'S CHAMBERS - DAY

Wolsey and More.

WOLSEY is standing with his back to MORE, apparently
looking out of his windows.

Wolsey is all business.

                    WOLSEY
          In a few weeks, the court will quit
          Whitehall for Hampton Court. There's been
          an incident of the sweating sickness in
          the city. You know how afraid the king is
          of any illness.

More nods.

A beat. Still WOLSEY has not turned round.

                    MORE
          How is the king?

A long beat. WOLSEY turns. His face is wet with
tears. MORE understands their cause.

                    MORE (cont'd)
          I was sorry to hear of Cardinal Orsini's
          election as pope.

                    WOLSEY
          You are perpetually sorry, More.

                    MORE
          I wasn't simply being polite.

                    WOLSEY
          Oh, really?

                    MORE
          I was not. As long as there is such
          blatant corruption in the church, that
          heretic Luther will continue to gain
          followers.
                    (beat)
          I know that if Your Eminence had been
          elected, you would have worked tirelessly
          to cleanse the church of all its evil
          practices.

A beat. Wolsey looks up.

                    WOLSEY
          Perhaps you think too highly of me, Thomas.
                    (beat)
          Perhaps you think too highly of the whole
          human race.

More bites his lip.

                                             CUT TO:

INT. COURT - WHITEHALL PALACE - DAY

MORE walks through the court. He pauses as he sees
ELIZABETH BLOUNT approaching, and bows.

                    MORE
          Lady Blount.

                    ELIZABETH
          Mr. More.

For a moment we favour ELIZABETH BLOUNT as she
moves past him.

As she passes the queen's private chambers, the
doors open. The chamberlain walks out and
announces:

                    CHAMBERLAIN
          The queen!

Katherine processes out, on her way to chapel,
accompanied by several of her ladies.

Both women catch sight of each other and pause.
Behind Katherine's eyes there is a terrible pain,
which is also a terrible bitterness.

Elizabeth curtsys.

                    ELIZABETH
          My lady.

Without responding, her head held regally high,
Katherine sweeps away.

                                        CUT TO:

EXT. AVENUE OF TREES - DAY

We are close on the throne with its canopy and
regal trappings. It appears to be floating on its
own through the English countryside.

As we widen the shot, we see that it is being
carried in a cart, together with pieces of the
king's bed and several of his chairs of estate.

A second cart also laden with hangings and carpets
and linen follows behind.

Two carriages rattle along in front: one
containing KATHERINE and two LADIES, the first -
flanked by mounted YEOMEN - carrying HENRY and
WOLSEY.

The court is on the move to Hampton Court.

                                        CUT TO:

EXT. SMALL CHAMBER - WHITEHALL PALACE - DAY

Two MEN are whispering together. As we get closer
we recognize Norfolk and Boleyn.

We don't hear what they are saying.

Someone else quietly enters the room and moves
closer to the two men.

From behind we see a slim YOUNG WOMAN with black
hair. She drops to her knees. Norfolk offers his
hand, and she kisses it.

                         YOUNG WOMAN
         Uncle.

                          NORFOLK
         Anne.

Norfolk smiles a little, then withdraws.

Then Boleyn raises her gently. We see again the
beautiful, dark-haired YOUNG WOMAN we saw in the
French pavilion, surrounded by French admirers,
when she was no more than 16 or 17. Now she's 18,
flowered to her full beauty, with deep brown,
magnetic eyes.

                          BOLEYN
         Sweet Anne.

                           ANNE
         Yes, Papa.

                          BOLEYN
         You know why you are here?

                           ANNE
         No, Papa. In Paris, no one explained.

                          BOLEYN
         Good. It is better that way.

A beat. Anne is curious.

                           ANNE
         What's happened?

                          BOLEYN
         His Majesty is tiring of his French
         alliance.

He pauses. It doesn't help her much.

                    BOLEYN (cont'd)
          It seems he is also tiring of your
          sister. He no longer invites her to
          his bed.

                    ANNE
          Poor Mary.

She tries to sound sympathetic - can hardly
conceal a grin.

                    BOLEYN
          Poor us! When she was his mistress, all
          our fortunes were made. Now most likely
          they will fall.
                         (beat)
          Unless . . .

He stares into those deep brown intelligent eyes.

His meaning is obvious - and not lost on his
youngest daughter.

                    ANNE
          Even if he had me, who is to say he would
          keep me? It's not just Mary. They say that
          all his liaisons are soon over. That he
          blows hot, he blows cold.

Boleyn smiles.

                    BOLEYN
          Perhaps you could imagine a way to
          keep his interest more . . . prolonged?
          I daresay you learned things in France?
          How to play his passions?

BOLEYN touches his daughter's cheeks softly, still
looking into her eyes.

                    BOLEYN (cont'd)
               (beat)
          There is something deep and dangerous in
          you, Anne. Those eyes of yours are like
          dark hooks for the soul.

She looks back at him.

EXT. KING'S CARRIAGE - DAY

INT. KING'S CARRIAGE - DAY

                    HENRY
          How was your meeting with the emperor?

                    WOLSEY
          Good. Productive.
               (beat)
          He makes no secret of his antipathy for
          the French. He wants to go to war with
          them and he is desperate for an alliance
          with Your Majesty.

Henry nods, thinks about it.

                    HENRY
          And in return for our alliance?

                    WOLSEY
          There will be a joint invasion of France
          for the overthrow of King Francis.

A beat. Henry is remembering being overthrown
himself in the wrestling match with Francis. And
it still hurts!

                    HENRY
          And I shall claim the crown, and once more
          truly be king of England, Ireland, and
          France, just like my forefathers!

Henry is pleased with the idea. At the end
of the avenue, Hampton Court appears and
sunlight glints off all the windows of the
great house.

Henry pauses and studies the effect.

>   HENRY (cont'd)
>   Your Eminence has built the most beautiful
>   palace here.

>   WOLSEY
>   Thank you, Your Majesty.

>   HENRY
>   Probably the finest house in England.
>   (beat)
>   I have nothing to compare with it. Nothing
>   to show more fair.

He smiles gently at WOLSEY.

Wolsey, too, gazes at his beautiful and beloved
house - then falls to his knees.

>   WOLSEY
>   Majesty - it is yours.

A beat.

>   HENRY
>   With the furnishings?

With a smile Henry gently raises Wolsey back into
his seat. The carriage rolls on.

End of Episode 2

Top:
Jonathan Rhys Meyers (Henry VIII)
and Natalie Dormer (Anne Boleyn)

Bottom:
Natalie Dormer (Anne Boleyn)
and Jonathan Rhys Meyers (Henry VIII)

Clockwise (from top left):
Natalie Dormer (Anne Boleyn) and Jonathan Rhys Meyers (Henry VIII);
Maria Doyle Kennedy (Katherine of Aragon), Sonya Macari (Lady-in-Waiting), Myia Elliott
(Lady-in-Waiting); Natalie Dormer (Anne Boleyn) and Jonathan Rhys Meyers (Henry VIII)

Top (from left to right):
Callum Blue (Knivert), Steward, Gabrielle Anwar
(Margaret), Sam Neill (Cardinal Wolsey),
Jeremy Northam (Thomas More), Maria Doyle
Kennedy (Katherine of Aragon), Natalie Dormer
(Anne Boleyn), Nobleman, Jonathan Rhys Meyers
(Henry VIII), Courtier, Henry Cavill (Brandon)

Bottom (left to right):
Jonathan Rhys Meyers (Henry VIII)
and Jeremy Northam (Thomas More);
Jeremy Northam (Thomas More)

Clockwise (from top right):
Sam Neill (Cardinal Wolsey); Jonathan Rhys Meyers
(Henry VIII); Henry Cavill (Brandon); Henry Cavill
(Brandon) and Gabrielle Anwar (Margaret)

Top (from left to right):
Steven Waddington (Buckingham), Henry Cavill (Brandon), Jonathan Rhys Meyers
(Henry VIII), Callum Blue (Knivert), and Kris Holden Ried (Compton)

Bottom (from left to right):
Sam Neill (Cardinal Wolsey) and Jeremy Northam (Thomas More); Callum Blue (Knivert)

Clockwise (from top):
Jousting; Kris Holden Ried (Compton);
Jonathan Rhys Meyers (Henry VIII);
Jonathan Rhys Meyers (Henry VIII)

Top:
Natalie Dormer (Anne Boleyn) and Jonathan Rhys Meyers (Henry VIII)

Bottom (from left to right):
Padraic Delaney (George Boleyn), Natalie Dormer (Anne Boleyn),
Jonathan Rhys Meyers (Henry VIII), and Bryan Murray (Jean de Bellay, the French Ambassador)

Episode 3

Created and Written by
Michael Hirst

FINAL SHOOTING SCRIPT
July 12, 2006

EXT. WHITEHALL PALACE - GREAT HALL - ESTABLISHING

INT. GREAT HALL - WHITEHALL PALACE - LONDON - DAY

In the great hall of Cardinal Wolsey's London
palace, a rehearsal is under way.

On a rudimentary stage, with a tower built of
scaffolding, a DOZEN or so WOMEN have been
stationed. They are STAND-INS and appear very
confused about their roles. Many other PEOPLE are
milling about in a chaotic fashion: MUSICIANS and
MUSKETEERS, SET DESIGNERS, and so on.

In front of the stage is a group of would-be
ATTACKERS - also extras, who simply look bored.

The producer, WILLIAM CORNISH (fifties, distracted),
is trying his best to organize the chaos. Finally
he claps his hands.

> CORNISH
> Let's rehearse again, everybody! Shut the
> gate. Concentrate, please.

> CORNISH (cont'd)
> (shouting)
> Ready, everybody! Attack!

He gives a signal. DRUMS start beating raggedly,
and then trumpets and cymbals join in, making a
horrible cacophony.

> CORNISH (cont'd)
> (screams)
> Well, go on! Attack!

Stirred at last, the EXTRAS run up to the stage
and try to mount it.

Then there's simply pandemonium. Some of the women
throw everything to hand at the attackers, while

others scream and jump out of the way. Everything
is frantic, slightly farcical.

And then, too late, the musketeers fire their
muskets for effect. Unfortunately one of them uses
live ammunition, and the ball narrowly misses
Cornish and smashes into the woodwork.

                    CORNISH (cont'd)
                 (shouts)
             That's enough, everybody. Stop, you
             idiots. STOP!

Some order is restored to the proceedings. Cornish
glares at everyone.

                    CORNISH (cont'd)
             Have you any idea of the cost of this
             production? Do you truly imagine that His
             Majesty will be happy to spend a small
             fortune - on such a large shambles!

He strides over to the musketeers.

                    CORNISH (cont'd)
             Who fired that musket ball?

A long beat. Then one of them timidly steps
forward.

                    MUSKETEER
             I think I did, Mr. Cornish, sir.

Cornish walks up and cuffs him round the head.

                    CORNISH
             What are you trying to do? If you can't
             entertain the envoys, then you're going to
             shoot them instead! Is that it?!

The youth hangs his head.

                    CORNISH (cont'd)
        Again!
                                        CUT TO:

EXT. ROYAL PARK - DAY

Henry and Brandon on horseback.

                    HENRY
        I have some business for you, Charles.

                    BRANDON
        As you desire.

                    HENRY
        My sister Margaret is to marry the king
        of Portugal. I want you to escort her and
        her dowry to Lisbon, and give her away in
        my name.

A beat. They ride slowly side by side.

                    BRANDON
        Why me?

                    HENRY
        I need someone I can trust.

Brandon grins.

                    BRANDON
        You trust <u>me</u> with a beautiful woman?

Henry reins in very sharply, and stares at him.

                    HENRY
        With my <u>sister</u>. Of course I trust you. Why
        shouldn't I?

A beat. Brandon, rather shame-faced, lowers his
eyes. Henry rides on again.

> HENRY (cont'd)
> In any case, you're already betrothed
> to . . . ? What's her name? I can't keep up.

> BRANDON
> Elizabeth Grey. She's a cousin of the
> marquess of Dorset.

> HENRY
> Exactly.

A beat. Riding on.

> BRANDON
> I'm honoured by Your Majesty's trust - but
> there is still a difficulty. I'm not
> important enough to give away the sister
> of a king - let alone the king of
> England.

Henry smiles, puts a hand on his shoulder.

> HENRY
> That's why I'm making you a duke.

For once Brandon seems genuinely taken aback,
surprised - much to Henry's delight.

> HENRY (cont'd)
> Duke of Suffolk. How does that please
> Your Grace?

And with a laugh, Henry canters away.

                                        CUT TO:

INT. COACH - LONDON ROAD - DAY

On the rough road from the port of Dover to
London, the coach lurches and bounces on its
rudimentary springs.

It contains THREE MEN: the first is Thomas More.
The other two are ENVOYS from the EMPEROR CHARLES V,
the nephew of Queen Katherine. The smaller, very
Spanish-looking envoy is MENDOZA. His companion, a
large, handsome, bearded fellow is CHAPUYS.

                    CHAPUYS
          The emperor sends his best wishes to
          the king.

                    MENDOZA
          We are most grateful to you, Mr. More,
          for coming to welcome us in person.

                    MORE
          No, it's my honour. His Majesty regards
          your visit as a thing of great moment.

The envoys smile gratefully, as the coach lurches
again over a rut.

                    CHAPUYS
          When shall we have an audience with His
          Majesty?

                    MORE
          Let me advise Your Excellencies on this:
          There is only one way to reach the king's
          ear, and that is through the good offices
          of Cardinal Wolsey.

A beat. The envoys glance at each other.

                    MENDOZA
                 (quietly)
          We heard some rumours, Mr. More, that the
          cardinal advocates French interests.

More meets his gaze squarely.

                    MORE
          Only when he believes them to be in ours!

A beat, then . . .

INT. COACH - DAY - CONTINUOUS

Outside, the English landscape slips past: mostly
wooded, with little signs of human habitation or
even agriculture. More brings up a pet subject.

                    MORE
          Tell me: What is the emperor's attitude to
          the rise of the Lutheran heresy through
          some of his territories? My friend Erasmus
          tells me that in Germany it's spreading
          like a forest fire!

                    MENDOZA
          His Highness does everything in his power
          to suppress it. But, as you know, Luther
          himself is the guest of one of the German
          princes unfortunately beyond his control.

                    MORE
          My king is writing a pamphlet demolishing
          Luther's arguments and defending the
          papacy and our faith.

The envoys glance at each other again, astonished.

                    CHAPUYS
          You mean - he is writing it himself, with
          his own hand? No!

More smiles (an unusual event).

                    MORE
          There are a great many things that my king
          can do!

EXT. HAMPTON COURT PALACE - ESTABLISHING

INT. WOLSEY'S CHAMBERS - HAMPTON COURT PALACE - EVENING

> HERALD
> The envoys from the emperor, Your Eminence.

Wolsey approaches, in his red robes and some magnificence, surrounded by SERVANTS.

Wolsey smiles warmly.

> WOLSEY
> Your Excellencies.

The envoys kiss his hand.

> WOLSEY (cont'd)
> This is indeed a happy day. We have planned many festivities in honour of this most welcome visit. And it's my devout wish and hope that, together, we can finalize the details of a treaty which will bind your master and mine in perpetual friendship.

> CHAPUYS
> That is very much our hope too, Your Eminence.

Wolsey smiles, gestures for them to follow him into a side chamber. But as MORE tries to join them, WOLSEY bars his way.

> WOLSEY
> Good, good.
> (quietly)
> Not you, Thomas.

                                        CUT TO:

INT. WOLSEY'S CHAMBER - EVENING

The door is closed behind them. Some wine is poured
out - then the SERVANTS dismissed.

Wolsey's manner is immediately less diplomatic.

                    WOLSEY
          I don't want to waste your time, or mine.
          Before we drink, tell me: Is the emperor
          in fact sincere about this treaty?

He looks them in the eye - rather unnervingly.

                    CHAPUYS
          Of course he is.

A beat. Wolsey almost seems satisfied, nods a little.

                    WOLSEY
          Then to cement it I propose that we also
          announce the betrothal of the emperor to
          Princess Mary, the king's daughter.

The envoys look at each other.

                    MENDOZA
          It is our understanding that she is
          already betrothed to the dauphin.

                    WOLSEY
          But she will now be betrothed to Charles.
                    (beat)
          Unless you have some other objection?

A beat.

                    MENDOZA
          On the contrary.

                    WOLSEY
          Good. We are agreed.

A beat.

                    CHAPUYS
                (almost whispers)
        The emperor told us to inform Your
        Eminence personally that he wishes to
        bestow upon you a very generous pension.
        He will also throw his weight behind your
        ambitions to be pope.

Wolsey hardly reacts. Keeps a straight face.
Raises his glass.

                    WOLSEY
        Let us drink to the success of Your
        Excellencies' visit.

                                        CUT TO:

EXT. PARKLAND - NORFOLK'S ESTATE - DAY

NORFOLK's hunting dogs proceed him. NORFOLK walks
with BOLEYN - some servants following - around a
great circular pond.

                    NORFOLK
        You have found some means to put my niece
        before the king?

                    BOLEYN
        Yes, Your Grace. It's already arranged.
        Anne is to appear in the pageant for
        the Spanish envoys. As is the king.
        She will find a way to draw his
        attention.

                    NORFOLK
        Good!

NORFOLK nods - says something to his dogs.

NORFOLK (cont'd)
After she has opened her legs for him, she
can open her mouth and denounce Wolsey.

He looks at BOLEYN - and laughs.

NORFOLK (cont'd)
They do say that the sharpest blades are
sheathed in the softest pouches.

CUT TO:

INT. GREAT HALL - WHITEHALL PALACE - DAY

Now we see that Cornish himself is wearing a quite
extraordinary costume of crimson silk with burning
flames of gold. As MEMBERS OF THE CAST, MUSICIANS,
and MUSKETEERS move quickly into position, we
continue to PULL BACK.

Revealing: that what had once been a stage and
some scaffolding is now a specially constructed
CASTLE with three TOWERS, all painted green. From
each tower flies a banner: one of the three broken
hearts; the second of a woman's hand holding a
man's heart; and the third, a woman's hand turning
away a man's heart.

But we're still PULLING BACK, revealing now that
all around the great hall are rows of tiered benches
already packed with DIGNITARIES, COURTIERS, and
NOBLES. There's an audible air of anticipation.

Wolsey escorts the two envoys - as guests of
honour - to their special, elevated places beneath
a canopy, where More joins them, people around
craning their necks to get a look at them.

Then, as the MUSICIANS begin to play, all
attention is focused on the stage. As the envoys
watch, EIGHT YOUNG LADIES, all wearing white satin

158

gowns and bonnets of gold encrusted with jewels,
appear at the top of the towers.

                    MENDOZA
                    (curious)
          Who are those ladies?

                    MORE
          The Graces, Excellence. They have names
          like Kindness, Honour, Constancy, Mercy,
          and Pity. They are prisoners in the
          castle. The tall, fair-skinned lady
          beneath the broken hearts . . .
                    (indicates)
          . . . is His Majesty's sister Princess
          Margaret.

                    CHAPUYS
          Who is keeping them prisoner?

By way of answer, another, larger group of YOUNG
WOMEN appears at the base of the castle, though
these are dressed in black with black bonnets.
The music changes to reflect their threatening
appearance, and from the audience there is some
booing and hissing.

                    MORE
                    (laconic)
          Danger. Jealousy. Unkindness. Scorn.
          Disdain. Strangeness . . .

The music abruptly changes tempo again - the drums
beating and the trumpets sounding - creating an
effect of excitement and expectancy.

There is applause, too, and EIGHT LORDS enter the
hall, all wearing great cloaks and hats of gold
cloth that partially hide their faces. Cornish, in
his crimson costume, leads the lords up to the
castle.

                    MENDOZA
                (whispers, excited)
        Is the king there? . . . Which one is
        the king?

In fact, Henry __is__ there, with Brandon, Knivert,
Compton, and others.

                    MORE
        The men represent Youth, Devotion,
        Loyalty, Pleasure. Gentleness . . .
        __Liberty!__
                (beat)
        And, yes, His Majesty is hid among them.

But which one? For example, Henry's and Brandon's
physiques are very similar. The envoys search for
clues.

                    CORNISH
                (shouting)
        As Ardent Desire, I demand you release
        your prisoners!

                    SCORN
        As Lady Scorn, I laugh at your desires.

                    DISDAIN
        As Lady Disdain, I reject them.

                    CORNISH
        These men are noble lords.

                    STRANGENESS
        No, they're just men dressed up!

                    CORNISH
        I say again: Release these fair damsels
        you keep so cruelly.

                    DANGER
        Never.

                    CORNISH
        Then you give us no choice but to attack
        and breach your defences.

                    UNKINDNESS
        No knight shall ever breach mine!

                    CORNISH
        Lady, Desire overcomes all!

Trumpets sound the call to arms. Shouting their
war cries, the lords run towards the castle, at
which there is a great sound of GUNFIRE, the music
rising again to a martial pitch. Other effects -
such as dry ice - add to the thrill.

The Dark Ladies try to repel the gallant knights
by throwing rose water, comfits, and sugared sweets
at them - at which there is general laughter.

The lords, in return, to the continuous sound
of gunfire, throw dates, oranges, and fruits at
the Dark Ladies . . . the audience cheering their
efforts, applauding wildly as the Dark Ladies
are overcome - and flee, with hissing in their
ears!

We are with HENRY now - as he and his victorious
comrades storm through the red doors into the
citadel.

Henry climbs the steps up to one of the towers.

At the top, he comes face to face with his destiny -
with a sharp intake of breath, like an arrow
through his heart.

A very beautiful, 18-year-old YOUNG WOMAN with
jet-black hair and dark, expressive, exquisite
eyes, looks back at him. Her name is embroidered
in gold on her head gear, for Henry to read.

                              HENRY
              Perseverance? You are my prisoner now.

ANNE BOLEYN modestly lowers her eyes.

                              ANNE
              Not yet.

She walks away, and Henry comes face to face with
his sister, Margaret. He takes her hand.

                              HENRY
              Sister.

                            MARGARET
              Brother.

We cut to - Thomas Tallis. In the moment of
victory he starts to conduct the gentle, divine
piece of music he's written for the occasion.

He smiles with real joy as the young boy we saw
practicing earlier now rises to the occasion -
and, with several other MUSICIANS, the sublime and
emotional music fills the great hall.

                            CORNISH
              And now all shall be unmasked.

The lords lead their captive ladies back to the
ground floor, where they unmask themselves - to
fresh and delighted applause.

Henry stares at Anne as if suddenly rendered
incapable of speech.

Then the musicians start to play a stately pavane.
The lords and ladies begin to dance in formal
patterns, constantly changing partners.

Henry can hardly tear his eyes away from Anne, but
his sister MARGARET intrudes into his private
world. Her eyes are beseeching.

                    MARGARET
        I must speak to you!

                    HENRY
        I trust you have settled all your affairs
        here, Margaret?

                    MARGARET
        Yes, but -
                    HENRY
                    (quickly)
        The king has written of his love for you -
        his great eagerness to set eyes upon you,
        having seen your portrait.

The dance forces them apart. Henry desperately
looks round for Anne. But she avoids his gaze.

                    MARGARET
        I beg you, plead with you, as your
        sister, don't make me marry him. He's
        an old man!

He looks away. His eyes fixed on Anne - and this
time she passes him closely, and he whispers:

                    HENRY
        Who are you?

And she whispers back.

                    ANNE
        Anne Boleyn.

And then she is gone again, and the dance
goes on.

SIR THOMAS BOLEYN meets Cornish's gaze, smiles -
and drops a small pouch of money into his hand.

                    BOLEYN
        Thank you, Master Cornish. I'm very
        grateful to you.

                         CORNISH
              Sir Thomas . . .

                                              CUT TO:

EXT. GARDENS - DAY

A pretty young CHAMBERMAID stands alone.

Then a MALE HAND, reaching out, touches the
chambermaid's shoulder.

                         BRANDON
              May I see your mistress?

Embarrassed and excited in equal measure - and with
envious glances - she leads Brandon into a green
space, and the presence of Princess Margaret -
tall, graceful, with reddish-gold hair . . . and a
glacial expression.

Brandon bows.

                         MARGARET
              Mr. Brandon! - You are not yet <u>invested</u> a
              duke, I think?

                         BRANDON
              No, Madam.

                         MARGARET
              I shall be taking with me, to Portugal, a
              company of two hundred persons. They will
              include my chamberlain, my chaplain, my
              laundress, and all of my ladies.

                         BRANDON
              Yes, Madam.

                         MARGARET
              If you have anything to discuss, please do
              so with my chamberlain.

                    BRANDON
        Yes, Madam.

A beat.

                    MARGARET
        I am surprised my brother chose a man
        without noble blood to represent him.
        Even Norfolk would have been better.

Brandon doesn't say anything.

                                    CUT TO:

INT. COURT - DAY

Pace, the king's secretary, leads the two envoys
through the crowded court towards Henry's private
chamber.

But as they pass the queen's private chambers, a
hurried message is sent.

                    PACE
        I will announce you to Queen Katherine.
                (beat)
        Her Majesty Katherine of Aragon, Queen of
        England.

                    HERALD
        Your Majesty, the envoys from Spain.

Katherine appears. She smiles delightedly, as she
welcomes them, and they kneel before her. She
raises them gently.

Pace observes the interchange.

                    KATHERINE
                (in Spanish)
        I know you have an audience with the king.
        I just couldn't let you pass without
        seeing you.

                    MENDOZA
                 (in Spanish)
        Majesty, your nephew the emperor sends you
        his love and filial regards. Always.

                    KATHERINE
                 (in Spanish)
        Tell him, if he loves me, he should write
        to me more often!
                 (beat)
        But I am happy from the bottom of my
        heart that you are here - and that there
        is going to be a treaty.
                 (whispers)
        Just beware the cardinal.

Still Pace is listening.

The doors to the king's chambers open.

                    CHAMBERLAIN
        His Majesty will receive you now.

They follow the chamberlain past the heavily armed
YEOMEN of the guard and into the presence chamber.

But for a moment we favour a thoughtful-looking
Pace.

INT. PRESENCE CHAMBER - DAY

Henry waits for them, sitting on a chair of estate
beneath a canopy of cloth of gold, flanked by
several of his noblest councillors, including
Norfolk and Derby.

With his rich clothes, golden chains, and
glittering jewels, not to mention his stature
and growing self-confidence in the role he is
playing, Henry has become a formidable, rather
awe-inspiring figure to behold.

He gestures the envoys forward, where they fall to
their knees.

                    HENRY
          Gentlemen, I welcome you to my kingdom. I
          know you will succeed in your efforts to
          negotiate a successful treaty. You may
          trust in everything that Cardinal Wolsey
          says; he speaks for me directly in all
          matters.
                    (beat)
          For my part I should like to invite the
          emperor to pay a visit here, as soon as
          it can be arranged. The visit would give
          pleasure both to me and to my queen.

Henry smiles. It's the end of the audience. The
envoys rise, bow.

                    CHAPUYS
          Your Majesty.

They have to withdraw backwards; you can't turn
your back on a king!

As the doors shut behind them we . . .

                                        CUT TO:

EXT. GARDENS - WHITEHALL PALACE - DAY

Henry is experimenting with gunpowder. He's
talking to Wolsey - but all the while he's loading
an arquebus, a large gun. In the background, an
ARMS MASTER looks anxiously on.

                    HENRY
          When is he coming?

                    WOLSEY
          At the end of this month.

                         HENRY
          So soon?

Henry considers it.

                         HENRY (cont'd)
          If he needs allies for his attack on
          the French, that can only mean that
          he intends to do so very shortly.

                         WOLSEY
          Indeed. The envoys told me in confidence
          that the emperor will strike first
          against the French occupation of Italy.
          He has a claim to the duchy of Milan.

                         HENRY
          And then?

                         WOLSEY
          And then, after he has driven them out
          of Italy, with your help he will invade
          France itself.

Henry is increasingly excited.

                         HENRY
          You will prepare all our forces for a
          joint invasion.

                         WOLSEY
          Yes, Your Majesty.

                         HENRY
          And I want another warship.

A beat.

                         WOLSEY
          Majesty, we have only just launched the
          <u>Victory</u>.

                    HENRY
          Then order another. Even greater. What
          we lack in men we can more than make up
          for in ships. We're an island race. I
          swear we have the best and bravest
          sailors in the world - and I will have
          the best navy!

                    WOLSEY
          Ships are expensive.

Henry pauses, moves closer to him.

                    HENRY
          My father was a careful man. A shrewd man.
          A businessman. He left me a great deal of
          money, Your Eminence.
                    (beat)
          And I intend to spend it!

Then, having loaded and primed the gun, he aims
it and fires at an archery target, and blows it
to pieces.

Wolsey, meanwhile, exits, passing Sir Thomas
Boleyn as he does so.

Boleyn bows, then is allowed through into the
royal presence. Henry is checking out some
beautiful pistols.

                    CHAMBERLAIN
          Sir Thomas Boleyn.

Boleyn enters and kneels.

                    HENRY
          Sir Thomas.

Raises him.

                    BOLEYN
        Majesty.

                    HENRY
        I - I feel I have been remiss. I never
        showed you my gratitude for all your
        diplomatic efforts on my behalf.

                    BOLEYN
        Your Majesty had no need. I am simply
        content to serve you, in whatever capacity
        I can be of use.

Henry smiles. There is, however, something
uncertain about his manner.

                    HENRY
        Nevertheless, I do intend to reward you.
        It pleases me to make you a knight of the
        garter. And I am also appointing you
        comptroller of my household.

Boleyn looks suitably surprised, even humbled, as
if he has no idea why he should be chosen for
elevation.

                    BOLEYN
        I think Your Majesty has a better opinion
        of my talents than I have.

                    HENRY
        I will be the judge of that.
                (beat)
        We shall talk more later.

He appears to dismiss Boleyn, who even bows -
before Henry calls him back.

                    HENRY (cont'd)
        Oh. I forgot. Your daughter. The one who
        performed in our masquerade.

170

                    BOLEYN
        Anne.

                    HENRY
        Yes.

And then suddenly he is tongue-tied. Boleyn,
diplomatically, helps him out.

                    BOLEYN
        As a matter of fact, she is soon coming
        to court, as a lady-in-waiting to Her
        Majesty.

Henry nods, then seems to dismiss it. Boleyn bows
again and walks out.

Alone, briefly, and thinking of Anne, Henry's
expression changes - to one of open longing and
yearning.

                                        CUT TO:

EXT. GARDENS - DAY

As he exits the gardens, Boleyn catches Norfolk's
eye. And smiles.

                                        CUT TO:

EXT. HEVER "CASTLE" - DAY

A sight of the Boleyn's "modest" family home.
Panning across we see a statue of a bird - a
<u>falcon</u> - holding in its talons a copy of the
family's falcon crest.

Pan on - into the trees and gardens. We HEAR a
YOUNG MAN'S VOICE:

                    YOUNG MAN (V.O.)
          And will you leave me thus? / Say no, say
          no, for shame. / To save you from the
          blame, of all my grief and grame? / And
          will you leave me so? / Say no, say no.

As if trying to locate the voice, the camera
TRACKS among the formal gardens, along gravel
paths beside clipped borders, past sun-dials and
falcon statues . . .

Coming at last to a beautiful walled garden, where
the ancient fruit trees are garlanded in blossom.

The YOUNG POET, tall, dark curly hair, and
handsome, rests his back against a bough as he
recites his verse. His name is THOMAS WYATT.

He glances down at Anne Boleyn, stretched out upon
the grass.

                    WYATT
          And will you leave me thus / And have no
          more pity / Of him that loves thee? /
          Alas, your cruelty! / And will you leave
          me so? / Say no, say no.

A beat. Anne sucks upon a blade of grass,
squinting into the bright sunlight.

                    WYATT (cont'd)
          Well . . . do you like it?

He kneels beside her. She looks up into his face
with a smile.

                    ANNE
          Should I like something that accuses me of
          being cruel?

                    WYATT
          You are cruel, Mistress Anne.

                        ANNE
                     (teasing)
          Am I?

Her eyes and lips are like an invitation. Slowly
Wyatt lowers his face towards hers . . . only for
Anne, at the last moment, to turn her head away,
with a small laugh.

                    ANNE (cont'd)
          You have no claim on me, Master Wyatt.

                        WYATT
          I have the same claim as every other
          lover, to whom a woman's heart has been
          freely given.

                        ANNE
          You are a poet, as I am a woman. Poets
          and women are always free with their
          hearts, aren't they?

Wyatt's expression grows serious. His eyes fix hers.

                        WYATT
          Anne.

He reaches out, to touch and stroke her hair. She
trembles a little - then shakes her head, and sits up.

                        ANNE
          You mustn't. Stop it, Tom!

A beat.

                        WYATT
          Then I was right? You <u>are</u> leaving me.

She doesn't answer.

                    WYATT (cont'd)
          Why don't you answer me?

Anne looks at him.

                    ANNE
          You're married.

                    WYATT
          I know. But I'm separated. I'm getting a
          divorce.
                    (beat)
          I mean, who isn't married?

A beat.

                    ANNE
          You must never ask to see me again. Do
          you promise?

                    WYATT
          Why should I? When I have just learned
          what promises are worth!

She turns away.

          Is there another? Is that it? Do you love
          another?

Anne looks back - now her beautiful eyes are
hooded and dangerous, like a falcon's. Her voice
is cold as winter.

                    ANNE
          Never ask of me, and never, if you value
          your life, speak of me to others. Do you
          understand?

A beat. Wyatt is almost too stunned to respond.

Anne turns away from him again and walks back up
the path. Wyatt calls after her:

                    WYATT
          Have you no pity?

But she ignores him and passes through a gateway, out of sight.

EXT. BUCOLIC PLACE - PALACE - NIGHT

KNIVERT and COMPTON are drinking wine. They are both very drunk.

> KNIVERT
> Can you just imagine what he's going to be like now.

> COMPTON
> I'll wager he's already ordered a bigger codpiece!

> KNIVERT
> (mimicking)
> Your Grace! <u>Yes</u>, Your Grace . . . <u>no</u>, Your Grace. Allow me to bottle Your Grace's farts and sell them for perfume.

A beat. More drink goes down. Compton belches.

> COMPTON
> I don't want to talk about it anymore. It makes me ill.
> (beat)
> What shall we do?

> KNIVERT
> Find women.

COMPTON shakes his head.

> COMPTON
> Even if she was a complete Venus, I couldn't satisfy her . . .

> KNIVERT
> Let's just drink more then.

A beat. Compton raises his cup.

                    COMPTON
          All right. To His Grace.

                    KNIVERT
          To Charles.

                    COMPTON
          His Grace.

And they clash cups, and drown their sorrows.

END OF SCENE:

**INT. QUEEN'S PRIVATE CHAMBERS - OUTER CHAMBER -
EVENING**

We are CLOSE ON - a wine cup. On the cup the
initials H & K have been engraved, the letters
intertwined.

Henry looks at the cup self-consciously, twisting
it in his hands. Both he and Katherine are
drinking from similar ones.

There's a long beat. A great awkwardness between
them.

                    KATHERINE
          Did the envoys leave in good cheer?

                    HENRY
          They were in excellent spirits. And the
          treaty is agreed.

                    KATHERINE
          And my nephew will come?

                    HENRY
          We wait for news. Wolsey will find out.

Another long beat. Henry can hardly look at her.

                         KATHERINE
          I had a dream. And in my dream, you came
          to me again, and held me in your arms,
          and you whispered that all would be well.
          That all would be well, and all manner of
          things would be well.

Henry is silent, brooding, uncomfortable. Aware,
perhaps, that tears are forming in her eyes.

                    KATHERINE (cont'd)
                      (softly)
          Henry. Sweetheart. Husband . . .

She reaches out a hand, and gently places it over his.

                    KATHERINE (cont'd)
          You must believe me. I never knew your
          brother - in that way. He was so young.
          And he was ill.
                      (beat)
          I have known no other man, nor ever want
          to. I love you . . .

Henry remains silent, but walks to her, kisses her
forehead, and exits.

                       HERALD (V.O.)
          The king.

                                                CUT TO:

EXT. COURT - EVENING

Henry strides through his court, agitated, with
GROOMS and SERVANTS in attendance.

COURTIERS bow before him, LADIES curtsy. His eyes
flicker over them.

Then he catches sight of a young and nameless
WOMAN, standing with a group of other WOMEN, but
probably just a little prettier than they are.

With a signal to a SERVANT who knows exactly his meaning, Henry continues on his way towards his own chambers. The servant walks across to the young woman and whispers into her ear.

                                        CUT TO:

INT. QUEEN'S PRIVATE CHAMBERS - BEDCHAMBER - NIGHT

The door opens and the young PRINCESS MARY is brought in by her GOVERNESS - who curtsys.
MARY walks over to KATHERINE, who smiles tenderly and takes her into her arms. There are tears in her eyes.

                    KATHERINE
          Have you said your prayers?

                      MARY
          Yes.

                                        CUT TO:

**INT. HENRY'S PRIVATE CHAMBERS - OUTER CHAMBER/
BEDCHAMBER - NIGHT**

Henry knocks back another cup of wine.

Then, dismissing his SERVANTS, he walks through into his candlelit bed chamber. He sits down on a chair of estate - looks into the darkness.

After a moment the young woman slowly emerges into the candlelight. She is wearing only a thin, flimsy robe. As she unfastens it, it slips from her shoulders to the ground.

                    YOUNG WOMAN
                     (whispers)
          My lord, how like you this?

                                        CUT TO:

INT. QUEEN'S PRIVATE CHAMBERS - NIGHT

Accompanied by two of her ladies, she walks back
into her private chambers, into her bedchamber.

For a moment she glances over at the doorway to
the hidden passage connecting her chambers to
Henry's.

> KATHERINE
> (quietly)
> Has the king sent any message or sign that
> he might visit me tonight?

A long beat. The ladies look at one another: It's
suddenly clear how many times she has repeated
this question.

> LADY
> No, my lady.

Nothing in Katherine's expression gives away her
emotions. But as we see her sitting patiently and
alone, having her hair combed and bed prepared by
these young women, we appreciate her devastating
loneliness.

INT. WOLSEY'S BEDCHAMBER - NIGHT

WOLSEY lies facedown but naked on his great bed.
His mistress JOAN, a plain-looking peasant woman
with enormous breasts, straddles his back and
pummels it with her fists. WOLSEY groans with
relief.

> JOAN
> I'm worried about you, my love. You work
> too hard.

> WOLSEY
> I know that.

Grunts beneath another blow.

                    JOAN
          It will kill you.

                    WOLSEY
          I know that, too. What am I supposed
          to do?

She stops pounding him, leans over to whisper
in his ear.

                    JOAN
          Stay alive.

                                        CUT TO:

INT. COURT - DAY

Thomas Tallis, the musician, is walking innocently
through the court, humming - probably composing
something in his head - when he becomes slightly
aware of a huge movement of young COURTIERS in one
direction. There is excitement in the air.

Suddenly one of them grabs Tallis's arm.

                    COURTIER
          Aren't you coming?

                    TALLIS
          What is it?

                    COURTIER
          The queen's new ladies have arrived.
          Come on!

They join the small stampede of young males, through
the rooms towards the queen's private chambers.

As they do so, getting as close as they can, a
group of about TWENTY YOUNG WOMEN are escorted by

180

a formidable-looking minder, SIR ASHLEY GROSS, through into Katherine's rooms.

It's an opportunity for the sexually frustrated young men to drool and dream. They try to catch the eyes of the young women - one or two even making vulgar signs.

Tallis himself is embarrassed by the whole business.

Among the young women, we notice Anne Boleyn.

                                        CUT TO:

INT. HENRY'S PRIVATE CHAMBERS - OUTER CHAMBER - PALACE - NIGHT

More reads aloud from Henry's manuscript - which he had mentioned to the two envoys.

                    MORE
          "What serpent was ever so venomous as
          to call the Holy City of Rome 'Babylon'
          and the pope's authority 'Tyranny,' and
          turn the name of our Holy Father into
          'Antichrist'?"

A beat. Looks up at Henry.

                    MORE (cont'd)
          It's very good. Strongly worded - but good.

Henry beams.

                    HENRY
          You're sure?

                    MORE
          You might consider toning the polemic down,
          just a little. Here, for example, where
          you describe Luther as: "this weed, this
          dilapidated, sick, and evil-minded sheep."

                    HENRY
        Tone it down?

                    MORE
        For . . . diplomatic purposes.

HENRY shakes his head firmly.

                    HENRY
        No, never. No language can be strong
        enough to condemn Luther, nor gracious
        enough to praise his Holiness.
                (beat)
        I will dedicate a copy to him, and you
        can take it to Rome.

                    MORE
                (surprised)
        Why me?

                    HENRY
        If there is anything good or true in it,
        then that is due to you. I could never
        have written it, or anything else, Sir
        Thomas, without your guidance and unfailing
        honesty.

A beat.

                    MORE
        Why did you call me that? Sir Thomas?

                    HENRY
        A knighthood is the least I can do
        for you.

                    MORE
        But a great deal more than I deserve.

Henry looks at him.

                         HENRY
        Now, don't be too modest, Thomas. You're
        not a saint.

He laughs, claps More on the back.

                         HENRY (cont'd)
        There is something else I want you to do for
        me. Seize all the copies of Luther's works
        you can find - and burn them. Burn them all.

More looks back at him.

                                        CUT TO:

INT. CHAMBER - HAMPTON COURT PALACE - NIGHT

WOLSEY's SECRETARY takes a letter to his master,
who, as always, is working at his desk, late into
the night.

He looks up.

                         SECRETARY
        From France.

Wolsey takes the letter. He warms the seal over
the flame of a candle until it softens, and then
slices it invisibly open. He reads. Anger quickly
clouds his face.

                         WOLSEY
        King Francis has already discovered our
        rapprochement with the emperor. He feels
        betrayed and angry - is making threats
        against our interests.

                         SECRETARY
        Who told him?

The question hangs there.

CUT TO:

EXT. ST. PAUL'S CROSS - LONDON - DAY

More holds a copy of one of Luther's works in his
hand. It's a windy day, and the leaves flutter. We
see Luther's name boldly on the cover.

More tosses the book onto a huge bonfire in which
thousands of books and manuscripts are already
burning.

A CROWD, including some BISHOPS and PRIESTS have
gathered to watch the ceremony. One of the BISHOPS,
in his full robes and holding a cross, chants
Latin orisons over the flames.

Day turns to night - though the flames still burn.

Then fireworks FIZZ into the night sky - and
EXPLODE, showering glittering trails of gold and
silver.

>   HERALD (V.O.)
>   My lords and ladies, his Royal Highness,
>   Charles, Holy Roman Emperor, King
>   of Aragon, Valencia, Naples, and
>   Sicily . . .

INT. DOVER CASTLE - NIGHT

The PARTIES start to enter the great hall, hung
with banners and heraldic devices: set-dressed for
the great occasion. Lines of COURTIERS wait eagerly
for their first glimpse of the emperor, craning
their necks towards the open doors and the
darkness outside.

But Wolsey, with his keen sense of theatre, enters
first, and addresses the crowd.

                    HERALD (V.O.)
          . . . Duke of Burgundian Territories.
     Archduke of Austria.

The trumpets blare a fanfare in homage to the most
powerful man in the world.

Then CHARLES himself steps into the light. He's
not exactly what anyone anticipated. Just 21 years
of age, his appearance is decidedly against him.
Small, with a black beard, he has the prominent,
misshapen jaw of the Hapsburgs, pale watery blue
eyes, a dead-white complexion.

Nevertheless he is applauded as he walks between the
lines of PEOPLE, smiling and bowing to all sides.

Wolsey, enjoying the occasion, proceeds him
towards the High Table, which is already
magnificently set with gold plate and gold cups.

Then suddenly Pace steps in front of Wolsey.

                    PACE
          Your Eminence - a moment!

                    WOLSEY
          Move away, Mr. Pace. Move away.

                    PACE
          Yes, Eminence.

Puzzled, irritated, Wolsey pauses and looks back.
There is a fresh stir at the back of the hall, a
loud and growing and excited murmur, the sound of
people quickly making way.

And, as the crowds part, suddenly there is Henry
striding forward, smiling widely.

                    HENRY
          Your Highness.

                         CHARLES
          Your Majesty! I did not expect -

                          HENRY
          I could not sustain the anticipation. I had
          to come straight down to Dover to meet you.

                         CHARLES
          Then I am most truly honoured.

The two princes embrace and kiss - to fresh and
sustained applause.

                          HENRY
          Tonight we shall feast and dance. Tomorrow
          you will see my ships. Come!
                    (beat)
          Music! Let's celebrate!

MINSTRELS start to play in the gallery. Henry
walks arm in arm with the emperor to their seats
at the High Table.

Wolsey steps over to a GUARD.

                         WOLSEY
          Remove that man.

The guard leads a puzzled Pace up the steps to the
gallery. Meanwhile with great courtesy, Henry
makes sure that the emperor is seated before him.

In the gallery, Pace finds Wolsey and other
guards. He seems utterly confused.

                     WOLSEY (cont'd)
          Mr. Pace - you knew, of course, that His
          Majesty was going to pay this surprise
          visit?

                          PACE
          Yes. As his secretary I would obviously -

Wolsey ignores him.

                    WOLSEY
          And you knew - of course - that the
          imperial envoys had come, privately, to
          make a treaty with His Majesty. After all,
          Mr. Pace, you speak Spanish. Almost as
          well as you speak French.

Pace is still struggling.

                    PACE
          I - I don't understand, Your Eminence.

                    WOLSEY
          I think you do, Mr. Pace. I really
          think you do. Because I think you not
          only spy for me - you also spy for the
          French.

Pace blanches.

                    PACE
          No. It's not true!

                    WOLSEY
          You are removed from all your positions.

                    PACE
          No, wait! I swear to you - I swear by
          everything that's holy: It's not true!
          His Majesty is held dear in my heart.

                    WOLSEY
          It is treason to plot against His Majesty.

Pace looks astonished, disturbed . . . and suddenly
very frightened.

                    PACE
          What - what are you saying? Wait, please,
          Your Eminence . . . Don't do this . . .

Wolsey doesn't say any more. He makes a signal. Pace is seized by two of the soldiers and - too shocked to offer resistance - taken out of another door.

CUT TO:

INT. COURT - PALACE - DAY

Henry and Charles approach something across the room. Perhaps there ought to be something slightly surreal about this space . . . as there was about shapes emerging from the foggy sea.

> HENRY
> This is my flagship, the <u>Mary Rose</u>. She's the largest warship afloat. She displaces seven hundred tons, fires ninety-one guns, and has a company of four hundred men.

Charles shakes his head in wonder.

> CHARLES
> I have nothing like this.

> HENRY
> You have vast armies!
> (beat)
> Together, we shall be invincible. How could the French withstand us?

> CHARLES
> With you beside me, there is no boundary or frontier or world we could not conquer.

Henry stares at him.

> HENRY
> I like you already.

> CHARLES
> Except for the chin - what is there <u>not</u> to like?

And both men laugh.

CUT TO:

EXT. TRAITORS' GATE - TOWER OF LONDON - DAY

The boat containing Pace passes under the
portcullis, beating oars gently toward the landing
stage, where a small reception committee is waiting.

> VOICE
> (shouting)
> Prisoner to the steps!

The boat is moored against the steps. It's dark
and dismal. The CONSTABLE OF THE TOWER oversees
the disembarkation, with some tough-looking
SOLDIERS in attendance.

As if he was in a dream - or nightmare - Pace is
bundled out of the boat, pulled forward by his
chains.

He stares at the constable.

> PACE
> You must believe me - I'm an innocent
> man. I don't know why I have been
> brought here.

A beat. The constable stares back at him,
expressionless. Then poor Pace is dragged on, up
the steps, towards the tower.

He screams out.

> PACE (cont'd)
> I'M INNOCENT!

It makes not a jot of difference to the constable.

The torches are extinguished with a hiss, in the
dirty waters of the Thames.

INT. ENTRANCE TO COURT - WHITEHALL PALACE - DAY

Henry escorts Charles into the court - both in
great good humour.

>   CHARLES
> You know, you and I are united by an
> indissoluble tie. Since you are married to
> my mother's sister, you are really my
> uncle.

>   HENRY
> It's an affinity which both delights and
> pleases me - nephew.

They laugh. As the doors open, they are confronted
by twenty-five of the queen's loveliest LADIES.

Henry pauses, indicates to Charles.

>   HENRY (cont'd)
> Your Highness - your aunt awaits!

Charles bows, proceeds through the doors. Henry's
eyes quickly scan the ladies-in-waiting. He sees
Anne - just as she turns away, with the others, to
follow Charles inside.

>   CUT TO:

INT. COURT - PALACE - DAY

>   HERALD
> Your Majesty, His Imperial Highness,
> Charles the Holy Roman Emperor.

Charles is escorted down a long corridor, lined
with PAGES dressed in gold brocade and crimson
satin.

He looks up. Katherine is waiting for him. Plump
and matronly, she still looks radiant, dressed in

robes of cloth of gold lined with ermine, strings of pearls wound around her neck.

Smiling, the Holy Roman Emperor walks towards her - and, unexpectedly, falls to his knees before her.

>   CHARLES
>   Majesty, I ask for your blessing, as a
>   nephew to an aunt.

Katherine, visibly thrilled, stands, lets him kiss her hand, then gently raises him, and kisses him - with tears in her eyes.

>   KATHERINE
>   I give you my blessing freely, my dear
>   Charles - as I give you my love.

Charles offers his arm, and they walk arm in arm into a chamber behind them.

INT. CHAMBER - PALACE - DAY

In the chamber another party is waiting.

>   KATHERINE
>   Your Highness, allow me to present my
>   daughter Mary, your future bride.

MARY TUDOR, 9 years old, walks out from her escort. She curtsys beautifully before Charles. Charles applauds.

>   CHARLES
>   Bravo. Come!

He gestures her closer, kisses her cheeks, kneels before her, looks into her eyes.

>   CHARLES (cont'd)
>   We must wait. To be married. Do you think
>   you have the patience?

Mary nods, eagerly.

                         MARY
          I have a present for Your Highness. Do you
          want to see it?

                         CHARLES
          I love presents. Show me!

Mary takes his hand, draws him to the window, and
points.

                         MARY
              There! Look!

Charles looks into the courtyard - where six
beautiful horses are being paraded.

                         CHARLES
              Are they for me?

                         MARY
              Do you like them?

                         CHARLES
          They're the best present I've ever had!
          Thank you, Your Highness.

He smiles, and Mary grins happily.

                                              CUT TO:

EXT. GARDENS - WHITEHALL PALACE - DAY

Thomas Tallis is among the musicians who play for
the kings during their feast.

Henry and Charles sit with Katherine and Princess
Mary at a high table, served by Norfolk and other
great nobles on their bended knees.

CHARLES
(to Henry and Katherine)
As soon as possible, you must both come and
visit me. I want to show you especially the
treasures of Montezuma, the king of the
Aztecs, that General Cortés recently
discovered in Mexico.

HENRY
We should love that. We have only heard a
little about those lands across the sea
that people call the Indies.

CHARLES
I swear to you - that's where the future
lies. So much undiscovered land. So much
wealth of gold and silver, salt, and
minerals.

Some more dishes are brought - by lords for the
kings, ladies for Katherine and Mary.

Henry glances across - and sees Anne Boleyn, just
a few feet away. His heart stops. For a few
seconds he can see nothing but her . . .

And Katherine notices it - sees his look.

Anne moves away. Henry looks over at Katherine,
smiles, and gently places his hand over hers.

HENRY
Sweetheart.

Now we favour BOLEYN, as ANNE passes him.

BOLEYN
(whispers)
Put yourself in his way.

She nods, almost imperceptibly.

We favour Henry and the emperor again. Henry leans closer to him.

> HENRY
> How are your preparations?

> CHARLES
> We are recruiting more German mercenaries.
> But everything is going well. I shall take
> Milan by next spring.

> HENRY
> And then . . . ?

> CHARLES
> And then, together, we shall invade
> France, bring an end to the adventures of
> that libertine monarch, King Francis.

Henry grins.

> HENRY
> That will make me very happy.

> CHARLES
> It will also make you the king of France!

Henry drinks it in.

The musicians begin to play dance music. Charles glances at Mary.

> CHARLES (cont'd)
> Will you dance, Your Highness?
> (to Henry)
> With Your Majesty's permission.

> HENRY
> Granted.

There is loud applause as the emperor leads his
diminutive bride-to-be on to the dance floor.

Henry soon follows with his sister Margaret, who
chews his ear off again.

> MARGARET
> (whispers)
> I've heard he also has gout. They say
> his spine is deformed. He walks like
> a crab.

Henry is not really there; he's looking around for
a glimpse of Anne.

> MARGARET (cont'd)
> All right. Promise me something, brother.
> I'll agree to marry him - but on one
> condition: after he's dead - which can't
> be long - I can marry whom I choose!
> (beat)
> Agreed?

A beat. Henry seems to nod, abstractedly.

We PULL BACK, to yet a third table - where Brandon
is staring fixedly at Margaret as she dances with
Henry. Knivert and Compton are nearby.

> KNIVERT
> Not drinking tonight, Charles - or should
> I say, Your Grace?!

> COMPTON
> You should definitely call him by his real
> name: which is "cunt," or "villain."

Brandon looks round at them.

> BRANDON
> Why?

                    KNIVERT
        We are supposed to be friends, Charles.

                    BRANDON
        Aren't we? Still?

                    COMPTON
        Not if you do not favour us. It's in your
        gift to ask the king to give us some
        titles, or at least some lands.

                    KNIVERT
        But it seems that all His Majesty has to
        give away - he has given to you!

A long beat.

                    BRANDON
            Jealous?

                    COMPTON
        Naturally. As you rise, so should we.

                    KNIVERT
                (ironic)
        What should we do - to please Your Grace?

Brandon - a powerful man - looks back at him.

                    BRANDON
                (after a beat)
            Show me some respect!

Now we favour Katherine.

She whispers to her nephew, Charles.

                    KATHERINE
        I am so glad to see you. It is often
        lonely here.

Charles is surprised.

                        CHARLES
    Lonely?

                        KATHERINE
    Things are not well between us: with His
    Majesty and I.

                        CHARLES
    But - I saw with my own eyes how attentive
    he is to you. He looks at you with such -
    devotion, it seemed with such love.

                        KATHERINE
    I fear that was for your benefit. Henry is
    a good masquer.

A long beat. She tries to control her emotions.

As Anne moves away, she does so in such a way that
her path is blocked by Henry. Lowering her eyes
demurely, she curtsys again.

                        HENRY
    Lady Anne?

                        ANNE
    Yes, Your Majesty.

He just stares at her, especially when she raises
her eyes and meets his gaze. His eyes are lost
in hers.

We favour Katherine and Charles . . .

                        KATHERINE
    I fear sometimes that he will ask me for
    a divorce.

                        CHARLES
    A <u>divorce</u>!? No, that's impossible.

                        KATHERINE
    Is it? . . .

. . . then return to Henry and Anne.

                        HENRY
                  (after a long beat)
        Forgive me.

And he steps aside to let her pass.

                                          CUT TO:

INT. COURT - WHITEHALL PALACE - NIGHT

Henry walks alone through the palace. Suddenly, in
the gloom ahead, he catches sight of a YOUNG WOMAN -
wearing the dress he has already seen her in.

Henry starts to pursue her.

He pursues Anne through the chambers and down the
corridors of the palace. It's a game - but it also
has elements of a dream. Why is Henry alone, for
example? Where are the courtiers?

- sometimes we glimpse groups of them standing
vaguely back among the shadows. Like ghosts.

The pursuit goes on. What it really reminds us of
is the deer hunt. Anne is the quarry.

Henry strides after her, both of them enjoying the hunt.

Finally, she is cornered, unable to escape from
the chamber she has found herself in, panting from
her exertions.

Henry has her at his mercy. As he walks in, she
sinks to the floor in obeisance - or like a
wounded deer. Henry ravishes her with his eyes.

                        HENRY
        Anne.

She gently raises her head, stares at him. He walks over to her, gently raises her. Their faces close now.

                    HENRY (cont'd)
          Will you . . . ?

She smiles, but shakes her head.

                    ANNE
          No. Not like this.

                    HENRY
     How?

                    ANNE
          Seduce me.

She is no longer there, but in a different part of the room. The sense of being in a dream intensifies.

He stares over at her, filled with longing and desire.

                    ANNE (cont'd)
          Write letters to me. And poems. I love
          poems. Ravish me with your words. Seduce me.

He smiles, infatuated - makes a move towards her. But she's disappeared.

He turns. The only door to the chamber is closed.

He walks over and opens it.

On the other side, she is naked.

But the image is subliminal.

Anne has gone.

                                        CUT TO:

INT. BEDCHAMBER - NIGHT

Henry sits bolt upright in bed with a gasp.

The GROOM who sleeps at the foot of his bed
immediately scrambles to his feet, reaching for
his sword.

                    GROOM
          Majesty!

He stares wildly about the room.

A long beat.

                    HENRY
          It's all right. She's gone.

INT. COURT - WHITEHALL PALACE - DAY

Witnessed by many leading NOBLES, including Brandon
and Boleyn, as well as by Katherine and Mary,
Wolsey presents the new treaty to Their Majesties.

                    WOLSEY
          For Your Majesties to sign this treaty
          between you of perpetual amity and
          concord, and to confirm with your seals
          and before these witnesses the betrothal
          of Charles, Holy Roman Emperor, to her
          Highness Princess Mary, upon her reaching
          the age of twelve.
                    (beat)
          I say to you again, in my power as papal
          legate and chancellor of England, that you
          should sign this treaty of friendship, one
          to another, and never break it, so help
          you God.

To great applause, Henry and then Charles sign,
and apply their seals to the manuscript - and then
embrace.

200

Then Charles bows to Katherine, and kisses her hand.

> CHARLES
> (whispers)
> I swear to you my honour and my allegiance.
> You must always trust in me. Always.

And he meets her gaze.

The meeting is breaking up. Henry, moving away,
draws Wolsey to one side.

> HENRY
> Where is Mr. Pace? He should have been here.

> WOLSEY
> Majesty, I have discovered, shamefully,
> that Mr. Pace did not deserve Your
> Majesty's trust. So I have removed him
> from his offices.

> HENRY
> (surprised)
> You're sure?

> WOLSEY
> The French were paying him a pension.

Henry is shocked.

> HENRY
> I see.
> (beat)
> Then I trust you will find me a suitable
> replacement?

Wolsey bows, watches Henry move away.

Now we favour Norfolk - who draws Boleyn aside.

> NORFOLK
> (whispers)
> Well? How do our affairs proceed?

                         BOLEYN
          Very well, Your Grace. The king makes no
          obvious declaration of interest . . . but
          it's possible to detect it in the way he
          glances at her - as if, in his mind, he
          could see her naked.

Norfolk nods. They are still looking across at
Wolsey.

                         NORFOLK
          Well, he looks at most young women that
          way. But it's a start. A beginning to the
          end of that insufferable prelate.

                         BOLEYN
          All in good time. One thing will follow
          another.
                    (beat)
          Perhaps it would be a good idea to
          include the duke of Suffolk in our
          schemes.

He indicates Brandon. Norfolk almost spits.

                         NORFOLK
          Charles Brandon!? He is barely a
          gentleman.

                         BOLEYN
          He is the king's closest friend. And
          I believe he hates Wolsey as much as we
          do. He would be a natural ally - at
          least for a time!

And he smiles.

EXT. AREA BEHIND TILTYARD - DAY

Henry, after a day's jousting, surrounded by his
friends, suddenly notices a STRANGER waiting for
his attention.

Eager to see him. Henry immediately walks over, and CORNELIUS HEYS bows.

> HENRY
> Mr. Heys, do you have those pieces I asked for?

> HEYS
> Yes, Your Majesty.

Very carefully he removes a piece of velvet cloth, and opens it out upon a table.

Inside are four magnificent gold brooches. Henry smiles, picking them up in turn.

> HEYS (cont'd)
> One, rubies set in circlets of gold. A second, a precious stone upon a bed of gold and pearl. Third, small and large drops of pearl, with gold and purple and the detail of a lion's head.

He pauses, as Henry picks up the last and largest of the pieces.

> HEYS (cont'd)
> And lastly - feathers of silver, gold, and amber.

This last, Henry holds in his palm, admiring the genius of the craftsmanship.

> HEYS (cont'd)
> Jewels fit for a queen, Your Majesty.

CUT TO:

INT. CELL - TOWER OF LONDON - EVENING

Pace has been imprisoned in a dark, dank cell near enough to the water line for him to be

able to hear the water sloshing up against
the wall outside.

There is hardly any furniture. A single candle.

There's some dirty straw on the floor. The floor
moves, twitches.

When Pace moves the straw with his foot, a rat's nest
explodes. Pace - a man of a nervous disposition -
cries out in alarm, fear, and revulsion.

He rushes to the door and bangs on it with all his
might, banging and banging until his hands bleed,
and all the while screaming out:

> PACE
> It was Wolsey! Not me! It was Wolsey!
> Listen to me. It's Wolsey who has a
> pension from the French. Ask him. Ask him.
> It's not me. I didn't do anything. I'm
> innocent. It was Wolsey. Wolsey. Wolsey.
> He told them! Wolsey told them. Listen to
> me. It was Wolsey.

His terrified voice drifts out across the cold,
silent waters of the river . . . unheard.

End of Episode 3

THE TUDORS

Episode 4

Created and Written by
Michael Hirst

FINAL SHOOTING SCRIPT
July 10, 2006

INT. COURT - WHITEHALL PALACE - DAY

Gathered in the court are many of the PEOPLE who are going to accompany PRINCESS MARGARET to Lisbon for her marriage to the king of Portugal. They include her private CHAPLAIN, a LAUNDRESS, CHAMBERLAIN, her LADIES, WARDROBE MISTRESS, MEN SERVANTS - and so on.

MARGARET waits for the king, with Brandon withdrawn a little behind her. She is in an emotional state, and wipes tears from her eyes.

> HERALD
> His Majesty, the King.

Henry enters, with Wolsey in attendance. Margaret curtsys and kisses his hand. Henry embraces her.

> HENRY
> My dear sister.
> > (beat)
> Fare you well on your journey. Remember the king of Portugal, your future husband, respects and loves you, and you must love him in return.

Margaret stifles a loud sob. Then suddenly pulls Henry close, as if fervently embracing him - but, in fact, to hiss into his ear.

> MARGARET
> Remember your promise! When he dies, I marry whom I choose.

Henry's expression is noncommittal; it can be read either way.

With some difficulty he disengages himself from his clinging sister and moves to Brandon, who bows.

                              HENRY
                Your Grace, Charles, as you love me, take
                care of her.

                             BRANDON
                I will. You may have no doubts. I shall
                treat her as if she was my own sister.

Henry smiles, pats his shoulder, looks round at
the room.

                              HENRY
                God be with all of you. And remember your
                duties to my lady and to England.
                              (beat)
                Let us pray.

As they all cross themselves and bow their heads,
Wolsey begins a Latin prayer.

                                                    CUT TO:

INT. HENRY'S PRIVATE CHAMBERS - OUTER CHAMBER - DAY

Henry with SIR THOMAS MORE.

                              MORE
                His Holiness thanked God for raising up
                such a prince to be a champion of the
                church. And he expressed astonishment that
                you had found time to write the pamphlet.

Henry beams.

                          MORE (cont'd)
                Furthermore, in order to show his
                gratitude the pope has decided to honour
                you with a new title: "Fidei Defensor."

                              HENRY
                Fidei Defensor: Defender of the Faith.

He seems genuinely moved, almost humbled (a very rare event).

There's a long beat.

                    MORE
          But Your Majesty should know that Martin
          Luther has also responded to your work.

Henry's eyes narrow.

                    HENRY
          What did he say?

                    MORE
          He accused you -

                    HENRY
          Yes?

                    MORE
          He accused you of raving like a strumpet
          in a tantrum.

Henry is genuinely shocked.

                    HENRY
          What!?

To prove it's true, More takes out Luther's
pamphlet. Quotes from it.

                    MORE
          "If the king of England gives himself the
          right to spew out falsehoods, then he
          gives me the right to stuff them back
          down his throat."

A beat. Henry is truly enraged. Picking up a
large plate he hurls it across the chamber so it
shatters.

                              HENRY
          He ought to be burned!

                                              CUT TO:

EXT. MARGARET'S SHIP AT HARBOUR - ESTABLISHING

INT. STATE ROOM - SHIP - PORT - DAY

MARGARET's chests of clothes and the chests
containing her dowry are being stowed in the
generous-sized state room with its wooden
panelling and good furnishings.

MARGARET enters with BRANDON.

                              BRANDON
          This is your state room. I hope it meets
          with Your Highness's approval.

MARGARET gives it a cursory glance.

                              MARGARET
          It will serve.

                              BRANDON
          The beds are narrow - but adequate. In case
          of action all this panelling will be removed.

She looks at him.

                              MARGARET
          Action?

                              BRANDON
          If we are attacked.

                              MARGARET
          Who will attack us?

                              BRANDON
          Pirates.

BRANDON is enjoying himself. She suddenly sees
it - his game.

                    MARGARET
        It seems to me, Your Grace, we have more
        to fear from the pirates already onboard!

She turns from him, and starts to organize her
LADIES.

                                        CUT TO:

INT. CHAPEL ROYAL - DAY

Henry, dressed in a suit of black velvet lined with
sable, his studs and buttons made of diamonds and
pearls, processes to Mass in the Chapel Royal with
Knivert, Compton, and Courtiers in attendance.

People bow before him. Queen Katherine waits for
him, with several of her LADIES.

With a pang, Henry sees that one of them is Anne
Boleyn. But she won't catch his eye. Henry smiles
at Katherine and offers his arm.

                    HENRY
        Good morning, Madam.

                    KATHERINE
        Your Majesty.

Henry and Katherine take their seats before the
rood screen. Behind it is the altar, Wolsey and
the priests, the wine, bread, and chalice.

We start to hear sacred music. Tallis conducts a
boys' choir, their high countertenor voices
blending in soaring and intricate harmonies of
his own increasingly sophisticated making.

Katherine - by now even more religious than she was
before - sits humbly, her eyes downcast. But Henry -
though he tries - can't sit still. He keeps trying
to look round and catch a glimpse of Anne.

He imagines that Katherine is unaware of his
endeavours - but she isn't; we can see it in her
eyes, every time his body twists away from her.

Then Wolsey, having offered the host, signals them
to the altar, where they kneel together.

CUT TO:

INT. HENRY'S PRIVATE CHAMBERS - OUTER CHAMBER - DAY

Henry sits, unable to do or think of anything else.

The door opens and the chamberlain appears, bows.

> CHAMBERLAIN
> Your Majesty, Lady Anne . . .
> (Henry's heart misses a beat)
> Clifford.

Another YOUNG WOMAN, with bright red cheeks,
enters, curtsys. She has something in her hand.

> LADY
> Your Majesty.

Shyly hands Henry a folded piece of cloth of gold,
then curtsys again, and is silent. With a gesture,
Henry dismisses her.

He unfolds the cloth on a table, finding inside it
the four gold brooches he had commissioned for
Anne . . . and a letter. He tears the letter open
quickly, takes it to the window so he can read it
better.

                    ANNE BOLEYN (V.O.)
          Your Gracious Majesty. It causes me such
          pain and grief to return the gifts you
          gave me. Alas, they are too beautiful, and
          I unworthy to receive them . . .

                                          CUT TO:

INT. COACH - DAY

Anne travels in the coach with a young female SER-
VANT. She rests her head back against the seat,
smiling a little.

                    ANNE BOLEYN (V.O.)
          I think I never gave Your Majesty cause to
          give them to me, since I am nothing and
          you are everything. Give them, I pray you,
          to a lady more deserving of Your Majesty's
          affections.

                                          CUT TO:

INT. HENRY'S PRIVATE CHAMBERS - OUTER CHAMBER - DAY

Henry's hand shakes slightly as he reads.

                    ANNE BOLEYN (V.O.)
          I am leaving now for my family's house at
          Hever. I shall think of you on the journey
          there.

                         HENRY
                        (reads)
          "Your loving servant, Anne Boleyn."

Henry stares at her handwriting, and gently touches
her signature.

                                          CUT TO:

                                             213

INT. CELL-TOWER OF LONDON-DAY

The heavy door is unlocked and opens, and the
constable enters. There is a single feeble light.

Pace is inside. His courtier's clothes are dirty
and threadbare. But he is still courteous.

> CONSTABLE
> Mr. Pace.

Pace bows.

> PACE
> At your service, sir.

> CONSTABLE
> You are to be released.

A beat.

> PACE
> I don't know anything.

> CONSTABLE
> What's that? I said - you are to be
> released.

> PACE
> I told my wife. I told her: I don't know
> anything. Anything at all.

> CONSTABLE
> You - told your wife, Mr. Pace? When?

> PACE
> Yes, sir, hush. She's sleeping.
> (laughs softly)
> We talk together. I thought she had
> died giving birth to our son. I was

                    sure I went to her funeral, and wept.
                    But now I see she is alive, and as
                    well as I.
                              (hesitantly)
                    Do you not see her?

Disconcerted, the constable holds the candle up to
Pace's face. Pace's eyes stare back at him
blankly; he's quite mad.

He puts the candle down.

                         CONSTABLE
                         (quietly)
               Yes, Mr. Pace. I see her.

Pace is reassured, and smiles broadly.

                                             CUT TO:

INT. WOLSEY'S CHAMBERS-DAY

WOLSEY, carrying a sheaf of papers, moves through his
chambers - pauses when he sees a MAN very diligently
at work at a desk. The man appears to be doing some
accounting, writing down lists of figures.

He is in his thirties. Slender, sharp-looking.
Intelligent.

                         WOLSEY
               Mr. Cromwell!

THOMAS CROMWELL looks up from his work.

                         CROMWELL
               Eminence.

He is soft-spoken, unassuming almost. Who could
guess what he will become?

                    WOLSEY
        I have long noticed your aptitude for work
        and your diligence in carrying through my
        affairs. And your discretion.

                    CROMWELL
        I am grateful to Your Eminence.

                    WOLSEY
        You are from obscure stock - but so am I.
        It should not be held against you.

A beat. He's thinking.

                    WOLSEY (cont'd)
        I may have a proposition to put to you.

                    CROMWELL
        Thank you, Your Eminence.

Cromwell watches Wolsey walk through into the next
chamber.

                                            CUT TO:

**EXT. WOLSEY'S PRIVATE CHAMBERS - INNER CHAMBER -
HAMPTON COURT - DAY**

Henry with Wolsey. He's still distracted.

                    WOLSEY
        By the terms of our treaty with the emperor,
        we are obliged to support his war effort
        financially. At present his armies are
        fighting the French in Italy. Near Milan.
                    (beat)
        Unfortunately, I have calculated that to
        honour our obligations we shall be obliged
        to raise taxes.
                    (Henry doesn't respond.)
        A bill will be presented to Parliament in
        its next session.

Henry nods absently.

                    HENRY
        Good. Good.

                    WOLSEY
        I trust the bill will pass successfully.

                    HENRY
        I am sure, Your Eminence, that with your
        guiding hand - it will be so.

                    WOLSEY
        At least our alliance with the emperor is
        popular. I ask myself, sometimes, why that
        should be so?

Henry looks at him.

                    HENRY
        Because he's not French!

Henry doesn't smile - moves away, restless.

                    WOLSEY
        Right. The new warship is commissioned at
        Portsmouth.

Even this doesn't bring the king round.

A beat. Wolsey thinks.

                    WOLSEY (cont'd)
        I forgot to mention to Your Majesty: we
        have a new visitor at court, Princess
        Marguerrite of Navarre. I received her
        yesterday and thought her indeed a very
        beautiful young woman, with a very sweet,
        and yielding, disposition.
                    (beat)
        She confessed a great admiration for Your
        Majesty.

A beat. Henry's at least half-listening.

                    WOLSEY (cont'd)
          Shall I arrange . . . ?

                    HENRY
          Yes. Do it!

                    WOLSEY
          With Your Majesty's permission, I intend
          to appoint a new secretary, instead of
          Mr. Pace.

Henry, still absently, nods.

                    HENRY
          Yes.

                                        CUT TO:

EXT. SHIP AT SEA - NIGHT - ESTABLISHING

INT. SHIP - NIGHT

Margaret lies in her narrow bunk beside her state
room, dimly illuminated by a swinging lantern. The
ship pitches and rolls slowly in the swell, its
timbers creaking.

Some of her LADIES sleep nearby, cramped into even
smaller bunks in the overcrowded vessel.

But Margaret is awake. Through the thin partition
that divides the state room from the captain's
cabin, she can hear male VOICES and laughter, the
clink of glasses, suggesting another world. And
Brandon's distinctive voice.

Around the table that almost fills the cabin
are the CAPTAIN, two of his OFFICERS, and
Brandon. They play cards, gamble, and drink -
and laugh.

The players bet on their cards - dropping pennies and shilling into a pot. The "trumps" are ace, king, queen, and knave.

They play a round as the ship continues to roll gently, and the wind whistles. Margaret, kneeling up, finds a small hole in the wall between the cabins and has a partial view of Brandon and the captain as they play.

> CAPTAIN
> (plays a card)
> There we are, Your Grace. My king has your queen.

A beat. She sees Brandon shrug.

> BRANDON
> I was rather hoping, Captain, that the knave would get the queen.

They laugh. Brandon raises his eyes and looks straight back at the wall, as if he knows that Margaret is watching him from the other side. She springs back, embarrassed.

> CUT TO:

INT. COURT - NIGHT

Music is playing - as Wolsey approaches Henry. He is escorting a pretty YOUNG WOMAN in a velvet dress, her dark hair caught in a net behind her white neck.

Henry gestures them forward.

> HENRY
> Eminence.

> WOLSEY
> Your Majesty, may I present Princess Marguerrite of Navarre.

                    HENRY
          Madame.

The PRINCESS curtsys, her dress cut so low that
Henry cannot fail to appreciate her very large
breasts.

Henry raises her gently. She fixes him with a gaze
that is almost feral.

                    PRINCESS
          Majeste.

A beat.

                    HENRY
          You are visiting here?

                    PRINCESS
          Oui, Votre Majeste, the count, my
          husband, had to stay behind in France -
          regrettably.

She flirts with him outrageously.

                    HENRY
          Indeed. Very regrettable, madame. But you
          must be compensated. You must enjoy some
          pleasures whilst here.

The princess smiles a little.

Now we favour Norfolk. A man of rather simple
appetites, he is eating heartily - when Boleyn
quietly joins him.

                    BOLEYN
                (after a beat)
          I have some news which may interest Your
          Grace.

Norfolk looks up at him, his mouth full of half-masticated food.

                    BOLEYN (cont'd)
          The bishop of Winchester died six months
          ago. Winchester is the richest parish in
          England. Wolsey is supposed to appoint his
          successor.
                    (beat)
          And he just did. He appointed himself.

                    NORFOLK
          How much more wealth does that man want?

They both look across at the cardinal, as he moves
away from Henry's table.

                    BOLEYN
          There's more.

                    NORFOLK
          Tell me!

A beat. Boleyn leans even closer.

                    BOLEYN
          It appears that he has been using some
          of the king's money to invest his new
          college in Oxford, and his own personal
          foundation. He closes down the worst
          monasteries, strips them of their assets,
          as he is supposed to do - but instead of
          transferring all the profit to the privy
          purse, he makes all the profits
          disappear.

Norfolk stares at him.

                    NORFOLK
                    (spluttering)
          You must tell the king! Right away.

                         BOLEYN
          Forgive me, Your Grace, but we must judge
          the time - exactly! Such is Wolsey's hold
          over the king that, whatever the evidence
          against him, the king won't believe it.
                         (beat)
          But there will come a point. When the
          king's belief in his minister will hang in
          the balance. And then, Your Grace, we
          shall drop our truth into the scales, and
          the scales will fall.

A beat.

Now Henry spots MORE moving through the crowds.
Going over, he embraces him warmly and drunkenly.

                         HENRY
          Dear Thomas!

                         MORE
          Majesty.

                         HENRY
          Come on, stay at court. I need you. I'll
          give you great chambers. Compton has great
          chambers. You can have his!

He laughs. MORE smiles.

                         MORE
          Much as I love Your Majesty, I like my
          chambers to have my family inside them.

HENRY smiles - then is abruptly distracted again.
He sees someone - and wants to talk to him. He
moves away.

For a moment MORE remains with KNIVERT and COMPTON.

                        KNIVERT
          His Majesty loves you above anyone else,
          Mr. More, you know that.

A beat. MORE looks back at them.

                    MORE
          That may be true. And yet - if my head
          were to win him a castle in Spain, I
          think he would cut it off.

Smiling enigmatically, he moves on. Now we
favour HENRY again. He gestures to the young
man he saw - the poet THOMAS WYATT (whom we
saw earlier with ANNE). WYATT bows. As HENRY
talks to him, we realize that he's not drunk
at all!

                    HENRY
     Mr. Wyatt.

                    WYATT
     Your Majesty.

                    HENRY
     I hear you're a poet.

                    WYATT
     I write poems. I don't know how to be
     "a poet."

                    HENRY
     I have read some. I like them.

                    WYATT
     My lord, I don't know what to say.

A long beat.

                    HENRY
     Were you in love with Anne Boleyn?

Wyatt is taken somewhat off guard.

                    WYATT
        I -

                              HENRY
          Cardinal Wolsey tells me you were once
          engaged.

                              WYATT
          No! That's not true.

A beat. Henry stares at him.

                              HENRY
          Did you love her?

Wyatt must weigh this up very carefully. The wrong
answer and his head will soon be missing.

                              WYATT
          Lady Anne is so beautiful that it is the
          duty of every man to love her. Of course
          I loved her - but from a distance.
          Personally, I have a wife.

A long beat. Then suddenly Henry seems to accept
his explanation. He dismisses Wyatt.

                              HENRY
          Enjoy the feast.

Now we favour Thomas Tallis. He is not yet such a
great star that he can eat at the big tables. But,
typically, he's not really thinking about that. He
eats with other lowly servants, though he's not
interested in the food. He annotates music with a
scratching quill, locked into his own world.

Two young SISTERS, ladies-in-waiting, watch him,
they whisper together, and giggle - obviously
attracted. They egg each other on to talk to him.

                         FIRST SISTER
          Thomas? . . . Thomas Tallis!

He looks up reluctantly. The two very PRETTY GIRLS
treat him to a smile.

                    TALLIS
                 (embarrassed)
          Hello.

                 FIRST SISTER
          We just wanted to say - we love your music.

Tallis almost blushes.

                    TALLIS
                 (whispers)
          Thank you.

He lowers his eyes. The girls move closer along
the bench.

                 SECOND SISTER
          We share a room. Do you want to come back
          with us?

A beat. Tallis looks, from one to the other. Maybe
they're actually twins. Certainly very attractive.

But then he shakes his head.

                    TALLIS
          I want to finish this song.

                 FIRST SISTER
          You could finish it tomorrow.

                    TALLIS
          I'll have forgotten it by tomorrow.

                 SECOND SISTER
          And you'll forget us, too.

Tallis smiles, rather apologetically

The girls move away.

Tallis goes back to his musical annotation. Then a
shadow falls over the paper and he looks up.

William Compton, one of Henry's best friends, has
paused to look at him. Like most of Henry's best
friends, Compton is devastatingly handsome and
beautifully dressed.

Tallis looks back at him - and his heart,
surprised, misses a beat.

Then Compton passes on his way.

He finds HENRY with KNIVERT, and bows.

They are drinking and HENRY is eating tidbits
from bowls brought by SERVANTS.

HENRY looks over at the PRINCESS.

> HENRY
> Compton, my friend, what do you think
> of Princess Marguerrite of Navarre?

KNIVERT and COMPTON look her over.

> COMPTON
> She's well-built, Your Majesty - a
> little heavy in the top decks for my
> taste though.

They laugh.

> HENRY
> She's Francis's sister. I happen to know
> that.

He winks at them suggestively, and they laugh again.

EXT. KING'S BEDCHAMBER - NIGHT

In the outer room, several of the king's GROOMS
and SERVANTS listen to what is going on in the
king's bedchamber.

The wooden bed is shaking violently, and everyone
can hear the princess's unabashed and very vocal
pleasuring.

                    PRINCESS (V.O.)
          Oui Henri . . . C'est ca, Henri . . .
          oui Henri . . . Oh . . . C'est ca . . .
          Mon Dieu!

As the bed is heard to rock more violently, the
servants, vastly amused, can hardly contain
themselves.

                    PRINCESS (V.O.) (cont'd)
          Mon Dieu, Henri . . . ou . . . ou . . .
          Mon Dieu . . . ah oui . . . ah oui . . .
          Henri . . .

The servants, this time not bothering to pretend
they can't hear anything, begin to mimic her
strangulated English.

                    GROOM #1
                 (quietly)
          Ah oui . . . Henri.

There's quiet laughter.

                    GROOM #2
          C'est ca . . . oh . . . ah . . .

The pitch of her voice rises from the other room.

                    GROOM #1
          Mon Dieu, <u>Henri</u>!

They hear a final shriek.

It goes quiet.

                    GROOM #2
          C'est <u>fini</u>!

CUT TO:

INT. STATE CABIN - SHIP - EVENING

Margaret can hear Brandon moving about on the
other side of the partition. She is already in
her nightshirt.

Unable to help herself, she looks through the
spyhole to see Brandon getting ready for bed.
Removing his shirt he lies in a bunk just beneath
her eye level, his naked torso almost close enough
for her to touch.

She feasts her eyes on it.

INT. COURT - DAY
Knivert personally leads one of the RIDERS through
the court - though the man is literally covered
head to foot with mud.

The courtiers, sensing something in the air, rush
to witness the event.

CUT TO:

INT. PRESENCE CHAMBER - DAY

Henry strides eagerly into the chamber - sees
Knivert with the figure covered in mud.

                    KNIVERT
        A messenger from the emperor, Your Majesty.

The muddy fellow sinks, exhausted, to his knees.

                    HENRY
        Well . . . ?! What is it?

                    MESSENGER
                 (after a beat)
        The emperor has won a great victory
        against the French.

Henry's eyes light up, but he can hardly believe
what he's hearing.

                    HENRY
          What are you saying?

                    MESSENGER
                (recovering a little)
          At the Battle of Pavia, five days ago, the
          emperor's army totally overcame those of
          the French. The French army was destroyed.

Henry begins, happily, to understand.

                    HENRY
          My God! Is this true?!

                    MESSENGER
          Not only that!
                (beat)
          The French king himself was also captured
          on the battlefield.

It takes a moment.

                    HENRY
          Francis? . . . King Francis was captured?!

                    MESSENGER
          Yes, Your Majesty. He is now the emperor's
          prisoner.

Henry strides down and embraces the man, beaming
and almost laughing.

                    HENRY
          You are as welcome here as if you were
          the angel Gabriel.

Looks at Knivert, the others in the chamber.

                    HENRY (cont'd)
          What great news! We must celebrate!

We HEAR the sound of trumpets.

                                        CUT TO:

EXT. TILTYARD - DAY

Done up in its usual flambuoyant way. Pennants
fluttering in the breeze, brightly colored
pavilions and heraldic devices.

The drama and theatre of it.

Katherine watches beneath a royal canopy on which
her initials are interlaced with Henry's. Sitting
next to her, in a place of honour, is the
messenger who brought the good news to Henry.

Great CROWDS cheer and applaud as two KNIGHTS run
a course, their lances shattering.

Wolsey and MORE are among those watching as Henry
rides out into the tiltyard, to applause and
cheering (for it is always a special thing to see
the king of England ride into battle!).

We quickly favour Knivert, who has just jousted
and passes - either on foot or horse - Compton,
who is preparing to enter the list.

                    COMPTON
          Well done.

                    KNIVERT
                 (grimly)
          I tell you, William. I will be called a
          knight today, or I never will be.

                    HERALD
          His Majesty, the King.

We cut back as Henry approaches the platform . . . and
the cheers are multiplied as Katherine rises and ties
her colours to his lance, so that he is her champion.

                    HENRY
          My queen.

                    KATHERINE
          My lord.

                    HENRY
          My lady.

We favour Wolsey, watching this. Leans closer
to MORE.

                    WOLSEY
               (rather contemptuous)
          You see how popular the queen is with
          the people!

                    MORE
          She is the daughter of Isabella and
          Ferdinand - so perhaps they think she
          is what a queen should be.

WOLSEY frowns, lacks his usual air of congeniality.

                    HERALD
          William Compton, riding against His
          Majesty.

For a moment we favour Compton, as he rides out
to joust with Henry.

Then cut back.

                    MORE
          You seem out of sorts today.

                    WOLSEY
          I have reasons to be downcast and pained.
          They needn't bother you.

A beat.

                    MORE
                  (quietly)
      Why should we not have pains? Some people
      seem to think that we ought to go to
      heaven in featherbeds! It's not the way -
      for our Lord himself went there in pain
      and tribulation.

Another pause. MORE gives one of his laconic
smiles.

                    MORE (cont'd)
      Not that I'm suggesting that you're
      like that.

We favour Compton and Henry.

                    COMPTON
        Are you ready?

                    HENRY
        I was born ready, William.

There is a sudden explosion of noise . . . as
Henry and Compton thunder towards each other down
the list. Cheers and applause as their lances
break.

                    HERALD
        A point for His Majesty, the King.

We favour Katherine. She speaks quietly to the
messenger.

                    KATHERINE
        Do not look at me - but I ask you
        privately to do something for me. Take
        this letter to the emperor.

She slips the letter to him, unseen, and it
vanishes into his clothing.

KATHERINE (cont'd)
You will do this for me - and not show it
to anyone else, or say a word about it?

He nods, almost imperceptibly.

Meanwhile Compton and Henry run their second course.

HERALD
A second point for His Majesty.

CUT TO:

INT. KITCHENS - HEVER - DAY

The kitchens of the castle; stone floors, an open
fire, rows of ovens, slate surfaces . . . great
copper tureens, copper plates, rows of knives,
dead pheasants and partridges and jugged hares
hanging upside down from iron railings.

Anne reads aloud a letter.

ANNE
"I was distressed you would not accept
the brooches. They were made for you,
not for anyone else. And why are you
not worthy when I deem you so? For
certain, it must be plain to you now
that I desire to find a place in your
heart . . ."

MALE VOICE
Wait! Give it to me!

A YOUNG MAN, a few years older than Anne, with long
blond hair, turns away from the fire where he's
been listening, and tries to snatch the letter.

For a moment Anne holds it out of reach - then
hands it to him.

                          YOUNG MAN
                          (reads)
              ". . . and your grounded affection!"

He looks up at Anne.

                          YOUNG MAN (cont'd)
                    Grounded affection?

                          ANNE
                    Grounded.

And whistles appreciatively.

                          YOUNG MAN
                          (reads)
              "Tell me at least that we can meet in
              private. I mean nothing more than a
              chance to talk to you."

Again, the young man grins, and raises his
eyebrows.

                          YOUNG MAN (cont'd)
              "I beg you, come back to court -"

                          ANNE
                    Come . . . Give it back, brother.

                          YOUNG MAN
              "- soon. And meanwhile, accept this new
              gift . . . and wear it, for my sake."

He looks at Anne again.

                          YOUNG MAN (cont'd)
                    What gift? And where is it?

Anne indicates her neck. Around it, she is wearing
a double string of pearls with a small, solid gold
cross, inset with a diamond.

YOUNG MAN (cont'd)
Holy Jesus!

CUT TO:

EXT. TILTYARD - DAY

There is a fresh stir, of interest and
amusement . . . as two SERVANTS carry a long tree
trunk into the list. They are big guys, and the
trunk is clearly heavy.

Compton hands his lance to the page, and the two
servants heave the heavy timber over the saddle,
so that Compton can hold the end just like a
lance. Only this is longer and weighs a ton!

Watching, the crowd has become more and more
curious - then amazed. Naturally they like
novelties of every kind, but this is something new!
They watch almost open-mouthed as Compton gives the
signal - and takes the whole weight of the trunk.

Grimacing with the effort, he starts to rise slowly
from the list. The crowd almost holds . . .

Now we favour Boleyn and Norfolk. They talk quietly.

                    NORFOLK
        When will you bring my niece back to court?

                    BOLEYN
        Soon, I think. Now the king's appetite is
        whetted.

Smiles.

They turn, hearing the rising sound of applause.

Compton has very nearly reached the end of the
list. The tension is visible in his face, how he
tries to keep his arm locked and steady.

It starts to tremble. He almost shouts out in pain . . . but the crowds are CHEERING him on now, willing him on.

And he makes it! Dropping the trunk with relief . . . and taking the salute of the crowd as he rides around, taking off his helmet and grinning widely.

He passes Henry.

> HENRY
> What's this?

Compton grins.

> COMPTON
> Just a trick, Your Majesty. Just a trick.

> HERALD
> Anthony Knivert riding against His Majesty.

We favour Henry, about to enter the list again. He puts on his helmet, his page gives him his shield and lance - and he rides out to ringing cheers and applause.

So does his opponent. Henry spurs on his horse. But something's wrong.

> BOLEYN
> The king's forgotten his visor.

Many other PEOPLE have seen it too.

> VOICES
> (shouting)
> HOLD! HOLD! HOLD!
> (beat)
> THE KING! THE KING! HOLD!

But Henry can't hear the cries beneath the tumult of noise, the thundering of hooves . . .

And Knivert's lance strikes the front of his helmet, forcing, snapping his head backwards with a sickening sound - and shatters, and as Henry puts his hand to face and slumps forward - there is a sudden, shocked silence.

Katherine rises to her feet in alarm - as GROOMS and SERVANTS run towards the stricken king. Henry is helped from his horse. Knivert, Norfolk, and Boleyn are among those who attend him.

Someone gently removes Henry's helmet. His face is bloody, the skin gouged with splinters. Boleyn carefully plucks out the seven or so splinters that still protrude from the flesh of his cheeks and forehead.

                    HENRY
          I'm not hurt.

                    BOLEYN
          Not your eyes, thank God.

                    HENRY
          A cloth!

He is given a cloth and wipes the blood away with his own hand. Then grins at their appalled faces.

                    HENRY (cont'd)
          You see?!

Knivert has tears in his eyes, bows his head.

                    KNIVERT
          Will Your Majesty ever forgive me?

                              HENRY
              It's not your fault, Anthony. It's all my
              fault. And to prove to you - and the people -
              that no harm has come to me, I shall run
              again. Come, Anthony! Run against me!

They are astonished, but can't contradict him. Henry
walks - a little gingerly, it's true - over to the
dais and Katherine, who is still in a state of shock.

                          HENRY (cont'd)
              Madam, have no fear for me. I intend to
              show you and everyone that I am perfectly
              well and unharmed.

                            KATHERINE
                        (with genuine concern)
              If you insist - but I would much rather
              you did not.

                              HENRY
              My lady.
                        (to Anthony)
              Arm yourself!

People begin to realize what he is doing . . . and
from a slow and worried murmur, the NOISE grows
and grows into wild cheering and applause.

Henry, enjoying himself, calls out.

                          HENRY (cont'd)
              Are you ready for me, Anthony? People of
              England, your king is unharmed.

He rides to the top of the list. Moments later
Knivert has ridden to the far side, and they are
given fresh lances.

And now again the crowds fall silent - apprehensive.
The whole atmosphere is different: It's not just a
game now, it's something between life and death.

Henry and Knivert rush towards each other.

They come together. Knivert's lance glances harmlessly off Henry's shield (deliberately), but Henry's lance strikes Knivert's helmet - and from inside there's an EXPLOSION of blood. Knivert is blinded and unable to control his horse, sways sickeningly in the saddle.

> HENRY (cont'd)
> (shouting)
> Knivert! Anthony!

People rush towards Knivert, as he slumps forward and blood pours out of his helmet.

> CUT TO:

INT. STATE CABIN - SHIP - NIGHT

Brandon is escorted through to the state cabin. With its oak-panelled walls and velvet furnishings the cabin more resembles a room at court.

Margaret is seated at a table, playing patience. Brandon bows to her.

A long beat.

> BRANDON
> You wanted to see me, Your Highness?

Margaret continues to play the cards.

> MARGARET
> Only to ask how much longer we must be at sea?

> BRANDON
> With a fair wind, two more days.

Margaret doesn't respond.

Another long beat. Brandon bows again, starts to
leave.

                    MARGARET
          Do you play cards, Your Grace?

                    BRANDON
          Sometimes . . . Your Highness.

Margaret gestures for him to sit down in the chair
opposite. She gathers up the cards - and for the
first time looks at him.

                    MARGARET
          What game shall we play?

A beat. Their eyes on each other.

                    BRANDON
          You choose.

A beat.

                    MARGARET
          French Ruff.

Brandon nods, but keeps his eyes on hers.

Margaret deals them each five cards, puts the
stack in the middle.

                    MARGARET (cont'd)
          You pick trumps.

Brandon reaches forward and turns over the top
card in the stack - and shows it to Margaret.

                    MARGARET (cont'd)
          Kings.

                    BRANDON
          How appropriate . . . Your Highness.

They start to play - it's like whist - picking up
cards from the pack, discarding others, perhaps
not really concentrating.

Margaret gestures to one of her ladies.

                    MARGARET
          Wine?

                    BRANDON
          As you please.

Two glasses are poured. The game goes on.

A long beat.

                    BRANDON (cont'd)
          Your Highness must be looking
          forward with great anticipation to
          your wedding?

Margaret shoots him a warning glance, but stays
silent.

                    BRANDON (cont'd)
          I heard that the king was a great
          horseman-in his time. And famous for
          his beautiful mistresses.

                    MARGARET
                 (quietly)
          Don't tease me. I don't like it.

                    BRANDON
          Will you like it when an old man tries to
          make love to you?

Her eyes flare.

                    MARGARET
          Your Grace goes too far. Already.

                    BRANDON
          It says in the Gospels that the truth will
          make you free.

                    MARGARET
          Now you are blasphemous! My poor ladies
          should not hear you!

With a gesture, she dismisses them.

Suddenly they are alone. Margaret has a high colour.

Abruptly she pulls Brandon towards her and kisses
him passionately.

                    MARGARET (cont'd)
          I want you to leave.

                    BRANDON
          Do you?

She looks at him, her eyes bright with lust.

                    MARGARET
          Yes. Now!

                    BRANDON
          A pity. I had a winning hand.

But she doesn't mean it. And he crushes his mouth
against hers and feels her body.

                                        CUT TO:

INT. STATE ROOM - SHIP - NIGHT

Brandon presses Margaret up against the wall of
the cabin, as the boat pitches. Kissing her
passionately, caressing her.

He starts to lift her dresses. Her lips tear at his.

242

And Brandon enters her, as passionate as his kisses, and fucks her, and she wants it.

                                        CUT TO:

INT. COURT - EVENING

Henry walks through with Wolsey, courtiers bowing to left and right.

                    HENRY
        Send a message to the emperor. Tell him of
        our joy and contentment at his great victory
        at Pavia, and his capture of the French king.

                    WOLSEY
        Yes, Your Majesty.

                    HENRY
        Ask him what he intends to do with
        Francis. And whether or not, with Francis
        captive, it may not be a good time to
        think of striking at France itself? Tell
        him we have gold, men, and ships at his
        disposal, and that are eager to do battle
        and share some of his glory.

                    WOLSEY
        I shall.
                (beat)
        Ah! Your Majesty - this is your new
        secretary.

They pause while Thomas Cromwell detaches himself from the crowd, and comes forward. And bows.

                    WOLSEY (cont'd)
        This is Thomas Cromwell. He is a trained
        barrister, and a scholar and a diligent
        man. I pray he will prove most useful to
        Your Majesty.

Henry looks Cromwell up and down, and nods.

                    HENRY
          Mr. Cromwell.

                    CROMWELL
          Your Majesty.

Henry and Wolsey move on. Henry blithely unaware
of what Cromwell will mean to him one day!

They enter a hall, equally crowded. Katherine, at
the far end, is waiting for him, holding the hand
of their daughter Mary. But her ladies, including
Anne Boleyn, stand in front of her, and as they
sweep aside to make way for the king, Henry has a
second or two to whisper to her, even noticing that
she is wearing the pearl necklace he sent her.

                    HENRY
          You are back at court.
               (beat)
          May I see you privately?

Anne nods, both of them looking the other way.

Then he's moving forward again, and Katherine
releases Mary. Now Mary runs to Henry, who sweeps
her up in his arms.

                    HENRY (cont'd)
          Sweetheart.

                    MARY
          Le roi! Le roi! Comment ça va?

Henry laughs.

                    HENRY
          Très bien, ma petite. Et toi?

244

MARY
(prettily)
Comme ci . . . comme ça!

Henry laughs again, and kisses her, and puts
her down . . . and catches Anne's eye briefly.

Katherine glances coldly at Wolsey, then falls
into step with Henry.

HENRY
My lady.

They are all smiles, to their public.

KATHERINE
(under her breath)
Why does Wolsey open my letters? Am
I not the queen of England?

HENRY
Are you sure he does?

KATHERINE
I am sure.

A beat.

HENRY
Then I shall stop it.
(beat)
Cardinal Wolsey can be too zealous. But
it is always in our interest . . .
(beat)
Unless you have secrets!

He looks at her.

There's a beat.

Then Henry catches sight of Anne. She is talking
and laughing with the long-haired blond young man

we saw her with in the kitchens at Hever. There is
no doubting their obvious intimacy.

Henry stares, forgetting to pretend otherwise.
Katherine could not miss that look.

She lowers her eyes. Is deeply wounded. But says
nothing.

INT. PRESENCE CHAMBER - CONTINUOUS

>   HERALD
>   Anthony Knivert.

Norfolk and the other courtiers are already
assembled. Knivert's wound is still visible near
his eye, which is also deeply bruised.

>   HENRY
>   Anthony.

>   KNIVERT
>   Majesty.

Henry glances at the wound.

>   HENRY
>   You almost lost an eye.

Knivert shrugs.

>   KNIVERT
>   Never use that one much anyway.

Henry smiles, gestures Norfolk forward. Norfolk
holds a velvet cushion upon which sits a ceremonial
sword. He bows - as Henry takes the sword.

>   HENRY
>   (to Knivert)
>   Kneel.

Knivert kneels at Henry's feet. Henry touches him
on both shoulders with the blade of the sword.

> HENRY (cont'd)
> I dub thee Sir Anthony Knivert. Arise, Sir
> Anthony, and be recognized.

Knivert rises. Henry embraces him. Knivert is
overjoyed.

Norfolk looks disgusted. Another commoner getting
elevated!

Then the doors open again.

> CHAMBERLAIN
> Mr. William Compton.

Compton enters. Knivert looks between him and
Henry - and does a double take.

> HENRY
> Why so reproving a look, Sir Anthony?

> KNIVERT
> Majesty - I nearly lost an _eye_ for the
> same result!

Henry is enjoying himself.

> HENRY
> Ah - but you never carried a tree!
> (laughs)
> William! Kneel.

CUT TO:

INT. MERCHANT'S HOUSE - NIGHT

A servant opens a door - allowing inside two
gentlemen in dark cloaks, which they take off and

hand to the servant. These men, far from being
shady characters, look prosperous and important -
which, indeed, for the most part, they are.

They join an already gathered assembly in the main
room of the house, where a PASTOR in a plain,
undecorated gown, is already speaking. The pastor
is Dutch, but speaks English with a thick accent.

> PASTOR
> So that is why it is to be understood
> that the pope, far from being a descendant
> of St. Peter, is a sinner, a hyprocrite, a
> handmaiden to the devil, and the living
> Antichrist on earth. This is what Luther
> teaches us, in order to free us from false
> worship and false idols. In order that we
> might return to the true religion and take
> the true and fruitful path to
> salvation . . .

As he speaks - with passionate conviction - we
slowly scan the (male) faces in the room - dignified
and sober men, all of them dressed in black.

Then stop when we reach the figure of Thomas
Cromwell, listening with the rest.

> PASTOR (cont'd)
> Our message - of hope, of liberty, of
> truth - is already spreading throughout
> Europe, from one corner to another. Here
> in England, we have planted a seed that
> will, with prayer and with action, and
> perhaps even with sacrifice, one day grow
> to become a great tree whose branches will
> overreach the kingdom and destroy the
> putrid monastic houses of the Antichrist.
> And this tree will be called the Liberty
> Tree, and in its branches all the angels
> of the Lord will sing hallelujah.

                         CROMWELL
                        (mutters)
          Hallelujah.

                                                      CUT TO:

INT. CORRIDORS - PALACE - NIGHT

Henry walks alone through the corridors. This is
slightly strange - reminds us a little of his dream.
Anne is waiting for him, curtsys.

A long beat. Holds her gaze.

                         HENRY
          I have dreamt of this moment a long time.
                        (beat)
          Anne, you must know I desire you with all
          my heart.

Anne lowers her eyes. Henry gently cups her chin
and raises her face.

                         HENRY (cont'd)
          The young man you were dallying with
          earlier? Who was he?

                         ANNE
                        (with a smile)
          My brother, George.

Henry relaxes, smiles too. His hand is still upon
her face, and gently he draws her towards him.

Perhaps he expects some resistance - but there is
none. Henry kisses her lips, long and deeply. Then
looks into her wonderful eyes, which seem to shine
in that dull passage.

There is a noise from somewhere - footsteps,
perhaps - not far away, which causes them to

                                                         249

break, and withdraw a little, as if this was a guilty pleasure.

                    ANNE (cont'd)
          Her Majesty expects me.

Henry, drunk with love, nods, smiles.

                    HENRY
          Later.

Anne nods, drops a quick curtsy, and hurries away into the shadows.

Knivert and Compton emerge beside Henry - just in time to see Anne's disappearance.

They bow.

                    COMPTON
          Who was that, Your Majesty?

                    HENRY
                (softly)
          Just a girl.

                                        CUT TO:

EXT. LISBON HARBOUR - ESTABLISHING - MARGARET'S POV

INT. STATE ROOM - SHIP - DAY

Through the windows of the state room, MARGARET can see the town and harbour of Lisbon begin to materialize.

Brandon walks over, stands just behind her.

                    BRANDON
          Your new kingdom.

She is silent.

                    BRANDON (cont'd)
        The king must be -

                    MARGARET
        Don't! I forbid you.

He moves even closer. Margaret shivers slightly.

                    MARGARET (cont'd)
        I should hate you!

                    BRANDON
        But you don't. I know you don't.

A long beat. Margaret looks at him, her eyes wet
with tears.

                    MARGARET
        What will I do?

Brandon looks back at her.

                                            CUT TO:

EXT. PALACE - LISBON - DAY

Margaret, with Brandon a step behind her, walks -
with obvious trepidation - between rows of rather
severe-looking MONKS and NUNS, into the palace.

                                            CUT TO:

INT. PALACE - DAY

Inside, they are confronted by PORTUGUESE BISHOPS,
ARISTOCRATS, and OFFICERS in plumed helmets.
Nearly all of them are elderly men. But there are
strange-looking women, too, with high conical hats
or gauze over their faces. A shop of horrors! One
holds a chattering monkey!

MARGARET looks around in some alarm.

Then the KING OF PORTUGAL himself comes forward.
In his sixties, but looking older, his frame is
emaciated, and his thin hair sits on top of a
skull-like face. He walks slowly with a stick.

But the most bizarre thing about him is that he
has effected the dress of a much younger man.

As this apparition shuffles towards her, Margaret
almost visibly recoils.

> MARGARET
> (sotto voce)
> Save me.

But she is not to be saved.

We see the horror in her eyes and the king bows
to her . . . and the lascivious eyes set into
their bony sockets travel slowly up and down
her body.

Weak at the knees, she manages to curtsy.

> KING
> (in Portuguese)
> Margaret, you are even more handsome
> than your portrait. I feel so greatly
> fortunate that you are soon to be my
> queen. Everything here is at your
> disposal. I only want you to be happy,
> and to make me happy. And then we
> will make children together, you and
> I. Many children . . . with God's
> help!

Margaret, however, can't understand a word - and
looks even more horrified. Surely no one has told
her, either, that her new husband speaks not a
word of English.

Brandon's own face is expressionless.

Margaret suddenly, and dramatically, faints into Brandon's arms.

CUT TO:

INT. COURT - WHITEHALL PALACE - EVENING

Musicians play and COURTIERS dance.

Henry and Katherine watch the DANCERS.

Among the dancers is Anne Boleyn. Henry is fixated by the way she exchanges partner for partner . . . all the young BUCKS at court. How she smiles at one, rather than another. What signals her body gives out.

How terrible to be in love - to see your beloved in a public space, admired, even touched by other men.

Henry - the king of England - is being crucified.

Katherine knows it.

Anne knows it too.

Dancing into history.

CUT TO:

EXT. CHAPEL - LISBON - DAY

We HEAR the great pealing of bells.

At first we are really CLOSE ON Margaret's face. Her eyes are red raw from crying.

We HEAR solemn music.

But as we pull back slowly, we see she is wearing
her magnificent wedding dress, with TWENTY-FOUR
LADIES behind her holding up the heavy train.

She walks down the aisle, on Brandon's arm, past
throngs of Portuguese society people, and the
KING's relatives. They stare at her with obvious
hostility, and mutter in Portugese.

The CHILDREN just stick their tongues out at her.
So they process, slowly, towards the altar.

Behind it are the archbishop and bishops in their
robes.

And the king, cadaver-like, grinning back at her.
She falters, almost wants to draw back - but
Brandon propels her forward.

                    MARGARET
                    (hisses)
            What are you doing?

                    BRANDON
            What the king ordered!

They reach the altar. Then Margaret and the king
(the latter with some difficulty because of his
gout) sink to their knees on cushions - and, in
Latin, the archbishop begins to marry them.

                                        CUT TO:

INT. HENRY'S PRIVATE CHAMBERS - OUTER CHAMBER - DAWN

The king of England writes, in the early dawn, to
the mistress he doesn't really know.

                    HENRY (V.O.)
            Perhaps you don't understand. But I can't
            sleep, I can hardly breathe, for thinking
            of you. Your image is before my eyes every

waking second. I almost believe that I
would sacrifice my kingdom for an hour in
your arms . . .

CUT TO:

INT. ANNE'S BEDCHAMBER - NIGHT

Anne lies in bed in her nightdress, reading a letter
from Henry.

                    HENRY (V.O.)
          I beg you, name some place that we can
          meet, and where . . .
                    (beat)
          . . . where I can show you truly an
          affection which is beyond a common
          affection.
                    (beat)
          Written with the hand of your servant, H. R.

CUT TO:

INT. ANNE'S BEDCHAMBER - NIGHT

She smiles, tucks the letter inside her bodice.

From another angle - we see BOLEYN standing in
the doorway. Now he moves forward. With obvious
satisfaction he looks at his daughter.

                    BOLEYN
                    (quietly)
          Now he is "your servant." With some subtle
          care, and the lure of your flesh, he may
          become something even closer.

He smiles, then blows out the candle and walks
out. ANNE lies in bed, her eyes open. She isn't
smiling. Quite the reverse.

CUT TO:

INT. BEDROOM - NIGHT

LADIES prepare MARGARET for bed, like a
sacrificial lamb, lacing pearls into her hair
and spraying her with different perfumes - while
a PRIEST offers his prayers, and the bed is
anointed with holy water. Margaret is placed
inside.

More unbelievable still, MUSICIANS mark the entry
of the king. His dressing gown is removed. His wig
is removed to reveal a skull of grey stubble.

He dips his fingers in a bowl of holy water,
smiles at his beloved . . . and climbs into bed
beside her.

With great formality the curtains around the bed
are slowly closed. We are WITH Margaret for a few
moments, as she lies stiff as a board, the shadows
growing around her.

And then, as the curtains are finally sealed, we
CUT back to the outside, to the watcher and the
waiters. It's amazing how many people it takes to
witness this event.

There is some movement from inside the curtains. Then
the sound of heavy breathing. The bed creaks quite a
bit. Then it creaks a bit more. Then even louder.
Quite a considerable creaking. There are very
strange, odd noises that seem to come from the KING.
At one point his feet poke out through the curtains,
the soles alarmingly dirty. He is clearly trying to
get some leverage. His feet disappear again.

The people continue to look on solemnly.

Finally, after some more grunts and falsetto
trills from the KING - there's a solitary (kind
of) - squeak - from Margaret.

Then silence.

A long beat. No one knows what to do.

Then one brave soul steps forward and PULLS BACK
the curtains. The king is revealed, lying on his
back, red-faced from his exertions and actually
breathing with difficulty.

                    COLONEL
          Did His Majesty . . . ?

A beat.

Then Margaret nods. And everyone in the bedchamber
starts to applaud. And the noise and applause
grows and grows.

Now we're TIGHT on Margaret. She's looking at her
new husband. The physical effort of making love to
her has really taken it out of him. He's genuinely
struggling to breathe, his eyes are glazed, his
hand clutching at his chest.

Clearly it wouldn't take much to push him over
the edge!

                                        CUT TO:

EXT. FIELDS - DAY

Henry is out hawking with Knivert, Compton, and
other members of his immediate entourage, with
SERVANTS in close attendance.

A lazy buzzard circles in the afternoon sky.

The horses, richly caparisoned, canter down a long
field - a rather glorious sight.

At the bottom of the field, they come across a
sunken ditch - the first RIDERS pull up sharply.

                         COMPTON
          Hold! Hold!

Henry trots up.

                         HENRY
          What is it?

Compton rides around, testing the ground.

                         COMPTON
          The ground's too boggy for the horses.
          We'll have to go round.

He indicates somewhere in the distance. Even for
the naked eye it looks a long way.

                         HENRY
          Says who?

                         COMPTON
          We can't jump this ditch, Your Majesty.

HENRY looks at him.

                         HENRY
          You mean you can't jump this ditch.

Henry jumps off his horse, walks down to the
ditch. Some young trees are growing alongside it.
Henry weighs everything up-the size of the ditch,
the height of the young trees.

                         HENRY (cont'd)
                    (shouts)
          Flagpole!

A SERVANT runs forward with a flagpole.

                         KNIVERT
          Your Majesty.

                         HENRY
         Yes, Sir Anthony?

                        KNIVERT
         What are you doing?

Henry removes the flag from the pole.

                         HENRY
         I'm going to vault this stupid ditch. Nothing
         stands in the way of me and my sport.

Everyone laughs.

                        COMPTON
         You're sure?

                         HENRY
         Just watch and see what the king of
         England can do.

Amused, they do watch as Henry takes a few paces
back, measuring out his run. Tests the flexibility
of his pole.

Then starts to RUN at the ditch.

With the greatest agility he spears the pole into
the centre of the water and TAKES OFF.

In midair the pole snaps. Almost in slow motion
Henry falls to the earth, head first. And his head
and shoulders disappear beneath the mud.

Knivert, Compton, and the other courtiers cannot
restrain their mirth. They laugh out loud at the
comical sight of the king of England with his head
buried in mud and his legs waggling about.

It takes one of the SERVANTS to realize how
critical the situation really is.

Throwing himself into the ditch, he struggles
and powers through mud and water to reach his
master.

Then he frantically digs and pulls. Too late
the others realize that Henry must already be
suffocating. And even as they hurry to
dismount . . . the faithful servant has PULLED
Henry clear.

With one desperate movement the servant has
scooped the mud away from Henry's mouth . . . and
then actually reached into his mouth to clear out
even more mud from his windpipe.

And suddenly the air is SUCKED BACK into Henry's
body, with a great SHOCK of noise.

And Knivert and Compton and all the rest are
silent, frozen, and look on, utterly shocked.

There is no more laughter.

                                        CUT TO:

EXT. WHITEHALL PALACE - NIGHT - ESTABLISHING

INT. BEDCHAMBER - WHITEHALL PALACE - NIGHT

Henry roars with pain and sits up in bed, clutching
his head.

Grooms hurry into the chamber.

                    GROOM #1 (V.O.)
                      (alarmed)
              Your Majesty! Your Majesty!

Henry grunts, bangs his head against the bedpost
to try and ease the tearing pain obviously caused
by his violent accident in the tiltyard, although
there are no visible wounds to his face.

GROOM #2 (V.O.)
Fetch a physician! Quick! Hurry!

The first groom runs off.

Henry is in agony, banging his head, thud, thud,
thud . . .

INT. PALACE - LISBON - NIGHT

There is dancing here - to celebrate the royal
wedding.

The king's gout prevents him from dancing
personally. He sits next to Margaret - and they
are admired by, and bowed to, by all at court.

Brandon approaches, and bows.

                    BRANDON
          With Your Majesty's permission, may I
          dance with your wife?

The king has to have Brandon's words translated -
but then nods, in a not altogether friendly way.

Brandon escorts Margaret onto the dance floor -
and they start to dance.

                    MARGARET
               (after a long beat)
          When do you leave?

                    BRANDON
          Tomorrow.

Margaret looks panic-stricken.

                    MARGARET
          You can't.

Brandon smiles a little.

                    BRANDON
     Why can't I? I've discharged my duty. Why
     should I stay? You have a life to lead.

A long beat. The king is watching them like a
sparrow-hawk watches a sparrow.

                    BRANDON (cont'd)
     It's strange, but some men, who seem at
     the peak of health, who are still young
     and full of life - suddenly collapse and
     die. And by the same counter, some old
     men, whose bodies look worn out, whose
     race seems run . . . they can go on for
     years.
                    (beat)
     Don't you think that's strange?

A long beat. Margaret is trying hard not to give
anything away, conscious that a whole kingdom is
looking at her.

                    MARGARET
     Do you tease me because it amuses you?

                    BRANDON
     Why else?

A beat.

                    MARGARET
     Because you love me.

Brandon suddenly has no reply. He stares into her
eyes, as they dance.

And the king watches them. And he's visibly angry,
noticing their inappropriate intimacy.

                                        CUT TO:

EXT. BEDCHAMBER - NIGHT

Henry continues to groan, while three PHYSICIANS
whisper about his state. There seems to be some
disagreement - then reluctant approval.

They approach the bed.

                    PHYSICIAN
          Your Majesty, we would like to bleed you a
          little to drain away the bile that is
          causing Your Majesty so much pain.
                    (beat)
          With your permission?

Henry nods.

                    HENRY
          Yes.

The physicians - watched, of course, by several
COUNCILLORS summoned for the occasion (the king's
health being a matter of state) - swing into
action. A silver bowl is produced. A sharp knife.

Henry's sleeve is rolled up and a tourniquet
applied to his arm.

There is a tension in the room. Many of those
present cross themselves, their lips moving in
prayer.

There is also a pause as the physicians quarrel in
silence as to who will cut the king, passing the
knife from one to the other. Finally, one of them
draws the blade across the distended vein - and
blood spurts, and pumps into the silver bowl - the
physicians examining its colour and consistency.

Henry himself lies back on the pillow, his face
bathed in sweat, but clearly enjoying some ease.

Everyone in the room relaxes a little.

The thudding slows and ceases.

CUT TO:

INT. BEDCHAMBER - PALACE-PORTUGAL - DAWN

Margaret stares out of the window as the dawn sun rises over the city.

CUT TO:

EXT. HARBOUR - DAWN

Out in the harbour is the English ship, waiting to take Brandon back to England.

CUT TO:

INT. BEDCHAMBER - PALACE - PORTUGAL - DAWN

Margaret looks out at the harbour.

CUT TO:

INT. HENRY'S PRIVATE CHAMBERS - OUTER CHAMBER - DAY

Henry stares at Wolsey.

There's a very long beat.

                    HENRY
         I almost died.

                    WOLSEY
         Yes, Your Majesty.

A beat. Henry walks up to Wolsey and eyeballs him.

                    HENRY
         No! Not, "Yes, Your Majesty." I ALMOST
         DIED! DON'T YOU UNDERSTAND?

A long beat. Wolsey is silent, cowed. We have rarely seen this.

Henry paces about.

>   HENRY (cont'd)
>   Since that moment, I've done a great
>   deal of thinking. If I had died, what
>   would I have left? I have no heir - only
>   a daughter, and a bastard son. You
>   understand, Wolsey? The Tudor dynasty -
>   gone, all my father's work - finished.
>   And it's my fault. I have lived too long
>   for pleasure. I never even thought of
>   the future. I married my brother's wife,
>   and God has punished me. I've been such
>   a fool.

Another beat. Slowly he moves closer to Wolsey again. Stares at him.

>   HENRY (cont'd)
>   Now everything has changed. Everything.
>   I want a divorce. And you will get one
>   for me!

A beat. Then Henry walks out of the room.

                                             CUT TO:

INT. BEDCHAMBER - PALACE - PORTUGAL - DAWN

Margaret walks back to the bed. Her husband, the king, is asleep, but troubled.

He is still having difficulties breathing. And his face, as it lies on the pillow, seems particularly skull-like.

Almost as if he was already half in the other world.

Carefully and quietly, Margaret takes a pillow and presses it hard over his face.

She goes on pressing until the king of Portugal is dead.

End of Episode 4

THE TUDORS

Episode 5

Created and Written by
Michael Hirst

FINAL SHOOTING SCRIPT
August 1, 2006

EXT. WHITEHALL - ESTABLISHING - DAY

                    CROMWELL (V.O.)
          Sir Thomas Boleyn, you are, by order and
          permission -

INT. PRESENCE CHAMBER - WHITEHALL PALACE - DAY

The presence chamber is packed with COURTIERS and
foreign ENVOYS and is intolerably hot. Henry is
investing the new PEERS of the REALM. He stands
under his cloth of estate attended by Wolsey,
Norfolk, the earls of Oxford and ARUNDEL.

The doors are opened.

Boleyn walks in, and kneels at Henry's feet as
the patent of creation is read out by the king's
secretary, Thomas Cromwell.

                    CROMWELL
          - of His Majesty, King Henry today created
          Lord Rochford.

Boleyn is invested with a sword and cap of estate,
as befitting his new rank. Henry smiles at him.

                    HENRY
          Arise, my lord.

                    BOLEYN
          Majesty.

Bowing again, Boleyn moves over to join the small
group of new peers already created.

But now there is a significant stir in the room -
as if something important, or unusual, is about to
occur.

Then, to a FANFARE OF TRUMPETS, a small BOY is
ushered into the room. No more than 3 years old,
he looks around in some dismay . . . but is then
prompted towards the king.

> CHAMBERLAIN
> Henry Fitzroy.

We have a sense of his identity when we suddenly
see Elizabeth Blount watching events discreetly
from inside a darkened closet.

The boy is Henry's bastard son. He kneels,
obediently, before his father.

But someone else is also watching discreetly. From
another closet on the far side of the room, Katherine
is observing the events, with sadness and with anger.

> CROMWELL
> Henry Fitzroy, you are, by order and
> permission of His Majesty, King Henry,
> today created duke of Richmond and of
> Somerset, and earl of Nottingham.

The little boy is clothed in a crimson-and-blue
mantle, a sword is placed in his hands . . . but,
just as he is about to be invested with a little
cap of estate and a duke's coronet, Henry suddenly
steps forward and places them on the boy's head
himself. Henry kisses him.

> HENRY
> Arise, Your Grace.

Then, smiling broadly, places the boy beside him
on the dais.

Elizabeth wipes away her tears.

Katherine's jaw tightens, as she stares at Wolsey
with hatred.

The symbolism of the event is only too obvious.

Now we are CLOSE ON Henry. What is he thinking about?

INT. QUEEN'S PRIVATE CHAMBERS - OUTER CHAMBER - DAY

Wolsey is conducted through to one of Katherine's audience chambers.

> LADY-IN-WAITING
> His Eminence, Cardinal Wolsey.

Wolsey bows.

> WOLSEY
> Your Majesty.

Katherine tries to control her emotions.

> KATHERINE
> I see His Majesty's bastard son is made a duke!
> (beat)
> Does it mean he is now next in rank to His Majesty? Next in line to the throne? Above my daughter?

A beat.

> WOLSEY
> Yes. Technically. He is set above all others - except for a legitimate son.

This wounds Katherine in two ways. She stares at Wolsey, tears welling in her eyes.

> KATHERINE
> His Majesty loves our daughter. He has shown it on many occasions. I cannot believe he means to place his bastard child above her.

Wolsey doesn't rise to the bait. Katherine, deeply
upset, almost wringing her hands, paces away from
him, as if unable to look at him.

> KATHERINE (cont'd)
> I do not believe His Majesty was personally
> responsible for this action. After all,
> our daughter is engaged to the emperor!

She looks back at him.

A beat.

> WOLSEY
> Then Your Majesty has not heard? The emperor
> has married Princess Isabella of Portugal.

Katherine hasn't heard and finds it hard to
disguise the fact. Wolsey twists the knife.

> WOLSEY (cont'd)
> Apparently he decided it was not worth
> waiting for your daughter to grow up.
> And - who is to say - but perhaps he was
> influenced by the fact that the beautiful
> Isabella brought with her a dowry of one
> million pounds.
> (beat)
> He broke his word.

A long beat. Katherine, almost dumbstruck, stares
back at Wolsey, as at some loathsome toad.

                                        CUT TO:

INT. HENRY'S PRIVATE CHAMBERS - OUTER CHAMBER - DAY

Henry eagerly opens and reads Anne's letter.

> ANNE BOLEYN (V.O.)
> My dread lord. How your tokens and signs
> of affection frighten me. How can I be to

you what you think me to be? You know I
am a commoner.

A beat. Henry's own voice takes over.

                    HENRY
          "You have flattered me with so many and
          such wondrous gifts. Allow me to send you
          this token in return - small though it
          is. And allow me to remain, in all
          things, your ever loving servant. Anne."

Henry opens the small package - and takes out a
silver locket. After a moment he realizes that it
opens. And when he opens it, he finds inside a
small miniature portrait of Anne.

Lovestruck, he stares at her image.

INT. CHAMBER - JERICHO - DAY

Little Henry Fitzroy - now the duke of Richmond -
is escorted by his own CHAMBERLAIN, CHAPLAIN, and
GOVERNESS into the room where his mother is
waiting for him.

She curtsys to him.

                    ELIZABETH
          Your Grace.

Then smiles, and the little boy flies into her
arms. These two have a natural and loving
relationship. She kisses him, wipes away a tear,
looks at him.

                    ELIZABETH (cont'd)
          Now, Henry, listen to me: You are going to
          own your own house now, and have lots of
          servants to help you and look after you.
          But you must promise me to be a good boy -
          and thoughtful and kind to those around

you. You may be set above them, but if I
find you have grown too proud, I will be
sad and displeased.

The little boy looks serious.

                    FITZROY
          Yes, Mama. I promise.

                    ELIZABETH
               (with a smile)
          And I promise to come and see you as
          often as I can. I am sure your new house
          will be very grand!

Overcome a little, she hugs him tightly again and
whispers into his ear, so that nobody else can hear:

                    ELIZABETH (cont'd)
          I love you, my darling boy. I love you.

                                        CUT TO:

EXT. SHIP - ESTABLISHING - NIGHT

INT. STATE CABIN - SHIP - NIGHT

The gentle creaking of the timbers, and the gentle
roll of the warship upon a placid sea.

Two FIGURES lie squeezed together in a narrow
bunk: Charles Brandon, now the duke of Suffolk,
and Princess Margaret, Henry's sister and, for a
few days, queen of Portugal.

They enjoy their intimacy. Brandon kisses her
gently.

He smiles.

                    MARGARET
          Do you think they were suspicious? Ever?

                    BRANDON
Of course they were suspicious! Didn't you
see the way his servants looked at you?
                    (beat)
But his son was overjoyed! I mean: His
Majesty was overjoyed. After all, he had
waited many years for the crown. The old
man had hung on grimly.

                    MARGARET
You don't need to tell me about that!

They laugh, softly, quietly. They brush lips.
These two, they're alike - and they know it. And,
in a way, that makes them even more careful.

                    MARGARET (cont'd)
                    (after a beat)
What are we going to do?

                    BRANDON
Isn't this enough?

                    MARGARET
No! . . . Well, yes. And no.
                    (beat)
We shall come to England eventually.

A long beat. Brandon turns her face, looks into
her eyes.

                    BRANDON
                    (whispers)
Marry me.

                    MARGARET
What . . . ?

                    BRANDON
You heard me. Marry me!

Margaret stares back at him.

CUT TO:

INT. CHAMBER - HAMPTON COURT PALACE - DAY

Henry paces about. He is holding something in
his fist.

>   HENRY
>   My poor sister.

>   WOLSEY
>   Indeed. To be made queen for just a few
>   days. It seems incredible. A tragedy.

>   HENRY
>   (nods)
>   Upon her return she is to be treated to
>   every comfort and kindness, while she
>   mourns.

Henry passes on.

>   WOLSEY
>   As for the great matter of Your Majesty's
>   annulment. I have set up an ecclesiastical
>   court with Archbishop Warham to consider
>   and decide on the matter. It will meet in
>   secret, if Your Majesty agrees.

Henry looks at him.

>   HENRY
>   Make sure they come to the right decision
>   quickly.

Wolsey inclines his head.

>   WOLSEY
>   I have some further news. About the
>   emperor.
>   (beat)
>   He has released King Francis.

Henry stops dead.

                    HENRY
     What?!

                    WOLSEY
     I have it on good authority.

                    HENRY
     Under what terms?!

                    WOLSEY
     I have yet to find out.

                    HENRY
          (angrily)
     Why wasn't I consulted? We are supposed to
     be allies! What's he playing at?
          (beat)
     Tell his ambassador I want to see him!

                                        CUT TO:

EXT. KING'S HIGHWAY - DAY

Henry rides fast down the hard-baked earthen road,
escorted by two YEOMAN OF THE GUARD, their hooves
churning up clouds of dust.

In the distance we see Hever Castle.

                                        CUT TO:

INT. GALLERIED CHAMBER - HEVER CASTLE - DAY

                    HENRY
     Anne . . . Anne!

Through a long chamber, Henry climbs the steps
up to the galleried chamber - and sees Anne
across the far side. He walks over. She falls
to her knees.

He lifts her. He is almost shaking with passion.
Stares into her eyes.

He crushes his mouth against hers, greedily . . .
a man intoxicated. His arms encircling her,
drawing her ever closer.

> HENRY (cont'd)
> Anne.

He looks at her, smiling, his eyes bright.

> HENRY (cont'd)
> I want to say something to you. If it
> pleases you to be my true, loyal mistress
> and friend; to give yourself up to me,
> body and soul - I promise I'll take you
> as my only mistress. I won't have a
> thought or affection for anyone else.
> (beat)
> If you will agree to be my maitresse en
> titre, I promise I shall serve only you.

A pause. Anne has stiffened a little. Her eyes are
troubled.

> ANNE
> Maitresse en titre? . . . Your official
> mistress?

> HENRY
> Yes! And you will have everything you
> need. Everything within my power to give
> you. It's yours, just ask.

Anne has moved away a little, her face downcast.

> HENRY (cont'd)
> (softly)
> What is it?

She looks at him, visibly upset.

                         ANNE
          What have I done to make you treat me
          like this?

                         HENRY
                      (confused)
          Done? . . . What fault have I committed?
          Tell me! Tell me.

                         ANNE
          Your Majesty - I have already given my
          maidenhead into my husband's hands. And
          whoever he is, only he will have it.

                         HENRY
          Anne . . .

                         ANNE
          Because I know how it goes otherwise. My
          sister is called "the great prostitute" by
          everyone.

          Henry is stunned. Also confused, angry,
          frustrated . . . many emotions tussle inside
          him.

                         HENRY
          I'm sorry if I offended you. I did not
          mean to. I spoke to you plainly of my
          true feelings.

          Anne lowers her head again.

                         ANNE
                      (quietly)
          Your Majesty.

          What can Henry do?

          He turns and stalks away.

                                              CUT TO:

INT. HALL - "CASTLE" - DAY

Boleyn is waiting for the king down in the hall.
As Henry stalks up to him, red-faced and obviously
embarrassed, Boleyn's expression suggests both
surprise and concern.

                    HENRY
          Open the door!

Boleyn bows. But Henry doesn't say anything, and
walks quickly outside.

When Boleyn hears the sound of his horse's hooves
receding, he allows himself the luxury of a small
and satisfied smile.

Then he goes off in search of his daughter.

                                        CUT TO:

INT. QUEEN'S PRIVATE CHAMBERS - OUTER CHAMBER - DAY

Katherine plays with her young daughter, Mary.
They are laughing and fooling about - the laughter
infectious enough to spread to some of the queen's
LADIES.

Suddenly Katherine sees that Wolsey is watching
them - and freezes. She gestures Mary toward her.

                    KATHERINE
          Mary. Mary.

She kisses her, smiles at her.

                    KATHERINE (cont'd)
          Go to your room. I will come later.

She goes out. Katherine gestures for all her
ladies to leave too.

She looks coldly upon Wolsey.

                    KATHERINE (cont'd)
          Another visit, Your Eminence! You are
          always so . . . busy!

                    WOLSEY
          Actually, I have some good news. Since His
          Majesty has given the duke of Richmond his
          own establishment, he considers it only
          right and proper that his beloved Princess
          Mary should also have hers.

A beat. His manner is mild, confiding.

                    KATHERINE
          What do you mean?

                    WOLSEY
          His Majesty intends to send the princess
          to Ludlow castle in the Welsh Marches.
          She will be under the care of Lady
          Salisbury, her lady governess. Her tutor,
          Dr. Fetherston will also accompany her,
          along with three hundred members of the
          princess's household.

It takes a moment to sink in.

                    KATHERINE
          She . . . is to be taken away from me?

                    WOLSEY
          No. His Majesty is according her the true
          honours of a princess.

                    KATHERINE
                    (scathing)
          This is your idea.

Stares at Wolsey.

A beat.

> WOLSEY
>
> Madam, I am often accused of things that are not my fault, or responsibility. Some people are always prone to speak evil without knowledge of the truth. I fear they may have poisoned Your Majesty's mind against me.

> KATHERINE
>
> You are taking my child from me - my child. You are tearing her from me, as if you were tearing her from my womb.

> WOLSEY
>
> I do as His Majesty commands.

> KATHERINE
>
> No. You are my enemy.

> WOLSEY
>
> Your Majesty is unfair.

A beat.

> KATHERINE
>
> Get out of my sight.

Wolsey bows.

And leaves.

> KATHERINE (cont'd)
>
> Mary . . . Mary.

We are CLOSE on Katherine's distraught - almost devastated - expression. But she does not weep.

CUT TO:

INT. PRESENCE CHAMBER - DAY

Henry, flanked by Norfolk and other councillors, meets petitioners and envoys.

> CHAMBERLAIN
> The ambassador of His Highness the Holy Roman Emperor.

Mendoza walks in. We recognize him as one of the envoys from Episode 4. Saturnine, rather Spanish-looking.

Bows.

> HENRY
> Senor Mendoza, I am not pleased to see you.

Mendoza pretends astonishment.

> MENDOZA
> Majesty . . . ?

> HENRY
> Your master has broken all his promises. He has taken our money - but used it against our interests. He has negotiated a separate peace with the king of France and His Holiness the Pope . . . while neglecting his friend and ally. He has not kept faith.
> (beat - really angry)
> Charles has nothing but words for me! Deeds he keeps for others!

> MENDOZA
> The emperor would never betray Your Majesty. Never! He regards you as his uncle. He -

> HENRY
> His fucking uncle! How old am I?

A beat.

                    MENDOZA
        Well, Your Highness must consider that
        you, yourself, may not <u>always</u> have kept to
        your obligations. After all, we received
        only half the amount of gold that was
        promised . . .

It's almost too much for Henry. He steps off the
dais, jabs his finger in Mendoza's face.

                    HENRY
        Your accusations are totally false!
        Unacceptable. I will answer for my
        honourable conduct, <u>whoever</u> contradicts me.

Mendoza has nowhere to go. He manages to look
embarrassed, and hangs his head.

                    HENRY (cont'd)
        Leave.

                                          CUT TO:

INT. COURT - DAY

The very same Mendoza, looking far from sheepish,
walks through the court, seeking out someone.

And finds him - Boleyn. He makes a signal, drawing
Boleyn aside.

                    MENDOZA
        My lord Rochford.

                    BOLEYN
                  (curious)
        Yes, Your Honour.

                    MENDOZA
        The emperor sends you his warmest
        congratulations on your elevation.

                    BOLEYN
          What does the emperor care about my
          elevation?

                    MENDOZA
          He cares to have friends at the English
          court. And pays for the privilege.

A beat. Boleyn begins to see things in a different
light.

                    BOLEYN
          Does he have many friends here already?

                    MENDOZA
          Several.
                    (beat)
          You know them.

A beat. Boleyn's wheels are turning.

                    BOLEYN
          And - what does friendship pay?

                    MENDOZA
                    (with a smile)
          One thousands crowns a year.

Boleyn is aware that this is a great fortune - but
endeavours not to show it.

                    BOLEYN
          I will certainly consider His Highness's
          gracious offer.

Mendoza smiles, moves away.

Boleyn turns - sees that Norfolk is looking at him.

Is he on the gravy train too?

And who else?

Norfolk walks across. Boleyn bows.

                    BOLEYN (cont'd)
          Your Grace.

                    NORFOLK
          My lord! So how did you find the imperial
          ambassador?

                    BOLEYN
          Stimulating.

                    NORFOLK
          Indeed. I find him a man of great principle.

                    BOLEYN
          Indeed.

And Norfolk moves away. Boleyn bowing again as he
does so.

                                        CUT TO:

INT. CHAPEL ROYAL - DAY

Thomas Tallis composes on the organ. Thinking
himself alone, his beautiful composition evolves.
He stops . . . starts . . . refines. Is pleased,
very pleased, with a new phrase.

                    TALLIS
          Hallelujah.

                    MAN'S VOICE
                  (quietly)
          Hallelujah indeed.

Tallis hears footsteps, looks round - sees Compton
approaching. Gets to his feet quickly, to bow.

                    TALLIS
          My lord.

Compton smiles.

>   COMPTON
>   I was just listening.

>   TALLIS
>   Yes. I -

>   COMPTON
>   You have such a talent. Orpheus himself
>   would be jealous.

He has fixed Tallis with his gaze. Tallis blushes.

>   TALLIS
>   Sir.

A beat. Compton reaches out - and just touches his cheek. Smiles again, then turns and walks out.

After a moment Tallis follows him to the door and peeks through.

In the court outside, Compton is talking with three of the queen's LADIES-IN-WAITING. They are laughing - clearly flirting with him.

>   CUT TO:

INT. ANNE'S BEDCHAMBER - HEVER CASTLE - NIGHT

A still-emotional Anne reads Henry's entreaties. From the look in Anne's eyes, we see that these letters and emotions now mean something to her.

We may also notice, on the table in front of her, a tract by Luther, which she has also been reading.

Suddenly the letter is snatched away from her by her brother, George.

                         ANNE
            No, George! Please. Give it back!

But George skips away from her, reading aloud.

                         GEORGE
            "I have given you my heart - now I
            desire . . ."

Distressed, Anne tries again to reclaim the letter -
but George avoids her.

                         ANNE
            Don't! Please.

                         GEORGE
            ". . . to dedicate my body to you."

Anne has given up, slumps down. George finishes
the letter.

                         GEORGE (cont'd)
            "Written by the hand of him who in heart,
            body, and will is your loyal and most
            ensured servant, H. R."

A beat. George grins.

                         GEORGE (cont'd)
            And look! He has drawn a little heart
            between the letter H and R.

He laughs a little. Anne's face is red. George
moves close to her. Enjoying himself. Whispers.

                         GEORGE (cont'd)
            Just imagine: the king of England writing
            to my little sister - promising to be her
            servant! It's incredible.

                         ANNE
                      (quietly)
            Give me the letter.

He still teases her.

                    GEORGE
          He's in love with you.

                    ANNE
               (with passion)
          Give me the letter.

Something in her voice makes George stop laughing.
He hands the letter back to her - and she quickly
hides it away.

George studies her profile.

A long beat.
                    GEORGE
          You're not in love with him - are you?

Anne doesn't answer.

                                        CUT TO:

EXT. WHITEHALL - NIGHT - ESTABLISHING

INT. WOLSEYS'S CHAMBER - HAMPTON COURT - NIGHT

Wolsey with Thomas More . . . who is shocked.

                    MORE
          He wants a divorce?!

                    WOLSEY
          It's not a divorce. He wants an annulment
          on the grounds that he was never married
          in the first place. By marrying his
          brother's wife he has offended the laws
          of both God and man. He simply wants that
          recognized.

A beat. More ponders, disturbed. Shakes his head.

                            MORE
          The pope gave him a dispensation to marry
          Katherine!

Wolsey makes a dismissive gesture.

                            WOLSEY
          Indeed he did. No one denies it. But the
          king feels more beholden to God than he does
          to the pope. His conscience is genuinely
          stricken, and tender. He has disobeyed God's
          injunction and nothing His Holiness can say
          or do will alter that fact.

                            MORE
          The pope is God's representative on earth.
          He speaks for him.

Wolsey is suddenly tired of all this, and tosses
his quill aside.

                            WOLSEY
          Come, come, Thomas. What are you
          pretending? Kings get divorced all the
          time. And popes always find an excuse. I
          know you're an idealist - but you're not
          stupid! If Henry wants an annulment -
          who's to stop him?

A beat. More moves closer to Wolsey, looks him in
the face.

                            MORE
          All right. You talk of facts. Let me give
          you a fact: Katherine of Aragon is not
          only a great queen and the daughter of
          great kings, she is also immensely popular
          throughout the whole of the country. God
          forbid that the king should abandon her -
          just to ease his conscience! I don't think
          the English people would ever forgive him.

And he stares at Wolsey.

A long beat.

                    MORE (cont'd)
          Does she know yet? Does she know yet?

Wolsey doesn't answer. Still deeply troubled, More
goes to the window and looks out. There's a high
wind, masses of dark clouds gathering ominously
over the moon.

                                              CUT TO:

EXT. CHURCH - LONDON - DAY - ESTABLISHING

INT. CHURCH - LONDON - DAY

It's Good Friday. While the CHURCH CHOIR sings the
"Stabat Mater," Katherine watches the ceremony
known as "Crawling to the Cross."

Barefooted, the MEN of the congregation crawl on
their hands and knees towards an altar containing
an image of the Virgin. The image holds a large
crucifix "marvelously finely gilt."

After the last man has kissed the crucifix, a MONK
lifts it and carries it to the lowest steps in the
choir, placing it upon a velvet cushion. The
BISHOP FISHER himself - despite his age - crawls
barefooted over to it, and kisses it.

Then rising, he bows to Katherine and invites her
to follow him outside, through the church's open
doors. She processes with six of her LADIES.

                                              CUT TO:

INT. CHURCH - LONDON - DAY

A crowd - mostly of ordinary Londoners - is waiting.
As Katherine appears - beautiful, regal, and smiling -
they break into spontaneous and warm applause, which
she acknowledges freely.

Guided by Fisher, she approaches a small group of
particularly disadvantaged people - the very poor
and needy and mentally ill of the parish.

>   FISHER
>   Good people of Lambeth. On this Good
>   Friday the Queen's Majesty will distribute
>   alms to you unfortunate but true and loyal
>   subjects of Their Majesties . . . in the
>   Christian spirit of charity and love.

Katherine approaches the first thin and ragged
MAN, who falls to his knees before her, trembling.
One of Katherine's ladies passes her a golden
coin, which she presses into the poor man's hand.
She also whispers something comforting into his
ear . . . and tears roll down his cheeks. It's a
huge moment for him! Far above the value of the
money, is the significance of being touched - and
spiritually healed - by the royal presence.

Smiling, Katherine moves down the line distributing
the king's gift.

We PULL BACK slowly - and see Cromwell watching
these events. His face is expressionless.

                                        CUT TO:

EXT. STREETS OF LONDON - DAY

Compton walks through the crowded streets of
London.

INT. TAVERN - LONDON - EVENING

Compton comes in from outside, wet from the rain,
and makes his way through the crowded tavern. Many
of its customers look rather unsavoury CHARACTERS -
London lowlife - Compton himself standing out as a
gentleman in his rich suit, wearing a sword at his
side, his hand carefully on the hilt.

A DRUNK is playing a tin whistle, rather well,
with a WHORE sat upon his lap. Another WHORE
approaches Compton hopefully, but he moves away.

                    BRANDON
          My dear William.

                    COMPTON
          Charles, good to see you.

                    BRANDON
          Come, have a drink.

He pours two glass fulls.

                    COMPTON
          Why here? I don't understand.
                    (beat)
          We've been expecting you back at court.

Brandon's smile vanishes; he seems unusually
hesitant.

                    BRANDON
          How is the king?

                    COMPTON
          Anxiously awaiting his sister - to share
          her grief.

A long beat. Brandon almost drains his glass.

                    BRANDON
          We're married.

Compton isn't expecting that.

                    COMPTON
          What?

                    BRANDON
          She . . . and me! We're married.

A beat. Compton understands, looks at his old
friend in astonishment.

                    COMPTON
          You and . . . ?

                    BRANDON
          Yes. You have to tell him. You have to
          tell the king.

                    COMPTON
          I have to tell him? Why do I have to
          tell him?

                    BRANDON
          It will be better coming from you.

There's a long beat. Compton empties his glass,
then looks at his old friend again - and
unexpectedly grins.

                    COMPTON
          What's the matter, Charles. Lost your
          nerve?

A long beat. Brandon slumps onto the bench.

                    BRANDON
          This is no laughing matter.

                    COMPTON
          Then why did you do it?

Looks at him.

                    BRANDON
          You know me. I don't always think.

                    COMPTON
          Yes you do! Just not with your head.

Brandon looks back at him.

INT. QUEEN'S BEDCHAMBER - NIGHT

Katherine kneels in prayer before her small
shrine, with its icons and crucifixes.

Then, hearing a noise, she gets up. She is
surprised - astonished - to see Henry enter the
chamber through the private passageway.

> KATHERINE
> Henry.

For a few seconds, a mad hope flickers in her
eyes and illuminates her face. But then she
realizes that Henry is tense and awkward. She
curtsys.

Henry's awkwardness - almost embarrassment - comes
out as uncharacteristic bluntness.

> HENRY
> Katherine, I have something to tell
> you. As far as I am concerned our
> marriage . . . is at an end.
> (beat - swallows)
> Actually, there is no need to end
> something which has never been. You and
> I were never truly married. There was a
> misunderstanding of . . . of scripture,
> and a . . . a papal misapplication of
> canon law . . .

He can see Katherine's eyes begin to mist with
tears, and it starts to throw him off his obviously
prepared speech. Still, he's determined to go
through with it.

> HENRY (cont'd)
> It's true I didn't know about this before.
> But now . . . now these things have been

brought . . . brought to light by
learned opinion . . .

Tears fall from Katherine's eyes, streaking her
cheeks. Henry, stiffly, tries to get to the end of
his speech.

> HENRY (cont'd)
> . . . they weigh down my conscience.
> They . . . they force me to leave your
> bed and board once and for all.

Another pause. Katherine is openly weeping.

> HENRY (cont'd)
> All that remains . . . is for you to
> choose . . . to choose . . . where to
> live and to retire there as quickly as
> possible.

He waits for some response, as if that might help
him. But Katherine merely weeps, her tearful eyes
staring at him. Henry, suddenly hating himself,
hating more every moment of this scene (as men
do), softens his tone.

> HENRY (cont'd)
> I swear to you all will be done for
> the best.

Katherine cries piteously. Henry, unable to stand
it any longer, turns abruptly on his heels - and
walks out.

Katherine stays rooted to the spot, weeping long
and bitter tears.

CUT TO:

INT. CHAMBER - HAMPTON COURT - DAY

Wolsey has convened a secret meeting. Most of
the MEN gathered in the room are prelates - like

ARCHBISHOP WARHAM (fifties, tall and beaky) and
BISHOP FISHER (sixties, his body almost worn
out but his mind as sharp as ever) - all dressed,
like Wolsey himself, in their ecclesiastical
robes.

                    WOLSEY
     Your Grace . . . my lords . . . I
     believe you know why we are gathered
     here, in private. We are here at His
     Majesty's bidding. His Majesty has
     requested an inquiry into the nature of
     his marriage to Katherine of Aragon, for
     the tranquillity of his conscience and
     the health of his soul. For as it says
     in Leviticus: "If a man shall take his
     brother's wife, it is an impurity; he
     has covered his brother's nakedness;
     they shall be childless."

Wolsey pauses, glances around at his fellow
prelates, as if trying to judge their immediate
response. He meets a lot of carefully hooded eyes.

                    WOLSEY (cont'd)
     If, my lords, we are able to agree between
     ourselves that the marriage was, in fact,
     never legal, and was proceeded with against
     both canon and ecclesiastical law - as His
     Majesty, to his great regret, has come to
     believe - then it is my understanding that,
     as papal legate, I myself have the power
     and authority to dissolve and end it. But
     of course I would be grateful to hear your
     lordships' opinions on this great matter.
                    (beat)
     Your Grace?

                    WARHAM
     I am inclined to agree with Your Eminence -
     though I reserve judgement until I have
     heard all opinions.

                              WOLSEY
               My lord Fisher.

                              FISHER
               I see no merit in the king's case, so
               expressed. None whatsoever. If there was
               any obstacle to the king's marriage, then
               it was overcome by the pope's dispensation.
               The marriage was therefore legal, and as
               Your Eminence knows, divorce is disallowed
               by the church.
                              (beat)
               That is my opinion.

For once, Wolsey doesn't try to pull rank. Almost
in a flash, he sees how difficult this question
may turn out to be.

                                              CUT TO:

INT. QUEEN'S PRIVATE CHAMBERS - OUTER CHAMBER - DAY

A rather severe-looking aristocratic WOMAN is
brought into Katherine's chambers.

                         LADY-IN-WAITING
               Madam - Lady Salisbury.

LADY SALISBURY curtsys before the queen, with
elaborate formality.

                         LADY SALISBURY
               Your Majesty. I have brought your daughter -
               to say good-bye.

She signals. Mary is brought forward by another
LADY. Mary is dressed in very grown-up travelling
clothes - like a miniature lady. Almost a
stranger.

She has obviously been rehearsed. Instead of
running into her mother's arms, she curtsys to
her. It breaks Katherine's heart.

KATHERINE

My baby.

LADY SALISBURY

Your Majesty must be reassured. The
princess will be well taken care of, as
befitting her station. You will be sent
regular reports of her health and
accomplishments. And naturally you will
visit her during the course of Your
Majesty's progresses.

A beat. Katherine controls her emotions, not
willing to expose them to an inferior.

KATHERINE

You must make sure she practices her
music. She has a great facility for music.

Lady Salisbury bows again.

Katherine looks at little Mary.

KATHERINE (cont'd)
(in Spanish)
Be strong, my daughter. Remember who you
are - the descendent of Isabella and
Ferdinand of Castille, the only daughter
of the king of England. Be strong, and be
true, and one day . . .
(falters)
One day you will be a queen.

She kisses Mary tenderly. Then Mary curtsys to
her again.

MARY

Yes, Mama.

And then Lady Salisbury leads her away, into an
unknown future.

CUT TO:

INT. PRESENCE CHAMBER - DAY

Henry with Compton. His gaze is cold.

>   HENRY
>   Is he sorry? Does he repent of it? Tell
>   me! Does he beg my forgiveness?

>   COMPTON
>   Your Majesty knows His Grace.

Henry stares at him.

>   HENRY
>   You mean he does <u>not</u>?!

Compton is silent. Henry tries to control himself.

Then makes a gesture.

>   HENRY (cont'd)
>   Send in my sister.

Compton bows, and goes out. Henry puts his fingers
to his temple, as if his head is hurting him.

Margaret quietly enters, curtsys, keeps her head
and eyes lowered.

>   HENRY (cont'd)
>   You are not wearing black!

>   MARGARET
>   No, Your Majesty.

>   HENRY
>   But you are in mourning. Your husband is
>   dead.

A long beat. She doesn't respond.

>   HENRY (cont'd)
>   I said, your husband is dead!

She lifts her head, her eyes defiant.

                    MARGARET
          He's <u>alive</u>! My husband is alive.

Henry walks over to her, cups her chin.

                    HENRY
          I gave you no permission to marry Brandon -
          nor would I ever.

                    MARGARET
          You gave me your <u>promise</u>! I was free to
          choose.

                    HENRY
          I made no promise. You are mistaken.

He sees the defiance in her eyes.

                    HENRY (cont'd)
          How dare you look at me? I am your lord
          and master, not your brother.

A beat. Margaret lowers her eyes again, almost
obediently . . . deeply resentful. Henry steps
back on the dais, beneath his canopy.

                    HENRY (cont'd)
          You are both banished from court. You will
          relinquish your London houses. You will
          remove yourself from my sight. Do you
          understand?

                    MARGARET
                    (between her teeth)
          Yes, Your Majesty.

                    HENRY
          And Margaret?

                    MARGARET
          What?

                         HENRY
        I have yet to decide whether or not to
        make your new bedmate a head shorter.

Margaret lifts her eyes - and stares at him.

                                          CUT TO:

INT. COURT AND CORRIDORS - NIGHT

In a game of shadows, Tallis is followed into the
corridor, lit here and there by pools of light.

Holding a sheaf of music he hears footsteps
closing - and tries one of the doors to find it
locked. Like the next one.

                    MAN'S VOICE (O.S.)
        Say yes.

Tallis glances round, to see Compton approaching.

                    COMPTON
        Say yes.

Tallis shakes his head and moves away again, into
shadow.

Then as he turns the corner into the next
corridor, Compton appears again, but this time
in front of him. He stops.

                    COMPTON (cont'd)
        Say yes.

                    TALLIS
        You're married.

                    COMPTON
        So?

                    TALLIS
        So -

302

He tries to slip away again. There are distant
voices, echoes.

Compton suddenly grips his arm.

>   COMPTON
>   Why deny me?

>   TALLIS
>   I do not love you.

>   COMPTON
>   Is that all?

>   TALLIS
>   For me. Yes.

>   COMPTON
>   You're so beautiful, Tom.

>   TALLIS
>   (laughing)
>   You're a lord! What am I?

Compton's face is suddenly close.

>   COMPTON
>   A genius.

He leans in and kisses Tallis.

>   CUT TO:

**INT. HENRY'S PRIVATE CHAMBERS - OUTER CHAMBER -
NIGHT**

Henry on his own - the restless, frustrated lion.

A GROOM enters, bows.

>   HENRY
>   What is it?

                         GROOM
                A parcel, Your Majesty.

The groom holds out a small parcel.

                         HENRY
                Who is it from?

                         GROOM
                The lady Anne Boleyn.

Henry nods, without apparent enthusiasm, takes the
small parcel, dismisses the young groom.

But when he has left the chamber, Henry tears open
the package, almost trembling. And finds inside a
most exquisite jewel . . . a trinket in the shape
of a ship, with the small and sole figure of a
woman on board, and with a pendant diamond.

Still breathing heavily with excitement, Henry
stares at the jewel, trying to puzzle out its
secret meaning.

                         HENRY
                     (sotto voce)
                A ship . . . with a woman on board.
                What is a ship? What, but a symbol of
                protection, like the ark which rescued
                Noah.
                     (beat)
                And the diamond? What does it say in the
                Roman de la Rose? "A heart as hard as
                diamond, steadfast . . . never changing."

He paces around. It hits him.

                         HENRY (cont'd)
                She is the diamond - and I the ship.

A beat. His excitement is almost feverish.

                    HENRY (cont'd)
    She says yes!

His face is suddenly alive again.

                                        CUT TO:

INT. HENRY'S PRIVATE CHAMBERS - DAY

Wolsey with Henry. But Henry is distracted by
other thoughts, glancing down at the jewel Anne
has sent him - which, as usual, is good for
Wolsey.

                    WOLSEY
    King Francis is eager for a rapprochement
    with Your Majesty. He is disgusted by the
    treacherous behaviour of the emperor
    towards you - which behaviour he knows
    only too well at first hand, having
    suffered the same - and he offers you
    instead a true and lasting friendship.

Henry glances across at him.

                    HENRY
    It is true, the emperor has betrayed us.

                    WOLSEY
    Perhaps he was never sincere in the first
    place.
                    (beat)
    Even so, he still has friends at court.

Henry grows more attentive.

                    HENRY
    Which - friends?

                    WOLSEY
    My agents intercepted this letter.

                                              305

He produces the letter, and lays it before Henry.

                    WOLSEY (cont'd)
          The letter is from the queen. She asks why
          the emperor does not write to her more
          often.
                    (beat)
          But promises, as always, to be his true
          and humble servant.

Henry scans the letter, just to confirm Wolsey's
words. Then - much to Wolsey's unspoken satisfaction
- he angrily tears the letter up.

                    HENRY
          His servant; not mine!

And paces around.

                    HENRY (cont'd)
                    (after a long beat)
          Tell the French ambassador that we are in
          the mood for a rapprochement with King
          Francis. Tell him to send delegates. Let
          us be allies against this emperor.

Wolsey smiles.

                                        CUT TO:

EXT. WOODS - DAY

Henry gallops towards Hever Castle.

INT. BEDCHAMBER - HEVER CASTLE - DAY

Henry alone with Anne. They kiss passionately and
lingeringly. Henry's hands caress her body. He
kisses her breasts.

                    HENRY
          My lady.

He lifts his face to look at her. He seems groggy, as if drunk. But in reality, he is only drunk with love.

> HENRY (cont'd)
> I lay claim to your maidenhead.

Anne smiles, shivers.

> ANNE
> And I make you this promise: When we are married, I will deliver you a son!

It's what Henry wants to hear, above everything. It inflames his desire even more.

They fall upon the bed and their caresses become even more urgent and more intimate. Anne's eyes are bright with desire, her breath gasping, as Henry touches and kisses her.

His eyes meet hers. In his eyes is a question - and in hers an answer. The answer is yes.

He can take her now if he wants to.

Henry caresses her once more - but then strangely stops, rolls away. For a moment she doesn't understand - and can hardly cope with her rioting senses. And it takes a moment for Henry to control his.

> HENRY
> (after a long beat, quietly)
> No, I shall honour your maidenhead until we are married. No less can I do for love.

Anne looks at him, smiles.

> ANNE
> Oh, love. And by daily proof you shall me find, to be to you both loving and kind.

A beat. Henry leans up and kisses her, almost chastely on the lips - then quietly walks from the room.

CUT TO:

EXT. COUNTRY HOUSE - DAY - ESTABLISHING

      MARGARET (V.O.)
  I hate you!

INT. CHAMBER - COUNTRY HOUSE - DAY

Margaret throws a plate at Brandon. He ducks and it smashes against the wall.

      MARGARET
  You said it would be all right! You said
  he would forgive you! You told me! You
  promised.

From the bottles on the table we can judge that they are both quite drunk.

She picks up something else to throw at him.

      BRANDON
  For the love of God, wife!

      MARGARET
  I don't want to be your wife. I hate you.

Brandon tries to get closer.

      BRANDON
  No, you don't.

She throws the bottle, and only just misses his head. And it smashes.

      MARGARET
  Yes, I do! If it wasn't for you I'd still
  be queen of Portugal! Now what am I?

                    BRANDON
You are drunk. And you are foolish.
                    (beat)
Henry will forgive us. He's just standing
on his pride. We just wounded his vanity.

He grabs hold of her.

                    BRANDON (cont'd)
Believe me.

                    MARGARET
Why should I?

He leans in close, starts to kiss her. At first
she tries desperately to resist, to break
away . . . but then yields, and kisses him back.

                    MARGARET (cont'd)
I don't know if you're really brave - or
just a fucking fool.

A long beat.

                    BRANDON
Neither do I.

Brandon grabs Margaret. She resists - very physically,
even trying to kick him and slap him - as he forces
her towards the table. At the same time as trying
to hit him, however, she is also kissing him
passionately, and tearing at his clothes.

How the game goes on. How Brandon pushes her onto
a table, upsetting everything, and finds a way
into her clothes . . . and makes love to her with
wild abandon.

She climbs her register of pleasure.

                    MARGARET
Oh God . . .

Brandon grins. She slaps him again, and pulls him closer.

CUT TO:

INT. MORE'S HOUSE - CHELSEA - EVENING

Henry dines with More. The food is served by More's daughters and his wife, Alice.

She places a silver dish on the table, on which are two roasted pheasants.

>   MORE
>   Thank you, Alice.

Alice curtsys, and goes out, leaving them alone.

More pours wine for the king.

>   HENRY
>   I know you have talked to Wolsey. And I
>   know you do not approve of what I am trying
>   to do. It's against your conscience.

More tries to speak, but Henry stops him.

>   HENRY (cont'd)
>   I'm not going to try and change your mind.
>   That's unlikely, in any case.
>   (he smiles a little)
>   But I need you to understand, Thomas. I
>   need to explain. I have been living with
>   my brother's wife and I have come to
>   believe their marriage was consummated. If
>   that is true, then I have been living in
>   sin. Can you understand what that feels
>   like, Thomas?

Again, More tries to speak - and again Henry stops him, this time with a gesture.

HENRY (cont'd)
That is why I asked the cardinal to
examine the matter.

MORE
But what if it can be proved that the
pope's dispensation was valid, and that
there was no sin?

A beat. Henry musters a straight face.

HENRY
Then I shall be the happiest man alive. I
shall be content to live with Katherine
until the end of my days. Believe me.

More looks back at him.

CUT TO:

**INT. QUEEN'S PRIVATE CHAMBERS - BEDCHAMBER -
EVENING**

Katherine dips her hands into a bowl of warm water
held by one of her ladies.

Then she lifts them out. Anne comes slowly forward
with a towel. She curtsys to Katherine, and keeps
her eyes lowered as she offers her the towel.

There is a charge between them. Katherine's female
intuition is telling her something - and Anne's
obvious awkwardness, the fact she won't meet her
gaze, seems to confirm it.

Katherine dries her hands, hands the towel back.
Anne curtseys again, starts to move away.

KATHERINE
(quietly)
Wait.

Anne turns back, her eyes still averted . . .
then slowly lifts them. She meets the queen's
gaze . . . and for a long moment the two women
look at each other.

Then Katherine turns away, with a gesture to
another lady.

CUT TO:

INT. CHAMBER - HAMPTON COURT - NIGHT

Another secret meeting between Wolsey and the
religious leader. Even at first glance it
doesn't appear that Wolsey has made any
progress; indeed the prelates seem, if anything,
more intransigent.

> FISHER
> I ask you again: If the king is so
> troubled by his conscience, why has he
> waited so long to bring this matter to
> a head?

> WOLSEY
> Because of his love for the queen, he
> has denied the truth to himself. But her
> failure to produce a living son, is proof
> of it.

> WARHAM
> Then he wants to remarry?

> WOLSEY
> If his marriage is annulled, then, yes, I
> am certain he will remarry, in the hope of
> producing an heir.

> FISHER
> He has an heir!

                    WOLSEY
I do not believe for a moment that the
English people will accept his bastard son
as a legitimate heir. Nor does the king.

                    WARHAM
He has a legitimate daughter!

                    WOLSEY
My lords, English history is littered with
the tragedies of those who tried to pass
on their crown to a daughter.

A beat.

                    FISHER
Then - he has a new wife in mind?

                    WOLSEY
He has a mind to take one, yes.

A long beat. Fisher shakes his head.

                    FISHER
It stinks!

                    WOLSEY
I think you should be careful, my lord.

                    FISHER
As should you! One of the great advantages
of having a library, Your Eminence, is
that it is full of books. And some of
these books contain ecclesiastical law.
And according to those books - you have no
authority to judge this matter. It is for
the pope alone - or those whom he
appoints.
          (beat)
It seems that in this case, Your Eminence,
your reach has exceeded your grasp!

And he stares at Wolsey unblinkingly.

CUT TO:

INT. COMPTON'S CHAMBERS - PALACE - NIGHT

Compton, naked, lies asleep in his bed. Tallis
lies in the crook of his arm - but he's awake and
busy, scratching away with a quill on a piece of
paper.

He is composing music. Sacred music.

We might even hear some of it.

CUT TO:

INT. HENRY'S PRIVATE CHAMBERS - OUTER CHAMBER - DAY

Wolsey, in private, with Henry.

> WOLSEY
> So, I have invited a French delegation to
> visit Your Majesty's court, to discuss a
> new treaty, binding us together in the
> face of the emperor's intransigence and
> aggression.

Henry nods. Is in a good mood.

> HENRY
> Good. Excellent.

> WOLSEY
> And since the emperor has reneged on
> his promise to marry your daughter, it
> would perhaps be politic to resurrect
> her betrothal to the dauphin. Or, should
> the dauphin already be promised, then
> to the duke of Orleans, King Francis's
> youngest son.

Henry doesn't respond. But his silence seems to register his acceptance of the idea. And also that his mind is on other things.

                    HENRY
          And what of your secret sessions? Have
          they come to a decision? How soon can I
          expect my annulment?

For once, Wolsey is on thin ice here.

                    WOLSEY
          Your Majesty should not be concerned - but
          we were not able to come to a conclusion.

Henry stops - looks at him. This is also the first time that Wolsey has been unable to satisfy his requirements immediately.

                    HENRY
          Not able . . . ?

                    WOLSEY
          The matter is complex.

                    HENRY
          Really? . . . How?

A beat.

                    WOLSEY
          It is my considered opinion that we should
          apply to His Holiness, Pope Clement, for a
          ruling on this matter. Since he loves Your
          Majesty - I am certain he will rule in
          your favour.

Henry, not best pleased, stares back at him.

                    HENRY
          I hope so. I certainly do hope so. For
          your sake!

There's a threat in his eyes that Wolsey is not
used to.

INT. COURT - EVENING

Tallis is among the musicians playing to celebrate
the arrival of the French ENVOYS, who sit in a
place of honour. Tallis conducts the CHILDREN of the
Chapel Royal as they sing one of his compositions.

CLOSE ON: Henry and Anne. He can't take his eyes
off her, nor she off him. It's "that" look. They
are so plainly and evidently in love.

CLOSE ON: Katherine. Watching it.
We favour Boleyn and Norfolk. They stare at the
French delegates, in their very different, and
rather chic clothes.

> BOLEYN
> You can always tell the French.

> NORFOLK
> Yes. Ponces!

That's Norfolk's greatest insult.

Now they look at Wolsey - once again master of
ceremonies.

> NORFOLK (cont'd)
> But they never did anything so clever as
> giving Wolsey a pension. He has never
> failed them.

> BOLEYN
> We must wait and see. When the wheel of
> fortune has reached its zenith, there is
> only one way for it to go.

And, with his eyes, he indicates the fact that
Henry is now dancing with Anne.

And then, quite out of the blue, there are loud
SHOUTS from outside . . . shouts that seem to
presage something terrible, some news so urgent and
insistent . . . that everything in the room STOPS.

Dead.

Everyone waits - even Henry. Staring towards the
doors. They are all so quiet now that they can
hear the footsteps approaching on the other side.

Then the doors are flung open. A solitary KNIGHT -
a handsome youth, his eyes distraught - walks in.

                    KNIGHT
          Move aside. Out of my way. I bring most
          important news. Your Majesty! Rome has
          been sacked!

                    HENRY
          Let him through!

He walks up to Henry, and bows.

                    KNIGHT
          Your Majesty, I bring most terrible and
          calamitous news. Rome has been captured and
          sacked by the German and Spanish mercenaries
          of the emperor. They have plundered and
          befouled its churches, destroyed its relics
          and holy treasures, tortured and killed
          thousands of its priests.

People in the room have put their hands to their
mouths in horror at this new . . . this monstrous
and almost impossible sacrilege.

But Henry is thinking of something else, too.

                    HENRY
          What of His Holiness?

KNIGHT

The pope is a prisoner in the Castel
Saint'Angelo.

HENRY

He is the emperor's prisoner?

KNIGHT

Yes.

Henry looks shocked. Though a flicker of a smile
passes over Katherine's mouth.

But already people are beginning to leave. (Think
of getting the news of 9/11 at a public function -
but multiply it a thousandfold). No one is in the
mood to celebrate anymore.

The French envoys bow to Henry silently, as
they withdraw, following Katherine and her
ladies.

Anne casts a desperate look back at Henry - for
what chance now has his divorce?

CUT TO:

INT. LUDLOW CASTLE - WALES - DAY

A YOUNG WOMAN walks slowly down a dark stone
passageway. She is dressed in black, with a black
veil over her face. We have no idea who she is.

She is followed by a small retinue, some holding
flaming torches to illuminate the way.

Castles are not comfortable places. And this one
is cold and draughty and rudimentary.

The young woman is led into a chamber.

INT. CHAMBER - DAY

In the chamber there is a bed of state. Four
candles burn at each end. Around the bed are small
groups of PHYSICIANS and CHAPLAINS. Someone is
lying in the bed.

One of the PHYSICIANS comes forward, and bows.

                    PHYSICIAN
          Lady Blount.

She raises the veil - and we see the lovely face
of the king's ex-mistress Elizabeth Blount.

                    PHYSICIAN (cont'd)
          He caught the sweating sickness. There
          was nothing we could do. He complained
          this morning of feeling ill. By this
          evening he was in the hands of God.

Elizabeth, trying to control herself, moves slowly
to the bed, where her son - the bastard son of
Henry, recently created duke of Richmond -
lies still, as if asleep. Just a little boy.

Elizabeth touches his cold hand, then leans down
and kisses his cold eyes . . . and then breaks
down, and cries out in her grief, and sobs and
sobs until her heart must break.

                                        CUT TO:

INT. HENRY'S PRIVATE CHAMBERS - OUTER CHAMBER -
NIGHT

We track slowly in on Henry. He is sitting alone
and in almost total shadow. He has suffered two
enormous blows - and it shows in his eyes and in
his expression.

A single candle illuminates by its faint light two objects on the table in front of him.

They are a little cap of estate and a duke's coronet, small enough to fit a child's head.

End of Episode 5

THE TUDORS

Synopses of Episodes 6–10

Episode 6

Since the pope has been taken prisoner by the emperor, Wolsey decides to go to France and establish a new treaty with King Francis. He has also summoned a conclave of the cardinals for a meeting in Paris. With the pope imprisoned, he hopes to convince them to grant him the license and authority to annul the king's marriage. Wolsey, aware of the seriousness of his situation, heads to France with Thomas More.

Eagerly anticipating Wolsey's success, Henry continues his courtship of Anne. He sends her letters, pledging his love, which she reads aloud to Norfolk and Boleyn, her father. They instruct Anne that she must use her influence over Henry to bring down their enemy, Wolsey. Henry grows bolder in showing favor toward his new love, bringing her on a hunting trip with William Compton. Afterward, at Compton's home, Anne begins to place the seeds of doubt about Wolsey's ability to do the king's bidding.

Wolsey's arrival in Paris is a spectacle to behold, a magnificent train of wagons, guards, and musicians. He is greeted by Francis, who excitedly welcomes the new treaty and engagement of Mary to his younger son. Wolsey broaches the topic of the king's annulment and mentions that Henry might be interested in marrying Francis's sister.

In the court, Anne starts to enjoy the recognition of her newfound stature, angering Katherine. Katherine has already sent word to the emperor, her nephew, of her husband's intentions of a divorce. Now, she must watch the brazen attitude of Henry and his mistress in front of her very eyes, and she is powerless to stop it.

Thomas Cromwell gives the king some very good news; the pope has escaped and he is now holed up in a castle. Henry sends two letters to the pope. The first requests that after his divorce from Katherine he be permitted to marry any woman he chooses, even one who may be forbidden to him because of prior relationship to one of her relatives. The second requests that if his marriage to Katherine cannot be declared invalid, the pope must allow Henry a second wife.

Boleyn pays Charles Brandon a visit, on behalf of Norfolk. Norfolk will help Brandon gain the king's forgiveness if Brandon will help in their plot to destroy Wolsey. Norfolk and Boleyn reveal to Henry that Wolsey does not want the annulment, as he dislikes Anne. Boleyn also informs the king that Wolsey is stealing from the king.

Dr. Knight, on his way to the pope, is intercepted by Wolsey, who reads the letters. Wolsey suddenly understands that the king hopes to divorce Katherine so as to marry Anne. He sends the doctor on his way and heads for his meeting with the cardinals. He tries to get More to work with him, but More contends he will not compromise his values for anyone. In any case, Wolsey is to be bitterly disappointed, as not a single cardinal turns up to meet him.

Brandon comes to seek the king's forgiveness, and Henry allows his longtime friend back in the court. Wolsey returns, defeated, to break the bad news to his king and the king's new advisor . . . Anne Boleyn.

Episode 7

On shaky ground with the king, Wolsey works to regain Henry's faith. He invites Anne and Henry into his home for dinner. On even more important matters, he assures them that he has dispatched lawyers to the pope to argue the king's case. Wolsey meets with the lawyers and instructs them to do everything in their power to get an annulment, even if it means threatening the pope with the fact that the king is prepared to go outside the church's law. Meanwhile, Katherine has received word from the emperor that he will contact the pope on her behalf.

William Compton has caught the sweating sickness and soon dies from the disease. William's common-law wife, Anne, contracts the illness next, perishing within hours. Henry hopes any outbreak can be contained.

The French ambassador's arrival in court is well received. On a hunting trip with Henry and his companions, the ambassador meets Anne and treats her with the respect usually reserved for a queen. The ambassador also bears wonderful news; the emperor's forces are almost defeated. This report is tempered by the ominous realization that the sweating sickness has spread throughout the countryside.

When Anne's maid falls ill, Henry knows the disease has made its way into the palace. He immediately sends Anne to Hever and hopefully to safety. He orders Katherine to Wales to be with Mary and away from the contaminated court. Henry meanwhile shuts himself up in the palace with only a few servants. His plan fails, though, and Anne becomes deathly ill. Afraid, Henry races to a remote tower, trying to keep the sweating sickness at bay.

As England is ravaged by illness, the lawyers meet with the pope.

The pope listens to their argument and after much deliberation, appoints Cardinal Campeggio official legate. Once England is free of the epidemic, Campeggio will journey there and decide the case with Wolsey.

The disease grips the nation. Anne is close to death, and she is read her last rites. Miraculously, she recovers, and finally the epidemic is over. Henry returns to his court, whose numbers have been decimated. He learns that Emperor Charles defeated the French and gained control of Italy and Europe. Henry's first thoughts are with Anne, and finally, the two lovers are reunited.

Episode 8

Cardinal Campeggio arrives in England, hoping to convince the king to reconcile with Katherine. Wolsey warns him that that won't happen, and if Henry does not get his annulment, it will ruin papacy rule in England and destroy Wolsey himself. When Campeggio meets with Henry he has a new suggestion: perhaps the pious Katherine can be persuaded to abdicate the marriage and retire to a nunnery. Henry approves and Campeggio approaches Katherine with the proposal. She refuses to answer until she speaks with Henry, despite Wolsey's pleas. After asking Henry's permission to speak to Campeggio, she confesses to the cardinal that she was a virgin when she married Henry and she will not give up her marriage. Upon learning of this, a frustrated Henry orders Wolsey to expedite the court case.

Henry appoints Bishop Warham and Bishop Tunstall as Katherine's lawyers. Their meeting with the queen goes poorly, as they accuse her of acting against the king. Katherine fires them and demands that Bishop Fisher represent her. Henry goes to Katherine, asking her to reconsider her position. She begs him to attend chapel with her, like the old days, and he reluctantly agrees.

Anne, frustrated by the wait, grows jealous of Katherine. To appease her, Henry moves her into her own royal apartments. Anne approaches Henry, raising doubts about Wolsey's true intentions in the case. When Henry confronts Wolsey, Wolsey swears his loyalty lies with the king. Unfortunately for Wolsey, conspirators against him mount a plan to have him arrested and reveal his shady practices.

Wolsey implores Campeggio once again to give the king what he wants, but to no avail. The case begins in court, with Bishop Fisher representing Katherine. Katherine pledges her love and devotion to the king and leaves the courtroom. Her exit is greeted by thunderous applause from the great crowds outside. Henry listens to the roar, gets up, and stalks out the back door, glaring angrily at Wolsey, whose career and life now hang in the balance.

Episode 9

The court case continues, despite the queen's absence. Witnesses testify about Katherine's wedding night with Prince Arthur. The proceedings cause Henry great agitation and embarrassment, and Wolsey, sensing his master's anger, goes to Katherine to demand she surrender the matter. Katherine denies him, knowing that the case is taking a toll on Wolsey's relationship with the king.

Wolsey dispatches Thomas More to Cambria, where the French and imperial representatives are meeting to hammer out a treaty, along with representatives of the pope. Wolsey wants More to ensure no alliance is struck between King Francis and Emperor Charles so that the emperor and pope do not resolve their dispute. Otherwise, Wolsey fears the king will never get his desired annulment. The king goes to Katherine, entreating her to accept the inevitable. She denies him, standing by her principles. Angered, he retreats to Anne, hoping to find solace with her. Anne is not sympathetic, concerned Henry will eventually give in to the queen. Henry is unable to quiet her fears, and Anne leaves the court. Trying to force Campeggio's decision, Henry sends Brandon and Knivert to lean on the cardinal. Henry beseeches Boleyn to ask his daughter to come back to court.

It is judgment day in the court. Campeggio announces that the matter is too important to be decided without consulting with the curia of Rome. Since the curia is in summer recess, the matter will be delayed until October 1. Enraged, Henry leaves the court, and Brandon publicly denounces Wolsey. Henry takes comfort with Anne, who has returned to him.

A dispirited Wolsey welcomes More back from his journey, hoping for some good news. More informs him that the negotiations took place a week before he had even arrived. Francis and Charles negotiated a peace and both of them settled their differences with Pope Clement. Wolsey's worst fears are confirmed.

Thomas Cromwell suggests to Henry that there might be another way of obtaining his divorce. Meanwhile, Wolsey, in despair, writes to Cromwell, begging him not to abandon him. But Cromwell tears up the letter.

Wolsey, shunned by his king, is arrested by Brandon and Norfolk and stripped of his offices and wealth. Wolsey pleads guilty to the charges and is sentenced to imprisonment. Although Henry rescinds the punishment, Wolsey is banned from the court. Henry asks More to be his new lord chancellor. More reluctantly accepts only after Henry promises to not involve More in the Great Matter.

Episode 10

The judgment has caused great upheaval in the court. With Wolsey now out of the picture, Henry's new advisors, mainly Norfolk and Brandon, are put in charge of running the country. Anne introduces Protestant literature to the king, books considered heresy. Henry immediately adopts the teachings, latching on to the passages claiming that "the King is the representative of God on earth and his law is God's law." He is now speaking openly of reforming the church. Unaware of his king's new beliefs, the new lord chancellor, Thomas More, begins prosecuting heretics, burning the reformers at the stake.

Cromwell introduces his solution to the king. He believes the case is not a legal one but a theological one. Thus, Henry needs to canvas the opinions of theologians at colleges around Europe. After their sentence is pronounced, it could be implemented very easily by the king. The pope would have no jurisdiction over the decision. Excitedly, Henry encourages Cromwell to write up his thesis.

There are no longer any pretensions about Anne's status. She enters the court splendidly dressed in a purple dress, the color worn only by royalty, and openly insults the queen and the queen's native country, Spain. At a feast honoring the Boleyn family's new promotion in court, Anne sits in the absent queen's chair, and Henry, in full view of the entire court, kisses her on the lips. She will soon be his new queen.

Henry sends Cromwell off to present his thesis to the universities and dispatches Boleyn to inform the emperor and the pope of his new case. Meanwhile, Wolsey, trying to get reinstated in the court, writes to Anne, and after she denies him, secretly contacts Katherine and the emperor, hoping to help them resolve the annulment case and get himself reinstated as chancellor. Norfolk, warning Brandon that Wolsey is still a threat, has his fears confirmed. Henry, fed up with his new council's ineptness, decides to recall Wolsey.

Cromwell returns with his verdict, favorable from France and parts of Italy, denied in Spain. Boleyn, however, was refused audience with the emperor and simply given an edict from the pope. The edict instructs Henry to dismiss Anne from court and refuses him to remarry until after the papal curia decides his case. The king, angered, gets more news. Wolsey has conspired with the emperor and pope.

Acting quickly, Henry sends Brandon to arrest Wolsey on high treason. On his way to London for his trial, Wolsey cuts his own throat. Saddened by the news, Henry goes hunting with Anne. Meanwhile Norfolk, Boleyn, and Brandon celebrate Wolsey's death by staging a play in which the actor playing the dead cardinal is dragged down into Hell. Henry and Anne approach a remote tower, but passion overcomes them and they make passionate love on the forest floor. But at the last moment, Anne decides she is still not ready to conceive a child.

The spital fields

THE TOWRE

Printed in the United States
By Bookmasters